Love Under the Brooklyn Bridge

A Love Story Series

CAROLINE CHRISTIANSEN

Love Under the Brooklyn Bridge
Edited by: Julie Holt
Cover Design: Stacy Garcia
Interior Formatting: Alyssa Garcia

Content warning: Mentioned death of a parent, references/ flashbacks to physical and mental abuse by a parent, intensive and descriptive therapy sessions with a trained therapist, and alcohol abuse.

Love Under the Brooklyn Bridge

A Love Story Series

Let them eat Cake!

- Julie Holt

This book is dedicated to the mental, physical, and spiritual health community and their partners. For those who use their giftings to help others heal from trauma, abuse, and neglect. Also, to the survivors of mental, physical, and spiritual abuse/neglect. We see you and we hear you. We need you so desperately in our very, at times, fallen world. You are here for a reason! We Love You! Healing and Light is possible. Please reach out for help! There are references at the end of the book if you need to speak to someone. I pray you find hope, joy, and peace as you read Gemma's story. There is hope on the other side of pain and suffering. While Gemma's story is one of fiction. I pray you find solace and love in her healing process.

I Love You!

Much Love,
CC

Gemma

*"***M***ommy?" I hear the little girl scream in the near distance. I wander in the dark, trying to rescue the child by following her scared screams. I feel like I'm running as fast as I can, but I'm not getting anywhere. It's like I'm stuck in quicksand. I'm panicked because I can't find where the voice is coming from. I've checked every door in the hallway as the little girl's cries get louder and louder. I must be getting closer. "Mommy!!" she screams. My whole body feels tingly, like I'm watching a car wreck happen right in front of me. I come to the last door and behind it, the little girl is crying in her bed. I instantly recognize the room. I'm somewhere familiar. A faded purple paisley comforter with little white rabbits*

on it. I approach the bed because I can see the little girl is having a nightmare. I need to wake her up.

I pull the covers away from her face and she stops crying. She sits up, and I gasp as I see her bruised face and busted lip. She wipes her eyes, and I notice the Peter Pan collar of her white shirt is dotted with crimson. I reach up and touch my own lip. It's tender and there's fresh blood on it. She points behind me and I turn away from her, walking toward the white-framed mirror on top of the chest. When I reach in the hazy mirror, I blink a few times to bring my reflection into focus. The fog clears as I see my own reflection transform into the child's and I scream. I press my hand over my mouth and turn to look at the little girl.

She's gone because the little girl crying in her bed for her mommy is me.

"Ma'am?" the voice whispers as I'm startled awake. Oh shit! Thank God, it was only a nightmare. "Ma'am!" My eyes open and I try to find the voice. "Ma'am, are you okay?" I sit up, realizing I'm in a car that isn't moving.

"I'm fine!" I answer as I lean back against the seat of the town car. "I'm sorry. I had a nightmare."

"Are you sure you're alright?" the driver says as he drops me off at my apartment. Last night was one of our many night-shoots for the Frank Sinatra biopic I'm filming. This is my first film, and I'm not the star of the show but I've enjoyed playing a secondary character. Lana Turner is without a doubt a fun and energetic character. She and Frank had a very combative relationship. I'm wondering if all the tussling and fighting has dug up some memories that I've spent my entire life repressing. I'm no shrink, but I imagine it's related. I have a lot of material to pull from in that department.

Believe it or not, I was "discovered at work" by an executive producer. She thought I looked just like Lana Turner, but at the time I was a brunette. Now my hair is dyed platinum-blonde, almost white. It's bizarre how this whole thing came to life but I'm incredibly grateful. It's wonderful money, and my boss Blake has been so supportive. He gave me a six-week leave of absence so I could film my part in the movie. We are coming to the end of my time, and I have to say, as fun as this was, I'm kind of ready to get back to normal life. I am not used to staying up all night, so I must have fallen asleep on the way back to my apartment in Brooklyn. I grab my bags and open the door.

"I hope I didn't worry you?" I ask as I open the car door and my heart rate starts to normalize.

"You scared the hell out of me! Must have been some dream!" the driver says as I thank him for the ride from set. The long overnight hours are starting to get to me, so I'm glad a driver to and from set is part of the whole movie star gig.

I know I'm not like a lot of the other actors. I've never been in a movie or TV show. This is the first thing I've ever done in the entertainment industry. I don't have an agent or personal assistant on set. It's just me. My trailer is fairly quiet. The last two weeks I hung out in my co-star Ava's trailer, but now that she's gone it's just me. Dalton Calhoun, who is playing Sinatra, has been absolutely wonderful to work with. He's made some of the material we are shooting more comfortable and laid back. Otherwise, I'd be freaking out.

We haven't filmed our sex scenes yet, but I plan to "fake it 'til I make it." Everything with the sex scenes is very choreographed and rehearsed. That's happening two weeks from now so I'm nervous, but I know I can do this. There's a lot in my life that has been difficult to overcome, and this doesn't hold a candle. My early years were fraught with a lot of trauma, and I'm having more and more nightmares and flashbacks since filming started. I don't know where they're coming from, but I feel like I'm on the cusp of something. I don't know if it's a good or bad something yet. I'll just take it one day at a time.

I receive a text from Blake the next night as I'm sitting in my trailer after shooting for the day is done.

Come out tonight! I haven't

seen you in weeks!

I want to hear how everything is going. PLEASE!

I'm so bored without you!

Hey Stranger! Back from the highlands?

I was sorry to hear about your grandmother.

I don't have a change of clothes.

Where are you planning on going?

Just dinner and drinks! YES! It was beautiful.

Scotland in the summer is absolutely glorious. One day I'll take you! I want to hear all about the movie.

How is your life more entertaining than mine? It's not fair! PUH-LEASE!!

FINE! I'll meet you. Besides we just wrapped for the evening. I have an early call time tomorrow, so I need to leave by midnight. You know, turning into a pumpkin and all that!

Ah yes, my ill-fated Cinderella! Meet me at Perrone's at 7PM. I've got a table reserved under King. Small group of people so don't fret.

I'M SO DAMN EXCITED TO SEE YOU! IT'S BEEN AT LEAST A MONTH!!

Yes, I'm excited to see you too! I'll be back at work soon. Also, Perrone's is fancy Blake! UGH! I'll see what I can scrounge up on set.

That's awesome! Wear one of those silk nighties that you wore during your audition. That'll be fancy!

You've lost your mind! I'll figure

something out. I didn't drive to set so I'll have to get a cab. I don't have time to run home and then back into the city.

Do you want me to bring you something to change into? I think you have a couple outfits at my place.

I'm not doing a costume change at Perrone's Blake! You are too much sometimes!

Just trying to help Turner! DIVA!

I'm not being a diva! You're getting into your "Devil Wears Prada" zone, and you need to step out of it before I see you! Or ELSE!

I Love us!

Me too! See you soon!

I look through what wardrobe has left that I could possibly pass off as not 1950's attire. I find a red chiffon cocktail dress that is still somewhat modern. I text the wardrobe assistant and tell her I'm borrowing it for the night, but it'll be back in the morning good as new. She laughs, telling me people take things from set all the time. An actress isn't going to get in trouble for borrowing clothes. However, I'm not someone who just takes something without asking. My luck I'd get caught and fired! I slip on the cocktail dress and add a pair of tan heels. My make-up and hair are still done from set so I'm good to go!

I have the town car from the studio drop me off at Perrone's. I'm gonna miss the car service when I wrap my part in the movie. When I step out of the car, I'm immediately noticed by those around me. They don't know who I am, but when I'm all dressed up like this, they assume I'm "somebody." Well, joke's on them because I'm happy to be a "nobody." I walk in and tell the hostess that I'm with the King party. She gives me a strange look. Is there something in my teeth?

"I'm sorry, but he's already here with someone else," she whispers. Of course, he's with someone else. Blake said that he was having a few people.

"Oh, I know! He said he had a table. There might be a few of us. I'm sorry. I know I'm a little late. My driver had to wait to pull in front so I could get out. I'll call him," I start to say, and she shakes her head frantically.

"No no no, that's okay. We can pull up a chair,"

she explains as she tells the maître d' beside her to take me to table 31. He looks me up and down then nods, a little impressed. I'm confused. I receive a text message so I'm looking down at my phone when the maître d' stops, and I almost run into the back of him. He moves to the side saying he'll grab a chair. When I look up, it's not Blake and his friends. It's Brent King. THE. BRENT. KING! Blake's older and extremely attractive brother. The object of every woman and some men's desires. He also so happens to be the CEO of the company I work for. So, he's also my boss! Sitting across from him is who I assume is his date for the evening, looking super pissed at the intrusion. She looks me up and down and then glares over at Brent. I look at the fleeing back of the maître d' running to get another chair. OH SHIT! SHIT! SHIT!

"Oh. No no no no no no," I whisper-yell to his retreating back. Brent and I haven't been formally introduced. I've been working for his company for over a year now but he's in a different location than I am. I've seen him at functions and events, but he's never seen me. Life has taught me how to blend in. However, I'm not blending in now! He looks me up and down amused, but then smiles up at me. I think he finds this funny. I, on the other hand, do not. His smile could melt all the ice in Antarctica. Yes, he's that sexy. He's not just hot. He's scorching. I know I have to turn away from him, but his date interrupts my exit planning. I'm frozen.

"Can we help you?" his date says through gritted teeth. He snaps out of whatever was keeping him silent, and I don't give him a chance to speak.

"Um, no actually." I answer her, not making eye contact again with Brent, although I can feel his eyes on me. The maître d' comes back with a proud smile on his face, followed by a hostess carrying a chair. It feels like the entire restaurant is looking at us. WHICH THEY ARE! I grab the maître d's arm. "I'm sorry. Wrong KING reservation. I'm looking for BLAKE King's table," I whisper as his eyes widen in horror.

"Of course, of course. I'm so sorry," he says to Brent and his date. Brent looks more amused than put off, and I can't help but feel his eyes on my back. DEAR GOD, he's gorgeous. Like cross your legs and cover your tits in public sexy. "*Sex on legs,*" as some of my female, and male, coworkers call him. Behind his back of course. Having someone that beautiful watching you is not as thrilling as you'd think. I've spent most of my time here in New York trying to blend in with the crowd, so having the attention of the most attractive man in the world is thrilling in an almost painful way. The host motions for me to follow him, and I do so gladly.

Please get me the hell away from here. His date literally looks like she could rip my face off with her siren-red fingernails! I'm halfway back to the front of the restaurant when I stupidly decide to turn around. When I do, I meet the scorching gaze of Brent King watching me walk away. He's trying not to laugh and that pisses me off, so when our eyes meet, I do something I immediately regret. I wink at him! I'm given the chance to end this nightmare of an interaction AND I WINK! It must have worked though, because the smile falls off his face and he immediately turns back to his date who looks like she's eaten something sour. I can't help but laugh at myself. WHY THE HELL DID I WINK? Maybe it was sexy? Or maybe I just looked like I had something in my eye! I sigh and then see Blake standing at the front of the restaurant giggling like a schoolgirl at me.

"Holy shit, Gemma. You look amazing," he yells as he kisses both of my cheeks and then, as if this evening hasn't been embarrassing enough, spins me around so he can check me out. Then to add the cherry on top, he falls to his knees and pretends to worship me. "My GOD, you look so hot. You could turn a gay man straight. Look at your legs and that ass! Not to mention how great your tits look. Jesus, Gemma! Also, what's all the fuss about?" He's noticing that he's made even more of a scene than I just did. Which he LOVES. We need to leave NOW! Whatever he sees behind me, probably Brent and his date, makes him smile proudly at me. "Thatta girl! I would have made an introduction, but I see none is necessary."

"Well, damn it to hell, that was so embarrassing. Can we go please? Preferably to a different planet," I whisper as Blake takes my arm.

"Absolutely not! We are right where we need to be." The hostess apologizes and I wave her off. It's not her fault that two Kings have reservations at the same DAMN time, at the same DAMN restaurant. What are the odds? No wonder they were looking at me strangely. However, the one person who wasn't looking at me like that was Brent. I'll be remembering the way he looked at me for a while. Now that it's been burned permanently into my memory. I'll use it on a cold, sexless night in the near future!

"What happened?" Blake asks as we walk to our table on the other side of the restaurant. Luckily for me it's out of view from Brent's table. How embarrassing.

"As always, I didn't remember that you're always fashionably late. I said reservation for King, but they took me to your brother's table," I explain as Blake explodes into laughter. Jesus, he's loud. "Shut up, Blake. People are staring!"

"Well of course they are. You're a vision. What was my brother's reaction when he saw you? How about his date's? I've been dying to find the right time to introduce you to my brother. He's always out of town, or you're on set when he's in our office or vice versa. Oh my GOD! I love this!" he adds, leaning over and taking my hand. "Everyone's running late so we have time to catch up. Give me the blow by blow and don't leave anything out. I'll know!" I tell him everything that's happened, which takes maybe five minutes, and then he's howling with laughter again. "Darling. I'm surprised this doesn't happen to you more often. My family comes here all the time. You know we have a house account, lady love. I'm surprised you forget about this. I mean, how many reservations have you made for me here while you've been working at K.B. & A?" he asks, using the internal nickname for the firm.

Blake is co-owner now with his older brother, Brent. His father started King Brothers and Associates back in the 70's. He's retired now, and Brent has been running the show the last few years. Blake is over our uptown location, which is where I work. Brent works in the downtown office, but he's been gone a lot the last few years, traveling for the firm. Blake is speaking to the waiter about appetizers and I'm replaying the last 15 minutes in my head. Brent with his gorgeous smile, bluish-green eyes and dark hair. He's all kinds of tall and built like a linebacker. Except instead of a uniform, he comes pre-packaged in designer suits that give the air of someone destined to run a boardroom. Did I mention his accent? Melissa in our finance department is always droning on and on about his Scottish accent. Apparently, it's much more pronounced than Blake's, and much lower. I tell Blake all the time to read to me. Which he always answers by telling me to get my head checked.

"And yet," I say, taking a hearty sip of my Jack and Coke as I come back to the here and now. "It happened. To me. Tonight!" The waiter leaves, and I place the cold glass against my forehead. The food at Perrone's is delicious. I have only ever eaten here with Blake. He's here at least a few times a week and we always do brunch on Sunday.

"So, tell me," he says, whispering conspiratorially, "how mad do you think trampy-tramp is now that you've interrupted her dinner with King Casanova?" He gives me a suggestive eyebrow raise and sighs. "Ugh, I miss everything! I would have gladly died just to see his face take you in for the first time!"

"You didn't miss anything. It was an honest mistake and one I can tell my grandkids about when I'm old and wrinkly."

"Umm, hell no. We don't get old and wrinkly nowadays. Too many procedures to ensure that doesn't happen. Plus, I thought you didn't want kids?" he asks, moving back while the waiter puts our refills down. "Cheers, to us being reunited," he lifts his drink. "Also, you should have seen my brother's face when I kissed you on both cheeks. I think it's the first time in my life that he's been jealous of my date." We clink glasses as I fill him in on what's been going on at set, and he's enthralled. I tell him I'm a little nervous about the upcoming sex scenes, but he waves it off. "You'll be fine. How naked do you have to get?" He asks as I hear someone clear their throat beside us. We both look up at the same time and HOLY SHIT! It's Brent. DAMN. IT. TO. HELL!

"I'm sorry to interrupt," he says to Blake, who looks almost as shocked as I am. "I don't think we've been formally introduced. I'm Brent King," he says, putting his hand out for me to take, and somehow I have the decency to close my mouth. I take his outstretched hand as we make eye contact. The touch of his hand sends a delicious surge of energy up my arm, and I immediately let go and place it in my lap before I do something stupid with it. Like, I don't know, pull him in for a hot and scorching kiss. I clear my throat and give Blake an irritated smirk. Why? Why me? Also, DO SOME-THING! He looks back to me and then up at his brother, smiling like the cat that caught the canary.

"This is Gemma Williams," Blake tells his brother. "Gemma, I'm sure you've seen Brent at some of our events. He's right though, I don't think the two of you have been formally introduced. Such a pity. This is the infamous Brent King!"

Blake grins mischeviously, but Brent keeps his eyes on me.

"It's nice to meet you, Brent. I've heard a lot of wonderful things about you from your brother, and I'm sorry about earlier. They obviously sent me to the wrong table," I add, looking away from the Scottish god watching my every move. Blake is still smiling, as if we are here just for his entertainment.

"I'm sorry, but my two-favorite people in the whole world are finally meeting each other. This is great for me." Brent seems unfazed, and I sigh, resigned to my fate. Blake is going to be of no help in this situation.

"It's so nice to meet you, Gemma. I didn't mean to interrupt your dinner, but I wanted to formally introduce myself." A waiter walks behind him, and he has to press closer to the table. When he does, I get a whiff of his cologne. I cross my legs and pray to the gods I don't jump up and hump his leg.

"It's not a big deal." I say as I kick Blake under the table. "I guess it's only fair since I just interrupted yours. Also, I apologize for my friend here. Apparently, he doesn't know how to handle himself in public," I add as Blake gasps dramatically which makes Brent laugh. The sound could give angels their wings. Holy SHIT! I made him make that sound. Geezus!

"Thanks for stopping by, Brent," Blake says,

eyeing me cautiously.

"You guys have fun tonight. I hope to see you again, Gemma," Brent says as I turn to smile up at him before he turns to leave. His returning smile makes my heart skip a beat, and the breath I was holding rushes out. Blake stands up, gives his brother a hug and whispers something to him before he walks off. Blake sits back down, and I know that I should be courteous and stand to say goodbye as well. At the moment I just can't make my body do anything other than pant like a dog in heat.

"It was nice to meet you, Brent. I'm sure I'll see you around," I add breathlessly. Sweet Jesus did my voice crack too? Make it stop!

"I hope so," he adds as he turns to go. When he's out of sight I lean my forehead on the table and groan loudly.

"HOLY SHIT BALLS GEM," Blake bangs on the table rattling my forehead. "Are you kidding me right now? It was like he had to pry himself away to leave."

"Is it over? Is he really gone?" I ask as I groan into the polished wood of our table. Blake says my name, but I shake my head. "Sorry she's not home right now. Leave a message and she'll call you back," I laugh as he grabs a fist full of my hair, pulling my head up.

"He couldn't keep his eyes off you."

"I'm sorry," I whisper then take a large, unladylike swig of my cocktail. "God, what was that?" I ask as he smiles over at me. I'm saved from figuring it out because Blake's friends show up about that time. He leans over about halfway through dinner and squeezes my hand under the table.

"The conversation from earlier isn't over," he adds, and I roll my eyes. The hell it isn't. I hope we never talk about this night ever again.

A little after midnight I get up, giving everyone hugs and kisses even though Blake protests. It's already way past when I needed to be home. I push him away jokingly and tell him I'll call him tomorrow. The doorman hails a cab for me, and I hop in the back seat. I look down at my phone and already have a text from Blake.

Literally every man and woman in the restaurant was watching you as you left. Specifically, your ass in that dress, Gem. No wonder my brother was a mess over you.

You really did look divine tonight. Red is for sure your color.

Whatever Blake. I lost my head for a minute tonight. It won't happen again. Please know that I love you and only you!

I'm not at all offended Gemma. I know you love me. I know you didn't become friends with me for my brother. If you had, you would have stayed at his table tonight instead of doing the walk of shame to mine! LOL! I'm tempted to ask for the footage inside the restaurant tonight so I can see it for myself.

Jesus Blake. Don't remind me. Let me die in peace, please!

Kidding! Sweet dreams. Call me sometime tomorrow.

I've got dinner with the family Sunday night.

I can't wait to give Brent a hard time.

I'm sure he's home thinking about you right now!

You think he's having a HARD time too?

UGH! Will you stop! And please don't. Let's plan on getting lunch next week! I'm going to need the support! I'll be back in the office before you know it and everything will be back to normal! You'll see!

BORING! You know I don't do normal! And yes!

I'll have Helen make us a reservation since my 2nd assistant is too busy having fake sex with Dalton Calhoun!

God, I keep forgetting about that. You two together on the big screen is going to be hot! Can't Wait!

Good night Gem!

Good night!

Brent

I arrive home and nod to security as I come in. I used to not have security at the house, but I had a deranged woman break into my place one evening and since then it's been a necessity. I still have the vision of Blake's friend burned into my memory. She was the most stunning women I've ever met. There's just something about her that I can't shake. When the maître d' stopped at our table with her in tow I was speechless. It was adorable as hell the way she panicked. I'm not at all upset that my date was offended. She thought I'd had the interruption arranged because I had already told her that I wasn't interested in anything further than dinner. She was just telling me that she was hoping we could get together again but I declined. She wasn't pleased, but then she was really enraged when she thought I had another date on my calendar after her.

When I saw that the beautiful woman was with Blake, it was the first time I've ever been jealous of one of my brothers. Blake always has beautiful women on his arm, but this time was different. I could not stop stealing glances at her. Like was I really seeing someone this naturally beautiful in front of me? Was she all made up, yes, but not in the way I'm used to. Thick layers of make-up and plastic surgery shoved in my face. I've been traveling for the last two years, and I'm glad to be home for a while. I'm greeted by my golden retriever, Shadow, and I'm so glad to see him. As he's getting older, I don't travel with him as much as I used to. Luckily my schedule is clear for a while, so I'll be getting to come home to my boy more often. I have a trip the end of next week, but after that I'll be in town for a few months.

I head to strip out of my business attire for the night and hang up my suit jacket. It's getting quite warm in the evenings and even though I do enjoy the warmer weather, summer is my least favorite season in the states. For the most part I grew up in the highlands of Scotland, so I'm very much used to cold weather. I remember moving to the States with my parents when I was younger and being absolutely thrilled about the summer heat. It was a pool party every day. As I got older, I didn't have the time available to hang by the pool all summer since I was with my Da learning the business. I've really enjoyed taking over for my Da. There's so much I'm still learning and so much I'd still like to change or update with our company.

I pull on some athletic shorts and grab my phone to take up to the roof. I'm scrolling through social media when a picture of Gemma and Blake pops up on Blake's Instagram. I'm not on social media enough to know the ins and outs of Blake's friends. Most of the time I'm annoyed with them. The men normally want to get an in with business, maybe hoping I'll give them a job, a leg-up or something. They aren't as obnoxious as the women though. As Blake and I have gotten older it's gotten much better. He tends to surround himself with people who truly care about him and aren't using him to get to me. Tonight was the first night that a woman seemed shocked to run into me. It was quite refreshing. I don't play games with women, and I can't pretend that my interest hasn't been piqued.

I scroll through Blake's Instagram feed and smile at all the pictures of him and Gemma, some fairly recent. She has light brown hair in the photos, and I'm stunned. She was just as beautiful then as she is now with blonde hair. Her gorgeous sapphire blue eyes make my heart skip a beat in one of the pictures. She's in her pajamas, sitting in bed with Blake in his apartment. She has zero make-up on. I tap the picture and see that he's tagged her in the photo. Her account pops up as *Not Your Average Gem*. No last name, private account. I think about it for a minute and decide to text Blake. He's probably still out, maybe with her. It is getting late and maybe I can pass it off as checking to make sure they got home.

Hey Blake! You guys make it home okay?

What? It's like 12:30? The only personthat goes home earlier than you is Gemma.

I don't live in a retirement community Brent.

I'm not 90.

So I guess that means you are still out partying. Don't forget we have a 9:15 downtown tomorrow. You'll need to be bright and bushy-tailed. So don't stay out too long.

Thanks mum!

Oh shut up! I was just checking

on you!

Bull shit! You were wondering about Gemma and you know it. Do you want her number?

I'll see you in the morning Blake. Be Careful

Pathetic! Love you too!

Love you brat!

I put my phone down beside me and chuckle. Am I that obvious? Certainly I have more game than that. It has been a while since I've been in a relationship or with someone. I head down the elevator and decide to call it a night. As I'm laying in bed trying to fall asleep Shadow is snoring in the corner of my room in his dog bed. I can't stop seeing Gemma in that red dress. The way she turned around as she was walking away from my table and caught me checking her out. When our eyes met, I felt a crack in my rusty, jaded heart. A heart that's put love and relationships on the back burner for some time now. In that moment it wasn't just lust and attraction I felt towards her. It was something deeper. I was finding the situation incredibly humorous until she met my gaze and winked at me.

Something snapped in me. Something I don't really know what to name yet. But I do bloody plan on finding out.

Gemma

It's my last full week on set. Last week Blake came to support me, and it was so nice having him there with me. It was a closed set, due to the nature of what we were shooting, but he was able to be right outside when we wrapped. We spent hours in my trailer laughing and carrying on. He met Dalton, and I swear I've never seen Blake so taken by someone. Dalton really is incredible. I laughed at Blake for hours about his reaction to our "Frank Sinatra." He joked that the way he swooned over Dalton was how I swooned over Brent. That had me rolling and telling him it was a one-time encounter. I doubt I'll see Brent again for a while and next time I'll be prepared. No eye contact and for the love of God DON'T TOUCH HIM.

When we wrap the movie, I'm so thrilled to get back to normal everyday life. Shooting the biopic has all been very exhilarating but it's just not for me. I need more structure, and while it's been a wonderful experience, I'm in need of a break. I tell Blake he would thrive in the entertainment business because everything goes so late. I, on the other hand, like being in bed by 10 p.m. It's been nice having more money in the bank. I've been able to pay off some of my student loans and set a little aside to invest. Blake is supposedly going to help me figure out some investment plans.

Thursday afternoon I wrap early and see I've got 4 missed calls from Blake. I dial him back and he answers in a panic. "Oh, thank God!" Blake says dramatically and I roll my eyes. There's never a dull moment with this King.

"What's wrong?" I ask as the town car pulls up to my apartment. I thank the driver and get out. Blake is talking a mile a minute and I cannot understand a word he's saying. "Blake!" I interrupt and he pauses. "Buddy, slow down. What happened?"

"I said I've lost Brent's. Damn. Dog!" he yells, and I gasp.

"Who the hell would trust you with a live animal and how the hell did you lose his dog? You HATE anything that sheds! But also, why the hell are you watching Brent's dog? You don't even like animals! Which is still really freaking weird!"

"Seriously? This is the time you choose to have this conversation! I lost his dog and he's going to kill me!"

"Okay. Where are you?" I ask as I switch my phone to my other ear as he's busted the other one with his insistent yelling!

"In God-Forsaken Brooklyn!"

"Sweet Jesus, Blake. Like where in Brooklyn? It's not a small place!"

"I'm walking around outside Brent's apartment calling his stupid dog's name which I can't really remember since I don't like dogs! So, I don't know if I'm yelling the right name! It might be Arrow? Or maybe Shannon? They smell!" Blake says hysterically, and I want to laugh and strangle him at the same time!

"Do you see a street name?" I ask as I pinch the bridge of my nose. This is going to be the death of me. Knowing Blake, he's lost as well. "Can you drop a pin?" I ask and I can tell he is struggling. I take a deep breath and give him a minute. He drops a pin, so I walk to my car and head to the location Blake dropped.

It takes me about 10 minutes to get there, and when I do I find Blake sitting on the sidewalk with his face resting in his hands. I park on the curb and get out.

"He's going to kill me, Gem. He's been out of town this week and his normal pet sitter got like diarrhea halfway through or something. Probably from the dog. So, she called me, and I told her I could. He's never asked me to do something like this for him and now he never will."

"How long has the dog been missing?" I ask rubbing my hand over his arm to comfort him.

"An hour? Maybe a little less? I didn't put his leash on because I thought that he would stay with me. He's like really old. First thing that happened was he saw a damn cat and took off. You know I don't exercise well. I ran for a few blocks and then I lost him. I don't know what to do!"

"Did he leave a contact number for a vet in case of emergencies?" I ask as Blake looks at me, confused. "In case he got sick or injured? I'd leave it on a piece of paper. If I was him, I'd leave it on the fridge in the kitchen. Did you go inside and see if there was a vet's contact info up there?"

"Yea, but I don't have the damn dog, Gem. What's a vet going to do for me with no animal!"

"Seriously, Blake? Your brother is smart for not letting you pet sit for him. Is the dog microchipped?" I ask, and he shrugs his shoulders.

"I feel like you're starting to get political, and we need to like get back on track with the missing dog."

"Sweet Jesus, Blake. If the dog is microchipped, which the vet would know, then if the dog gets picked up, they'll check to see if he's microchipped. If he is it'll have Brent's information and they'll contact him to let them know they found him. Regardless if the vet or animal control picks him up."

"NOOOOO! Then Brent will know his pet sitter got sick and I'm watching him. Then he'll know I lost him!"

"Okay, at this point I think your brother would just want his dog found. Speaking of, what's the dog's name again?" I ask and he stands up.

"Shatter? Arrow, maybe? Shadow?"

"Oh my gosh! Let's just head to your brother's place so we can see if there's any information there that might help us. Can you at least get us back there?"

Blake starts leading me toward Brent's apartment. As we round the corner there's a guy in blue scrubs standing next to a golden retriever that is covered in mud. The guy looks like he just arrived, so Blake lets out a relieved breath and starts toward the man and dog in question.

"Are you Blake?" the guys asks as we get closer, and I smile. He's attractive in a scruffy mountain-man kind of way.

"I am! What the hell happened to you?" Blake asks the dog and I nod at the man as he waits for a response. "Where did you find him?"

"He was picked up about a mile from here and brought into the clinic. His microchip luckily had us listed as the emergency contact on top of Brent's information, so I thought I'd bring him back. We just got here. We didn't have time to give him a bath, but I figured you'd rather us bring him back this evening than leave him at the clinic overnight.

"Yes! Thank you," I say as the vet looks between Blake and I. He doesn't seem too keen on leaving the dog with us and I want to laugh. Probably not too far off. "We will clean him up."

"Yes," Blake says mirroring me. "Thank you so much for bringing him home. I promise we will do a better job next time!" *If there is a next time,* I want to say but decide it's better to keep that to myself.

"Call the office if you have any other issues. We have an answering service that will pick up at anytime, even if we aren't open."

"Yes sir," I answer, and the guy starts walking back around the corner. When he's out of sight Blake gives the dog a disgusted look.

"He stinks! Are we even sure that's mud?" he asks, leaning toward the dog and then backing away. "I think I may throw up!"

"Well let's give him a bath. That will for sure help with the smell!"

"We can't give him a bath at my brother's. He'll track mud everywhere. Brent has him groomed every other week. He'll know that something is up!"

"Well, we certainly can't leave him as he is,

Blake. Also, did you hear that thing about the microchip?"

"I did and shut up. We can fight about this later!" he groans and walks over to a set of garage doors. There are at least four of them and they span the entire side of the warehouse. He types in a code and the door closest to us begins to rise.

"What the hell?" I say as the dog and Blake start to walk inside. I hear Blake tell the dog to not touch anything and I have to laugh. I guess we are going inside. Blake grabs a leash from a drawer and secures it over the dog's head. "Oh! Now you put the leash on. Cool, cool!" A man steps out from an office looks us over and then down at the dog. He has a mind to keep his mouth shut, but he shakes his head and heads back into the office, closing the door.

"Shut up Gem, before I kill both you and the dog." We head up the elevator and I cannot believe he has an elevator. I mean sure he's the "King of New York" but are you kidding me? An elevator. We get out at the first floor and Blake takes the dog straight into one of the rooms on the main floor. I'm busy looking around at all the modern furniture when Blake yells my name. I walk toward his voice. I walk into a gorgeous bedroom. It's painted like the rest of the house in a light gray color. The furnishings and the bedding are all a darker or muted gray. I walk into the bathroom and there's a huge walk-in shower, and situated in front of the floor to ceiling window is a clawfoot tub. I smile, walking over and running my hand across the smooth surface. As I turn around Blake is standing there staring at me expectantly.

"What?" I ask as Blake is stands inside the glassed-in shower with the dog.

"I'm not giving him a bath. You can forget it. Brent can just kill me now. I'm not touching this dog."

"As ever, you are being so ridiculous and difficult! MOVE!" I say as I pull him out of the shower and take the leash off the dog. "Can you at least go find me some dog shampoo? I'm sure your brother has some somewhere. I'll start with washing the mud off him if you can find me some doggy shampoo."

"Is that a thing? They have specialty shampoos for dogs?" Blake asks as I turn the shower on and start to rinse off Shadow with the removable shower head. I've got his head cleared of mud when he shakes. Mud and water go everywhere, and I do mean EVERYWHERE. It's in my hair, eyes, clothes, you name it. I pause for a second and then look up at Blake who's howling with laughter.

"I'm so sorry, but if you could see you right now," he says trailing off. He looks at my face and decides it's probably best to go look for the damn shampoo. I finish washing the mud off of Shadow and then hold the shower sprayer over myself. Might as well. I have a change of clothes in my car but who the hell knows where I parked at this point. I'll figure it out later. For now, I'd like to be mud free. As expected, Blake is nowhere to be seen. I look down at Shadow, who's looking up at me with the same unimpressed expression.

"I hope that cat was worth it! Guess we're on our own bud," I say as I grab some shampoo from the shower and use it instead. It smells heavenly and I very much doubt that it's meant for dogs, but we don't really have many options here. Shadow is clean, but now I'm not. I decide to just go for it. I take off all my muddy clothes, tossing them in the corner of the shower. Then I tell Shadow to sit in the other corner and not to look at me. He does as he's told, and I laugh that he's better trained than most men I've been with. "Good boy," I say as I grab some shampoo and start washing my hair.

Brent

We pull into the garage, and as the doors are lowering, I release a deep, exhausted breath. I thank Paul for driving me back to the house and then start toward the elevators. My meeting ended early today, so I flew back tonight instead of tomorrow. That gives me a day to catch up on work for our New York office instead of working through the weekend. I step into the elevator and look down to see muddy tracks everywhere. Before the doors close, Paul places a hand on the doors and steps in.

"Sir, looks like your brother might have brought a visitor inside the house. Shadow looks to have had a field day in the mud." I groan and shake my head. Figures. I would never have asked my brother to pet sit, but my sitter got the stomach flu and after hearing from our vet earlier I figured things were out of hand. No surprise there. There's a reason I don't ask Blake to pet sit.

"Thank you, Paul. I can handle it from here. You said a visitor as well?" I ask and he nods.

"Unidentified female. They went into your master and that's the last I have eyes on them."

"Unbelievable. I'm sure there's no funny business, Paul. I'm sure it's fine and probably just a friend." I'm too tired for this shit.

"Are you sure?" Paul asks as I laugh and nod. Paul knows of Blake's sexual preference, so I know there's no funny business going on. He exits the elevator and I head to the first floor. When the doors open, I see it's just recently been mopped. At least he's taken care of his mess. I walk toward my bedroom and hear the water running. I'm assuming that means he's giving Shadow a bath, which is the least he should be doing. However, the laundry room is fitted with a tub specifically for Shadow, so why he didn't do it there is beyond me. Blake doesn't have a soft spot for animals like I do. I walk into my bathroom and it's steamy. I haven't seen anyone yet, so I'm assuming they are in my shower washing Shadow.

I open the door to my shower and almost jump out of my bloody skin. It's a soaking wet, and not to mention naked, Gemma. My mouth hits the floor. Bloody, Fecking Hell! I'm going to kill Blake.

"Holy Shit!" Gemma says as she tries to cover herself but there are not enough arms and hands to do so. I look away quickly so I can orient myself and see Shadow sitting in the corner clean as a whistle.

"Holy Shit!" I hear Blake say behind me and I want to strangle him.

"A word!" I grit out to Blake as I close the shower door leaving Gemma and Shadow to fend for themselves. I walk out of my bathroom, through my master bedroom, and into the kitchen. I'm so mad I could spit nails. I'm also extremely aroused by what I just saw and need to reel it in.

"It's not what you think!" Blake says defensively when we reach my large kitchen island.

"Not. What. I. Think!" I repeat as he has the decency to at least look embarrassed. "Blake, my vet called to tell me that someone had found my dog. Then I get home and see mud tracked all over the damn house. Thank you for cleaning that up at least. Then I walk into my bathroom, and not only is it not you giving Shadow a bath, it's Gemma giving Shadow a bath. AND she's completely naked! IN. MY. DAMN. SHOWER! With my damn DOG!"

"Okay, so maybe it is what you were thinking. Look, he got away from me earlier. Gemma, out of the kindness of her heart, met me to look for him. Then the vet brought him back covered in an inch of mud and we gave him a shower. I couldn't leave him covered in mud." Blake says, like I'm being unreasonable.

"WHY IS GEMMA NAKED?" I ask as I pinch the bridge of my nose.

"Well, the dog shook, and because it was her giving Shadow a shower the mud got all over her. So, I'm assuming she didn't want to be muddy either. So, she decided to have one as well? Two birds, one stone kind of thing?" I hear someone behind us clear their throat and I turn around and see Gemma wrapped in one of my towels. Jesus, Mary, and Joseph. I turn back around, and Blake has a sheepish look of amusement on his face.

"Sorry. I don't mean to interrupt, but Blake can I talk to you for a minute. NOW!" she grits out, and I almost laugh at the hilarity of all of this. Blake looks at me for help and I motion for him to go on. I can hear the two of them bickering in my room while I'm stuck out here in the kitchen. Blake comes out after a minute and says he's going to go try and find Gemma's car for her. He scurries out of the kitchen towards the elevator and now here I am stuck with the beautiful, and naked I might add, Gemma! She peaks her head out from my room and gives me a small, resigned smile.

"I'm sorry," she says, and I laugh. Dammit, she

looks amazing in my towel.

"What the hell?" I say as I look up to the ceiling. I look down at my watch and roll my eyes. "Let me get you a tee-shirt." I walk past her into my room and find my thickest tee-shirt and hand it to her. She thanks me and I can only nod in answer. I need to get the hell out of here. I hear her voice coming from my room and I know that she's speaking to me.

"We didn't plan this you know! Obviously, I was covered in mud, and it seemed like a good idea at the time to wash off. I promise I'll leave as soon as Blake brings me a change of clothes. My car is parked somewhere close, I hope."

"This has the stench of my brother all over it. I doubt you were involved in the main theatrics. I'm sure he will be back soon. If he isn't lost himself. DAMN HIM. Blake couldn't find his way out of a paper bag." I hear her giggle as she steps out of my room and walks towards the kitchen wearing only my shirt. My heart starts to beat a little faster, not only at the sight of her, but also her laugh is the sweetest sound I've ever heard. She sits on the stool next to mine and I admit I'm a little anxious. I can smell my shampoo on her, and I like it. "What do you think of my shampoo?" I ask, resigned.

"It smells amazing. I would have used the dog's shampoo, but Blake apparently never found any. Or he never looked. There's no telling with him!"

she adds with a small, annoyed laugh. I laugh too.

"He's a piece of work if ever there was one!" I add, and she smiles knowingly. "You know, when I said I was hoping to see you again, this is not exactly what I had in mind. Although, it is good to see you again." She smiles as she crosses her arms over her chest. I do keep my place fairly cool. So, I'm sure things are chilly when you are wet and only in a tee-shirt. Although it's starting to feel a little warm in here.

"I know! This isn't exactly how I envisioned our next run-in playing out," she says as she turns to face me. "Just my luck!"

"I do apologize for that. I didn't realize it would be you, naked, in my shower when I opened the door. At least I thought everyone inside would be fully clothed."

"One would think!" she adds sarcastically, and I chuckle to myself. "I do apologize for you finding me like that. I'm sure that's the last thing you were expecting to find in your shower. Even though you've probably had many naked women in there." I look over at her a little stunned, but I laugh anyway.

"I'm not sure whether to be offended or flattered?" I bark out and have to admit that she's being funny despite our current circumstance. I'm not sure what she thinks of me, but it's probably less women than she thinks. Not many women have come back to my apartment. Most of the women I've dated stayed with me at my apartment in Lower Manhattan. I haven't stayed there in a while. Brett, my youngest brother, is planning on moving into my old place later this summer. But I don't owe her a response even though I do find myself feeling a little defensive.

"How about we just forget about this part of the conversation and pray there's not a next time!" Gemma says as the elevator doors open, and Blake walks in with a small weekender. Gemma takes it from him and walks back into my bedroom. I imagine poor Shadow is still in the corner waiting to be let out. Blake looks over at my unamused expression and gives me a piss-poor job of a hopeful smile.

"Well, on a positive note you've now seen her naked. You know we are kind of working our way backwards but it's something, right? She's got a killer body, don't you think?" he asks as if I'm going to high five him or something.

"You are truly a nightmare sometimes, Blake. I don't even know where to start with you."

"I know! I'm sorry. This evening has been a nightmare for all involved." He didn't mean for any of this to happen anymore than Gemma did.

"Well!" I hear Gemma say as she walks out of my bedroom in a pair of shorts and a tee-shirt that isn't mine. She looks incredible, but I don't stare.

This is not how I saw my night playing out. "I think I've embarrassed myself enough for one night. I hope everyone in the room is okay if I get the hell out of here and go locate my car."

"I moved it. It's parked outside." Blake says timidly as Gemma looks at both of us and then takes her keys from Blake. "I'm sorry Gem!"

"No harm, no foul. I still have all my body parts and now everyone in the room can attest to that, since thanks to Blake, they've been on full display tonight."

"Thanks for coming out to help him, Gemma. I appreciate it!" Blake and I both watch her as she walks over to the elevator in silence.

"You know!" she adds as she turns around and looks at the two of us in the kitchen. "Things were going so well that I should have known something was bound to creep up and knock me back to reality!"

"Drive safe!" I add as she presses the down button for the elevator. I look over at Blake and he's watching her as well. Apparently, I'm not the only one mad at Blake. As the doors start to close, she yells, and my stomach feels like it's plummeted to the ground floor just as the elevator doors start to close.

"See you at work tomorrow, Blake!" she adds. It takes me a moment to process this, but I turn and see Blake is cringing. I slap him in the back of the head and swear I could punch him in the face, and I am not a confrontational person. I cover my mouth with my hand and want to escape my own body. I've never been this attracted this soon to anybody like I am to Gemma. And now I find she works for my company.

"OWW! What the hell was that for. I said I was bloody sorry!" he whimpers, and I walk out of the kitchen and into my bedroom to find Shadow. I'm now going to have to freaking blow dry him.

"See you at work?" I repeat as he lifts his head.

"Oh, so you did catch that last part!" Blake admits as he examines his fingernails.

"She works for us?" I ask, and he acts like it's no big deal.

"Yeah! What's the big deal? You just saw her naked," he responds, and I could throttle him!

"I can't!" I say as I walk away!

"What now? God, you are so emotional tonight!"

"Next time!" I say as I look behind me. "There's a dog bath in the laundry room. Use that instead of my bathroom and my shampoo. And GO HOME! I'll see you Sunday at Mum and Da's." Shadow is still in the corner of my shower, although he's now laying down. He looks up at me like he's in trouble when I open the shower door. He gives me his old puppy dog eyes, and I swear I haven't seen that look since he was a pup. I take him into the laundry room and begin the long process of blow drying him. This isn't what I expected to be doing tonight. I was hoping to order take-away and get into some comfortable clothing. At least I'll be able to sleep in tomorrow. I don't have to go into the office until Monday if I'm lucky.

Later that night as I'm winding down before bed, Shadow is nice and fluffed out on his dog bed snoring in the corner of my room. I'm channel surfing and the image of Gemma's wet and naked body in my shower comes to mind. I can still smell the mix of my shampoo and Gemma's skin. Her wet hair making a mark on the front of my tee shirt as we wait for Blake to return. I shake my head from those thoughts. No, I can't. She's an employee,

for Christ's sake. I need to lose that image forever. Easier said than done.

I make myself a drink. She works for me, and I'm extremely attracted to her. Not just her body but to HER. Her humor and the lightness that seems to be the vibe when she's around. I take a sip as I look out over the Hudson at lower Manhattan. The lights twinkle back at me. This view was the big seller for me when I was looking for a warehouse to buy. A view like this is worth millions. However, for the first time in a long time I feel very alone, and the person I want with me works for me. What the hell am I going to do?

Gemma

Friday evening Blake, Brianna and Helen take me out to dinner. We are at Perrone's. When I walk in it's the same hostess from the incident before. She recognizes me and takes me back to the table where everyone is waiting. Gosh I've missed them. We always have the best time. I get to catch up on what I've missed in the office, which is not much. Some client drama but we don't have a lot of drama in the uptown office. The real drama is the women in the Downtown office fawning and fighting over Brent. I laugh and Blake gives me a knowing smile. Brianna leans over to me and gives me a hug.

"We've missed you and that laugh of yours," she whispers, and I give her a kiss on the cheek.

"I've missed you guys as well. It was the opportunity of a lifetime, but I'm glad to be getting back to the real world next week."

"When does the movie come out?" Helen asks and I smile kindly at her.

"Not for at least another year."

We are talking late into the night when I feel like someone is watching me. I look over at the hostess stand and then scan the bar area. I spot Brent and a couple of friends having some drinks at the bar. He is surrounded by some "Upper East Side" type women. They are all really into him, but he doesn't seem to return their attention. He's not looking at me, but my god, even from here I can feel myself drawn to him. I'm mortified from the other night and haven't fully forgiven Blake for putting me in that situation. I'm not normally a person who takes herself too seriously or is embarrassed easily, but with Brent it feels different. One of the girls leans her head against his chest as he towers over most in his party by inches. He wraps his hand around her waist and leans down to whisper in her ear. She bites her lip and I become extremely aroused just watching them interact. What the HELL is wrong with me? I feel like he's whispering in *my* ear. I clear my throat and when I turn back towards Blake, he's got a conspiratorial smile on his face.

"What?" I ask and he shakes his head. "Did you know he was coming here tonight?"

"I did," he answers, taking a sip of his old fashioned. "I told him I had a hot date tonight. Dinner with business associates. He told me that he and some buddies were going to be up at the bar tonight. Some tennis or golf thing is on TV. He's also invited us to his place in the Hamptons for the 4th and I've accepted on your behalf." I've had one too many, but the thought of going to the Hamptons with Blake and his brother immediately turns my stomach. "Don't," he says, grabbing my hand. "It's going to be a fun weekend away with me. We will have the best time," he adds. We will. We always do. The thought of staying at Brent's though. Haven't I already humiliated myself enough?

"Thank you, but that's probably not the best idea," I say begrudgingly, and he squeezes my hand.

"Please! The other night is completely forgotten. Brent wouldn't have invited us if he was still sore over it."

"Am I at least staying in a room with you?" I ask, warming up to a weekend away with Blake but not completely sold.

"Umm… duh. I'm not leaving you with Brent's buddies. They're like vultures. If they haven't spotted you already they'll be swarming soon. I've already called the Queen Room at Brent's House. The house is big enough for us all to have our own bedrooms, but I told him I wasn't leaving you in a room by yourself. Just so you know he agreed that was a wise decision. He wouldn't let anything happen to you anyways. He'd beat the shit out of any guy who messed with you, and nowadays my brother is the least violent person I know."

"Why would he do that?" I ask, a little confused. I look back up and see Brent leaning down to listen to something the girl, in what I would call a micro mini skirt, is saying. Sensing that someone is watching him, his eyes lift and meet mine. I inhale as my heart skips a beat in my chest. I turn my attention back to Blake, but he's not looking at me.

"Please, Gemma. Regardless that he's already seen you naked, my brother has a good head on his shoulders. He's a stand-up guy. A true gentleman and don't you dare tell him I said that. Normally, I just give him crap, but you need to know what you're dealing with here. He's not going to let any of his buddies near you. He knows how guys are and how they think. Obviously, I wouldn't let that happen either, but I'm not as beefy as my brother. He hit me on the shoulder the other night, and I swear to God it left a bruise. I deserved it no doubt, but it still hurt. He's a strong dude." He turns his attention back to me and I feel a little down if I'm being honest. I don't understand why.

"Beefy?" I repeat and he laughs. "Your brother doesn't strike me as beefy."

"Really," Blake replies raising his eyebrows

and taking a sip of his drink. "How does my brother strike you?" he asks. I start to respond, but someone else beats me to it.

"I'm kind of curious to see how this conversation plays out," Brent says from behind me. I close my eyes and will myself not to do anything embarrassing tonight.

"Brent! Enjoying your sausage-fest tonight?" Blake prods as Brent swats him away. "See?" Blake adds as Brent slides into the chair across from me.

"Please continue," Brent says playfully to me. Blake throws back the rest of his drink. He lifts his empty glass to the waiter. Brent has already caught me staring at him. How much worse can it get?

"Guess I'm staying at your place tonight," I say as Blake shrugs his shoulders. He's already had too much to drink. I look over at Brent who's waiting patiently for my response. "I was merely disagreeing with your brother. He called you beefy," I answer, but I have a hard time holding his gaze.

"Beefy? In what world am I beefy?" He asks in disbelief to Blake, who seems bored with our conversation.

"Compared to me," Blake answers, taking a sip of his new drink.

"That's true," Brent and I say at the same time, looking at each other and then laughing. It's a harmonious noise. Blake is smiling into his drink, and I knock the bottom of his drink, so the ice cubes slam him in the face. He gasps for air like I've drowned him.

"And you were going to say I strike you as what?" Brent asks and I blush. I trail my finger down the side of my cup and then look up at Brent. I'm not sure how I'd describe Brent, to Brent.

"I was going to say something more elegant than beefy? Maybe more masculine?" He smiles at me and places his hand on my wrist. It feels electric but warming at the same time. I look down at his hand and then into his eyes. I bite my lip because I can't help how almost sexual the conversation has turned. I know I'm over my head with him. He has a magnetism that I've never experienced, ever. I feel like this could mean big trouble for me.

"I was kidding. Not trying to put you on the spot but thank you. Your answer is better than beefy," he answers in return. His voice is a little hoarse and I clear my throat as well. We stare at each other for a hot minute and then he snaps out of his apparent stupor. He taps the table a few times and then stands up. "Alright you two. Enjoy your night. Blake, please give Gemma my cell phone in case you end up getting too drunk tonight. You already look like you've had enough. I'm sure this will piss you off, but you need to be more careful, bud."

"I'm fine. Gemma is going to take me home. Don't be jealous brother," Blake slurs as I laugh. I cover my mouth and then remember I've probably had too much to drink as well.

"I can't drive! Remember you were supposed to be the DD tonight," I say as Brent looks from me to Blake and then sits back down. He grabs the stir straw out of my empty drink and puts it in his mouth. I look down at his full lips and then over to an empty table near us. "Don't worry about me. I'll get a cab back to my place. In my defense we were supposed to be celebrating me tonight," I add as Brent smiles. Blake gets up and heads towards the restroom but not before he lets out a ginormous belch. I roll my eyes but then fix them back on Brent.

"What are you guys celebrating?" Brent asks as he takes the straw out of his mouth. I try hard to focus. I'm buzzed for sure but being around Brent is also a heady experience.

"I've wrapped my part in a film," I answer, not knowing if he knows what I've been doing.

"I've heard about that. Blake told me about the biopic. Congratulations," he adds genuinely as I take another sip. I look back up at the bar and see a few females that are pissed that I've stolen Brent's attention. He turns around to see what I'm looking at and waves at the girls. They've all changed their facial expressions after he turns back around.

"Looks like I've pissed off some of your lady friends."

"Lady friends? Maybe a few, but also some of their expressions just look like that normally." I giggle and then cover my mouth. Brent has a grin on his sexy face that says he's enjoying this a little too much.

"Look, this happens a lot. I'm sure we will end up walking to Blake's. I stay there a lot after nights out with him. Don't tell him, but he snores when he's drunk so sometimes it's good to have a lot to drink to I can sleep too. It happens enough that I leave clothes at his house just in case." I sigh and Brent grins at me. He seems happy with my answer. One of his buddies comes over and pats him on the back saying they're heading out. He introduces me and then turns back to face me.

"I'm glad my brother has someone like you in his life. He deserves to have good friends," he adds as Blake comes back to the table and plops down gracelessly.

"Well don't we all look cozy tonight. And look, everyone has their clothes on! Don't hate me, Gemma," Blake says, looking ruefully at me. "I might have made an uh-oh."

"What did you do?" Brent and I say at the same time, looking at each other and then back at Blake. I'm sensing a trend here.

"I called Corey," he whispers loudly across the table. I groan and so does Blake. "I know! I know! But I had to, I couldn't help it. Forgive me," he adds as he reaches across the table, taking my hand in his. "Just add it to the list of things I need forgiveness for."

"I always forgive you, but you're going to hate yourself tomorrow. Is he coming to your apartment or are you going to his?" I ask as Brent watches us slightly entertained.

"He's coming to pick me up here," he answers as I finish my drink in one gulp. I put it down and then lift my hand up to the waiter. He comes by and I ask for the check. Blake and Brent both start to protest, but I put my hand up, stopping them. "You don't want to mess with her when she gets into 'Miranda Priestly' mode. She'll eat you alive. Which you might actually enjoy," he doesn't get to finish his sentence because I turn to look at him. He closes his mouth and when the waiter comes by, he quickly hands him his business credit card. "Celebratory dinner. Sorry Miranda, you can spank me later!"

I sit back and pull my phone out. I need to call an Uber. "By the way you are more Miranda Priestly than I am, and you know it!"

"Don't even think about it," Blake argues taking my phone away. "I will call you a town car. You aren't getting an Uber at this time of night alone to Brooklyn!"

"You live in Brooklyn?" Brent asks and I nod my head. "Did I know this?"

"Outskirts," I add, and he grins.

"I hate to say it, but my brother is right. You don't need to call an Uber. I'll drop you off on my way home. I have to make a stop first, but if you don't mind, I can drop you off after. Obviously, you know where I live." He adds and I feel myself blush. He winks at me, and I cringe internally. I start to open my mouth to protest but Blake interjects before I can.

"That's a wonderful idea. I'm surprised I didn't think of it first," Blake interrupts. "Don't be mad sugar tits! I really am sorry. I'll make it up to you! Hey I know! How about a trip to the Hamptons over the 4th? That sounds like a fun time, right?" He laughs, and I groan. Blake looks down at his phone, and I give him a nasty look. "Oh. He's here. I'll call you tomorrow! Thanks Brent!" Blake floats out of the restaurant without a care in the world. I know tomorrow he will be hating himself… for more than one reason.

"Sugar tits?" Brent asks aloud as I laugh.

"Wow. So, this night has taken a turn. My car is in the parking garage." I say as he nods.

"It's probably safer there. Let's head out. I'm going to say goodnight to some friends and then we can leave." We walk over to the bar, and I meet a couple of Brent's friends. A few are attractive, and the other half look like they've seen better days. A few girls are kind, but the others are forgettable.

Brent leans down, kissing a few of their cheeks and I could melt from jealousy, and I have no idea why. He's my boss! Well, maybe my boss's boss? I feel Brent's hand on the small of my back as he escorts me seamlessly through the restaurant and even through my clothes, I can feel a powerful connection between us. We walk out to the valet and pass the hostess on the way out. She does a double take, smiling at me and I shake my head.

"It's not what you think!" I say hoping to correct the narrative, and she smiles. It looks like I finally got myself a King. Which is not at all what's happening.

"None of my business," she whispers towards me as the car pulls up and Brent comes back inside for me. He really is quite the gentleman. He helps me into the passenger side of his Aston Martin, and I relax into the buttery seat. He slides in with a grace and elegance I know I don't possess. His long, muscular frame folds right into the seat like it was custom made for him. Which it probably was.

"How are you feeling?" he asks, and I laugh.

"I'm good. Not going to puke in your million-dollar car if that's what you were worried about?" I retort, and he laughs in response.

"That's not why I was asking. I was curious to how you were feeling. You seemed pretty pissed at Blake back there."

"Not pissed. Just disappointed. He deserves

better than Corey. I do like Corey, I just don't like them together. I think there are better men out there for him. I just wish Blake saw it that way," I add, and he looks over at me with a contented expression.

"I 100% agree with you. I don't really know Corey that well. He seems like a good guy. Blake will always deserve better in my book."

"Thank you for the ride, Brent. I hope it's not too far out of your way," I add as he looks over at me while we are at a red light.

"It's not!" he reassures me. "I'm happy to drop you off. I have to make a quick stop to my old place to leave something for my brother Brett to pick up. You sure you're okay with that?"

"Of course, you're the one driving. I'm just sorry you have to make an extra stop on your way home."

"It's no problem. It's not too far. How long have you been living in Brooklyn?" he asks.

"Since I graduated from NYU. I'm really in between Brooklyn and Queens. I stayed on campus for most of those years but then moved in with some friends after I graduated. I've only been at my apartment for a year or so. Both of my roommates are flight attendants, so they travel a lot. It's mainly me by myself a lot, which is an absolute perk. How about you?"

"I bought an old four-story warehouse when I

graduated from law school. About 10 years ago. I gutted it and little by little started to renovate it. Brooklyn is more of my style. I love the city, but I also love getting out of it."

We pull up to a high rise and park right out front. A valet comes around the car as Brent grabs something from his glove compartment before he gets out. He comes around to my side and opens the door for me. I get out and realize that I'm going in with Brent. A few people smoking outside look at Brent and I while I try not to make a big deal of it. This looks a lot different than what it is, but I need to learn that I don't have to explain myself to perfect strangers.

As we walk to the elevators, Brent places a hand on my back, and I let out a small whimper. He looks down at me, but I don't dare look at him. My body is betraying me and I don't know where I lost control. The doors to the elevator close, and I look over to Brent who's staring straight ahead, but also holding back a smile. By the time we arrive on the 11th floor I'm giggling. Brent shakes his head, and I have to admit that I'm in way over my head. He's literally dropping something off and then dropping me off. I'm such a dork.

The doors open to a beautiful entryway, and when I step inside, I can hear the doors close behind me. I know that we aren't here for any funny business, but I'm still very aware that he's close behind me. He whispers he'll be right back, and I walk straight ahead to the floor to ceiling windows. The view is incredible from up here. I've always felt so drawn to the lights of Manhattan, and it feels like I'm in the middle of it all, but at the same time safely away. I can hear Brent moving around in what I'm guessing is the kitchen. I turn around and he's holding up a bottle of champagne. I grin and nod my head.

"You don't mind?" I ask as I walk over towards the kitchen.

"I don't mind at all. It's been in here for a while."

"Were you saving it for one of your lady friends? I'm sorry if I put a damper on your plans," I add as he lets out an unguarded chuckle and I feel like I could fly if I wanted to.

"No. I had no prearranged plans for tonight. Actually, I'm grateful for that," he answers, and I blush. I'm a little tipsy but a lot turned on by him. I need to rein it in. He hands me a glass and I thank him. I walk back to the window.

"It's so beautiful up here. You could get lost taking it all in."

"It is beautiful. It's why I haven't had the heart to sell it. However, the view at night from my place in Brooklyn is better," he says, and I shake my head.

"I can't imagine anything more beautiful than this," I say taking a sip from my champagne flute. "This is amazing," I add, lifting my drink toward Brent.

"It's my favorite, and there's more where that came from, but I'm thinking maybe we should stick to this bottle and then head home," he adds, and I get a giddy feeling thinking of going home with Brent. What would that be like? To be romanced by Brent. I look over at him and he has his hand in his pocket looking out over lower Manhattan. He looks like he could get lost from the view as well.

"You're too much, Brent. I imagine no woman has a chance when it comes to you," I state as I take another sip of my champagne. I place it down as I look around his apartment, if you can even call it that. It's the nicest place I've been in in New York, nicer than Blake's place.

"I'm curious, Gemma. How am I too much?" he asks. Okay, we are going to go there. I've already bitten off more than I can chew, and he knows it.

"This!" I say, gesturing around his place. It's backlit and everything up here feels so amplified. "The view, the champagne, this apartment, YOU!"

"Whoa, whoa, whoa!" he says placing his champagne next to mine. He has an intrigued look on his face, and I feel like he's being honest. He has no idea. "I promise you I had to drop something off. You saw me pull the packet from my glove compartment. What was I going to do, leave you in the car?"

"I know!" I say as I go to pick up my champagne flute, but he grabs my hand first.

"Tell me," he asks as I look up at his beautiful face, and not only is he sincere he really doesn't have a clue. He releases my hand and looks down at me. I grab my champagne flute and turn back towards the window.

"I can't imagine anyone standing a chance against your charms, and you're not even trying." I answer, but I don't turn to look at him even though I can feel his eyes on me. "This place is a chick-magnet. I'm not the kind of girl to get swept away, but I'm sure this place works wonders on the masses of hopeful misses. Don't get me wrong, I know you're not trying to impress me. But you are."

"What? I am what?" he chuckles as he takes a sip of his drink. He sits on the edge of the chair near me. He could reach out a hand and touch me, he's that close. I know he's waiting for me to turn around, but I don't know if I'm ready yet.

"Impressive!" I answer as I turn around and lean my back against the window. I grin over at him and he shakes his head. "Don't get too cocky, Mr. King. I'm not that kind of girl. Well, that's not completely true. I'm not a hopeful miss though. I'm just saying that I'm sure this place holds top score for sealing the deal," I say, using air quotes.

I really shouldn't be allowed to drink and air quote at the same time. Blake tells me all the time I don't do them at the right time or I use them too much.

"Sealing the deal? Gemma, we are even talking about the same thing?" he asks laughing.

"Maybe?" I ask, now confused about where I was going with this.

"I feel like maybe we're heading in territory we shouldn't," he adds as he refills our glasses.

"Why? Because I'm right? Or is it because you're my boss?" I ask as he stands up and laughs. I finish off my champagne and hand him my empty flute. We are close. So close that I can see some scruff on his face. I can't look away though, and neither can he.

"Neither," he answers before he turns around and heads back to the kitchen. I join him in and lean against the counter. "I am your boss, but that would never keep me from having a conversation with you. This place was a bachelor pad for me 10, 15 years ago. I'm not that guy anymore, and I don't want you to think I brought you up here for any other reason than to drop something off. I offered you champagne because it's my favorite and I thought you might like it. I would like to get to know you better, Gemma, but it's a weird position for me to be in because you do work for my company."

"I don't think you brought me up here to woo

me. I was trying to point out that you don't have to," I add as he places the cleaned champagne flutes on the counter to dry. He turns around and rests against the kitchen counter next to me.

He turns to make deliberate eye contact with me. "If I was trying to woo you Gemma, you would know." I'm utterly speechless. He's looking down at me as I look up at him. He could lean down and kiss me, but he won't. "How did you work for us for over a year, and I never saw you? I know I would remember your face."

"I like blending in," I say as he moves a hair behind my ear. He smiles as he looks down at my lips and then back into my eyes.

"We should probably head out. It's getting late. Blake says you're an early bird like me," he adds, laughing. My answering laugh echoes through the mostly empty apartment. He's not wrong.

"Just because I turn into a pumpkin at midnight doesn't mean I'm less of a person, Brent," I joke as he chuckles behind me. As we leave, I turn around to take it all in. You never know the next time you'll be in such luxury. We make it back down to the lobby, and there are so many people down here. It's after 11 p.m., and I can't believe most of these people are just now going out on the town. "I'm not ashamed to be in bed at a reasonable hour Brent. If I'm keeping you from a party, just let me know. I could go back upstairs and sleep on the couch until you're done."

"Hell no," has answers as we take off toward Brooklyn. "Nothing good happens after midnight!" he adds, and I grin. My sentiments exactly. "Plus, despite what you've alluded to tonight, I'm too much of a gentleman to make a lady sleep on my couch."

I keep my unladylike response to myself, and we drive in silence for a while.

"What's your address?" I give him my address, and he plugs it into his GPS system.

We pull out into traffic, and I know I should be more embarrassed by where our conversation has gone tonight, but for some reason I'm not. As we're getting closer to Brooklyn a part of me is screaming to get out of the car. The other part of me is wishing the drive took a little longer. It's a crazy mix of wanting to spend more time getting to know Brent, but also feeling out of my element.

"About the other night," I say as he tries to speak at the same time. I laugh and so does he.

"Go ahead," Brent says as I bite my fingernail.

"I'm sorry about the other evening. Me, naked, in your shower," I add as I turn in my seat to face him.

"There's no need to apologize. I was going to say no hard feelings. I wanted to kill my brother, but I know you were only there to help him. He'll never pet sit for me but that has nothing to do with you."

"Plus, I also didn't think I'd run into you so quickly afterwards. I thought you'd have time to forget before we saw each other again," I add as we pull up to a red light. He turns to look at me.

"I didn't think so either, but I have to say I'm not that upset about it," he grins mischievously, and I can see how alluring he would have been back in his playboy days. "And as for the other thing, that's not something so easily forgotten."

"What? Running into each other so this soon?" I ask sarcastically. "Or me naked in your shower?"

"Both! If I'm being honest," he adds with a light chuckle, then turns back to look at the road as the light turns green. We sit in silence for a few minutes. Him smiling and me trying not to.

"How long have you had your place in the Hamptons?" I ask, breaking the silence.

"I bought the place about eight years ago. A friend of mine had asked if I wanted to go in on a place. I agreed, and then we had a pretty nasty falling out. He ended up backing out, and I purchased the place for myself. I go up there a couple times a year. I lend it out to other business partners and associates who want to take friends or clients on golfing trips or a weekend away. It's come in very handy for more than one reason."

"I'm sorry about the falling out with your

friend." I interject as I feel we are treading on a sensitive subject.

"I'm not. He was sleeping with a girl I was seeing seriously at the time. I tried to make it work, but it became too difficult to navigate." I snap my head back in his direction. What kind of idiot would cheat on Brent King?

"That sucks, I'm sorry. What an idiot," I add, and then wish that hadn't come out. He laughs, and I'm pressed back into my seat a little more as he accelerates. "I hope I didn't bring up any painful memories for you."

"Not your fault. It was difficult at the time, but my heart has healed, and I've found better friends. Plus, he saved me from a lot of heartache in the end. At the time I thought she might be 'the one'," he says using air quotes while we are stopped at another red light, and I smile sadly.

"Ah, the fated one," I whisper looking over at him.

"Have you ever had any big heart breaks?" he asks, and I wonder how much to disclose. I sigh and look back over at him. He's so easy to talk to, and he looks genuinely interested, so surprisingly I go all in.

"Honestly, no. I've never given anyone the opportunity to break my heart. I didn't grow up seeing healthy relationships. My mom died when I was little. I don't really remember her. My father didn't have conventional relationships. He had a lot of flavors of the week and a month-long tryst here and there. I decided a long time ago to forgo relationships. It seemed easier at the time. So far, it's worked in my favor. Some people would disagree, your brother being one of them. He seems to like falling in love. I, however, don't relish the idea of giving someone that much control over my emotions," I add with a little laugh. It's silent for a moment, and when I turn to look at him, he's watching me with an unreadable expression. The person behind us honks, and he returns his attention back to the road.

"I'm sorry, Gemma. About your mom," he adds as we get closer to my apartment. "I can't imagine how hard that must've been." I want to change the subject. Kind of wishing I hadn't doled out all that information about myself. "You're right. Sometimes not doing relationships has its benefits, but sometimes not so much."

"It's all good. I've made it this far on my own. Also, why is your Scottish accent so much stronger than Blake's? Not that I'm complaining. I could listen to you talk all night long," I add.

"I spent more time in Scotland growing up than Blake did. He's been in America a lot more than I have. I left after what you call middle school to head back to Scotland for schooling, my choice. I didn't come back until after I'd finished law school. I did my internships during the summer in New York, and at the time my Da had some international offices. I had my choice to stay there instead of coming back to New York. Although I did come back at times. I love Scotland. Have you been?" I laugh, shaking my head. Do I look like someone who would have traveled to Scotland?

"I've never even been out of the country. I have a passport. I had to in college to apply for some of the internships I wanted. However, I've never been west of the Mississippi."

"Well, I need to talk to Blake about that. He needs to take you on some trips," he says as we pull up to my apartment. He places a hand on my arm, stopping me as I reach for the door. "Wait one second," he gets out of the car and comes around to open my door. No one has ever done that for me. I close my eyes for a second, appreciating and soaking in the moment. What a gentleman, and he's done this twice tonight. He takes my hand, helping me out of the car and then closes the door, walking with me to the apartment entrance. I put my key in the door to the lobby and turn around, putting my hand out.

"Thank you, Brent. I hope it wasn't too far out of your way," I say as he smiles and takes my hand. We are both looking down at our hands clasped together, and we both stop laughing. When our eyes meet, it almost looks like he's trying not to laugh but also finding the moment intriguing. "I keep thinking I've embarrassed myself enough around you. Then I do something stupid like get drunk, and the owner of the company I work for has to drive me home. Then I shake his hand like I've just closed a business deal."

"Just sealing the deal, Gemma?" he jokes, winking at me, and I roll my eyes.

"I worry about what I'll do next!" Like invite him up for a "night-cap" or more?

"Everything's fine, Gemma. Have a good night and please take care of yourself." I look up into his eyes, and there's some silent promise hidden there. Something that tells me that maybe I'm not the only one that might want to get to know the other more. I reluctantly release his hand and turn around, unlocking my door. My hands are jittery, but I finally get the door open. I don't even bother turning around. I'm partially embarrassed at myself for putting my hand out for him to shake, but also in shock at how he made me feel. He never made me feel stupid. I feel like I'm heading towards dangerous territory here. Next time I need to insist on getting a cab. When I'm inside my apartment, I walk over to my window and peek between the blinds. I hear his car pull away and can feel it reverberate deep in my bones. That car was something else. I could have melted in those buttery seats. I have no problem falling asleep, and I dream of Brent King.

Brent

The entire week is a blur. I go between wanting to get Gemma's number from Blake and wanting to throttle myself for even considering crossing a professional line. Yes, she works for our company, but at the same time something feels so different with her. The way we can just speak and it's like we haven't just met. She's so funny and light-hearted, but I can tell that beneath the surface there's more than what she's projecting. Blake called me all in a tizzy about what they needed to pack and wear for the weekend. I hope he didn't make Gemma panic. She's perfect, regardless of what she packs. I haven't invited anyone who wouldn't welcome Gemma with open arms. I've been lucky in my friendships. As I've grown older,

I've learned what true friendship looks like, and I hope I can be that for her. By Wednesday I'm about to kill Blake. He has lit my phone up all week about the itinerary and he needs to chill out.

Thursday, everyone starts to arrive at the Hamptons House after lunchtime. I've got a large spread of sandwiches and appetizers so people can eat as they arrive and settle in. The master and the "Queen Room," as Blake calls it, are on the main floor. The other five bedrooms are spread between the_second and the_third floors. There's an open-concept kitchen that connects with the living space. What really sold me on the house was the floor to ceiling windows in the back of the house. When you open the front door, you can see the ocean immediately. There's a heated pool in the backyard and lots of space to entertain. I've got baskets of goodies and bath & body supplies for Blake and Gemma to enjoy in their room. I really wanted to make sure that both Gemma and Blake have a good time.

Most everyone is lounging by the pool or sitting on the deck drinking when Gemma and Blake arrive. I meet them inside, hugging them both before Blake runs outside to greet Elaine. She spotted him and it's been a while since they've seen each other. Gemma looks up at me with excitement in her eyes, and I have to say it makes me feel so good to be the recipient of it.

"Can I take your bag?" I ask, and she smiles at

me in awe as she takes in her surroundings. I take her weekender and show her where she'll be staying for the long weekend.

"Wow," she gasps, walking towards to the French doors that are open to the backyard. "This is incredible. I'm guessing all your places have deal-sealing views."

"If you say so," I joke back at her. "Would you like a tour?"

"I'd love that!" I show her around, and when we make it back to the main floor, we walk out back. The wind whips Gemma's hair around. "God this place is so beautiful. How are you able to leave?"

"I know. It's hard, but there's work to do and someone's got to do it." She and Blake head into their bedroom so I give them space and head out back to join my friends.

About an hour later they come out in their bathing suits. My breath leaves my chest when I see Gemma in a bathing suit. It's not even a tiny bikini like I'm used to seeing women wear around the pool. It's some kind of one-piece. It has one strap on her shoulder and a cut out in the center and the back. She's got a matching headband on keeping her hair out of her face and I smile when our eyes connect even, though she's wearing sunglasses. She looks like she's stepped out of a James Bond movie. I walk over once they are situated on one of the double loungers. They apologize for oversleeping, but I could care less.

"No need to apologize. I'm glad you're enjoying yourselves." I can tell her eyes are roaming over my body, and I let her take all of me in. I look over at Blake, but he's already back asleep. "Let me know if you need anything."

I walk back over to where most of the crew is hanging out, and my buddy Hugo bumps my shoulder as he's grabbing another beer.

"So, is she single?" he asks, looking over at Gemma. I smile to myself because I knew this was coming. I'd be asking the same question if I was him. I shake my head.

"Not sure. I think she's single, but she's not here for you, Hugo. She's here to hang out with Blake and enjoy a relaxing weekend away from the city.

"Oh, she'd enjoy herself. You can damn well count on that for sure." I turn to face him, and he takes a step back after seeing my expression.

"I'm not kidding, Hugo. She's not here to be messed with. Leave her the hell alone. I'm sure you'll find someone to warm your bed soon enough while you're here, but it's not going to be with her."

"Oh. Someone's a little touchy about the new girl," he whispers knocking me with his elbow. "I've got you, boss! I'll keep the others away." I'm dead set on them having a good time, and one of the ways I can do that is by ensuring that the guys leave her alone. An hour later Gemma and Blake are laying on their stomachs talking. Philip comes up to me, and I roll my eyes and shake my head.

"NO!" I say more sternly than I mean to, so he hands me another beer. We've got a long weekend to go. Blake gets up to get something to drink and approaches me.

"Gemma's pretty hot, huh? I know you've already seen her naked, but she fills out a suit like she was meant to wear them," he says, grabbing a bag of chips from the table and opening it. "You're used to women trying to impress you with a thread bare two-piece. It's pretty spectacular when one can wow you with a full suit on, don't you think?"

"Hot?" I repeat, trying the word out to describe Gemma. "I'd say she's stunning or beautiful. I've been approached by every male in the vicinity so far inquiring about her. I'm glad you guys are rooming together."

"Wow, stunning and beautiful. I like it. What's for dinner tonight, big daddy?" he asks, laughing.

"We're grilling chicken and shrimp tonight. Everything is in the downstairs fridge. I'll probably start prepping here in an hour. I'm not sure the crew will make it too late tonight. Most everyone here is already drunk. How are you feeling?"

"I feel great! I wonder who will make an ass of themselves first tonight? Hugo?" he says knowingly, and I laugh. Gemma looks over at us, and I smile at her.

"For sure it'll be Hugo," I answer as Blake, and I clink our drinks together.

I head in a little early to shower so I can change into some shorts and a button-down shirt for dinner. I roll my sleeves up as I start to prep dinner downstairs in the kitchen. Gemma comes in, asking if she can help, and I shake my head. She's in her bathing suit, so I try to focus on what I'm doing.

"No, I'm good. Go enjoy yourself, Gemma. You don't need to help cook."

"I know I don't need to do anything. I enjoy being in the kitchen. My apartment has the smallest kitchen, so I don't get to cook often. This kitchen has nothing on your lower Manhattan apartment, but I guess it will do," she laughs, and I shake my head. That feels like forever ago that we were there drinking champagne and she was calling me out. "How about this? I'm going to go shower, and then when I'm done, I'll help if there's anything left to do." She looks so happy with her idea that I don't dare take that away from her.

"That sounds great. Thank you, Gemma."

About 20 minutes later she comes out in a short blue seersucker dress. The mere sight of her makes my heart skip a beat as I take her in. She has very little makeup on, and her hair is recently dried. She smells like a dream. Vanilla with a hint of cinnamon. I'm making the chicken and shrimp skewers. Now that I have everything chopped, Gemma helps me assemble the skewers. Blake comes in a couple minutes later. He turns on some music and starts dancing around the living room, making both Gemma and I laugh. He comes around the counter and starts dancing inappropriately behind me so I kick him away.

"I know you can't tell from my brother's tight-ass persona, but he be a lot of fun. He can dance, he can sing AND from what I hear his dancing skills translate into the bedroom," Blake says as he shimmies himself into their bedroom. He kicks his bathing suit off into the hallway, making Gemma laugh. When I glance over at her she rolls her eyes.

"He's a hoot when he's drunk," she adds, skewering some veggies.

"He's something, that's for bloody sure," I interject. "He's full of himself even when he's sober, and despite what my idiot of a brother thinks, he knows nothing about my sex life," I add.

"He says a lot of things. He also said we were going to pace ourselves this weekend. I think you and I are the only two people not currently drunk."

"That's probably an accurate assumption," I agree as I place my skewer on the tray.

"So, is it not true then?" She asks as she continues to skewer veggies. I grin back, and curious to where her line of questioning is heading.

"What part of his statement are you referring to, Gemma?" I ask, moving to the sink and washing my hands. I hold up the soap, and Gemma joins me over the sink so I can put some in her hands. She washes her hands as I cover the skewers, placing them back in the fridge for later. I still need to go out and start up the grill.

"All of it," she answers.

When I turn around, she leans her hip against the counter facing me, and I lean back against the counter staring back at her. I can tell part of her is joking, but I'm curious if part of her is a little curious as well.

"Well. I've never had any complaints. About my dancing, singing or otherwise," I answer, grinning at her as she dries her hands. "I mean, it's hard to review myself. That would be kind of weird, don't you think? I don't have a Yelp account or anything to show you for reviews," she giggles, and I love that sound. She's so sweet.

"That's good to know. Do you need any more help?" she asks, and I see a sparkle in her eyes. Like maybe she's asking for something more than what she's actually asking. I'm not sure, but I shake my head to be safe. I need to be careful with her. Like me, she's a flirt. We could get into a lot of trouble if we aren't careful. There's nothing more I'd like than to kiss her. I'm not so sure she'd be averse to it either. I know she doesn't do relationships, and nowadays I'm a relationship only kind of guy. She turns and walks back to bedroom. I turn toward the door and see Hugo, Philip and Rhodes watching me with knowing grins.

"It's a good thing your brother's gay," Hugo says in his Texas drawl. "I think you'd kick your own brother's ass if he wasn't. I think our boy here likes her!"

"I give it 24 hours," Rhodes says in his Boston accent. "I'm not surprised he hasn't told Gemma he went to Harvard. That's normally what he leads with. I can already see how the weekend could play out." Hugo is drunk, but he might be right. There's just something about her. When she's in the room I can't keep myself from finding her. Hugo isn't known for being able to hold his liquor or beer. He's not a lightweight by any means, but even he has his limit. Once he reaches it, it's all downhill from there. They all stumble upstairs, and I smile at their retreating backs.

Gemma

My God, I had to walk away. He's starting to get under my skin, and I have to admit I like it. A lot. I smile at myself in the mirror as I fix my hair. I only dried it so I could get out to the kitchen to help Brent. I really wanted to be in that kitchen. It's fantastic. All-white, beach themed kitchens are a dream. The house is so tranquil and relaxing. Blake comes out of the bathroom as I'm curling my hair and smiles mischievously at me.

"How do you know your brother is good in bed, you weirdo?" I ask as he burst out with a giggle. I wonder if he even remembers he said that. It looks as if the shower sobered him up a little.

"I'm not sure you want to hear this, but a couple of my friends have slept with my brother. It's rare but there have been times when our social circles have overlapped. I've slept with a couple of my brother's friends. No one here this weekend, thank God, but it happens. The ladies have all been very vocal about my brother's talents in the bedroom." He clears his throat, and I give him disgusted expression.

"They say those things in front of you?" I ask, and he nods. "I can't imagine. That's so freaking weird."

"It can be, but I mean we're both adults, and we can be and do whatever and whoever we please. I'm not friends with any of the women he's been with anymore, and I'm not sure my brother is friends with any of the guys I've slept with. It's hard to be friends with someone who's actively screwing your sibling. Especially when they were never interested in being your friend from the get-go."

"I can only imagine. I'm sorry about that," I add as he shrugs nonchalantly.

"It is what it is."

"Flirting is still on the table though, right?" I ask as I spray my hair and then start to clean up my space. I start making the bed from our nap earlier and right when I'm fixing the pillows Blake jumps on my bed.

"You're damned right it is!" He exclaims as he jumps up and down on my freshly made bed.

"BLAKE!" I whine as he keeps jumping on my

bed. He's such a child!

• • •

"Hugo!" Brent yells as Hugo takes the platters of cooked skewers outside to the screened-in back porch. "Don't eat them before you make it to the table!"

"Yes, mom!" Hugo says as I giggle and start washing the lettuce for a salad. Brent is chopping some tomatoes and cucumbers when Blake comes in.

"Well isn't this homey," Blake comments as Brent and I both look up at him unimpressed. "What? I'm just saying this looks very natural."

"Be a dear Blake and get some plates and salad bowls out," I ask Blake before he can start any more trouble.

"It's supposed to be really nice tonight. The screened-in dining area of the back porch is great to avoid bugs. I'm not sure if you've seen Blake around bugs, but he screams like a little girl."

"I do not!" Blake squeaks back defensively as he grabs a tray full of plates and silverware heading to the screened-in porch. We hear him squeal, and I start laughing. "Okay! In my defense, I wasn't ready for it to attack me! It was like waiting for me." I hear Hugo tell him it was just a butterfly, and we all laugh. Blake is everything and more. I look over at Brent as he puts the final touches on the salad, and he smiles proudly when he looks up at me.

"Can I ask you a question?" I ask as he places the salad on the corner of the island.

"Anything," he answers.

"You've just recently been to London to close one of your international offices. Do you have a lot more traveling for that?" I ask and he sighs.

"Depends on your definition of a lot. I enjoy traveling. I love Scotland and New York, so it's no hardship on me to travel between the two. I can't imagine keeping any of the other offices up and running besides Scotland and New York! It was too much to oversee London and Paris on my own."

"Are you sad about that?"

"A little. They are still King Associates but not a part of our main branch anymore. We still offer support, but I don't oversee their locations. I don't know what the future holds, but I'd like to be around more so I can know who all works for our company," he says as he gives me a pointed look.

"It's not a big deal that you didn't know I worked for you guys! Don't beat yourself up about that. I've enjoyed working behind the scenes for you all, Brent." He walks closer to me, and even though I'm ready for it my breath still catches in my chest. We face each other, and he moves a stray hair back behind my ear, just like he did the other night in his old apartment.

"It's still not okay with me though. If I've missed the fact that you work for us, what else have I missed?" he asks, and I don't have an answer. "I will feel better about everything if I'm able to be more present. That's one of the biggest changes I want to make in the New York. To imagine that someone like you has been working full time in one of our offices and I didn't know it. Before that you interned for us, right? Yes, I've been traveling a lot the last few years, but I still missed this," he says as he runs the back of his fingers down my arm. He takes a step back, and I miss his touch immediately.

"I think you are looking at it differently than I am. There's been no reason for us to have ever met. I'm in a different location of Manhattan. When I was an intern, I prided myself on staying behind the scenes. That's where I do my best work. Most people want to be noticed. I think you and I were in the same vicinity maybe a handful of times and always with me behind the scenes at an event."

"I can't imagine you blending into the background."

"Well, like I said, that's where I flourish," I say as we see everyone is congregating on the screened-in back porch.

"I disagree," Brent whispers in my ear as he passes me with a few sides in his hands to add to the table.

We take everything out to the porch and place it on the table. Half of the crew is already seated. I stand back waiting for everyone else to sit. Blake saved me a seat at the end of the table, so I go to sit next to him. He grabs my hand under the table, and I look over at him.

"He can't keep his eyes off of you!"

"If I didn't know better, I'd say you wanted something to go down between your brother and I?" I whisper as he stops eating. He puts his fork down and turns to face me.

"Of course I do. My brother and my best friend. Can you imagine how incredible that would be?" he asks, more as a statement than a question. I blush and look down. He lifts my chin, and I shake my head. "I know you don't do relationships. Neither of you really have experience with relationships. You, mainly because you don't want to try. Him," he says, stabbing over his shoulder with his fork, "because he's not found the right woman. They've all been one-dimensional." He turns back around, and I see Brent watching us. "That's not you! You're definitely more than one-dimensional, Gemma."

"And what if things don't go as well as you hope they do? What if they end up going really bad?" I ask.

"You know what your problem is, Gemma?" he

asks as I giggle looking back over at him.

"What's that?"

"You've never met the right man." I roll my eyes, but deep down I know he's right. I haven't. I haven't even tried. What a wonderful world that would be if there was a right man or right woman for everyone. That shit doesn't exist in the real world, but that's not where Blake resides.

Later that evening after we've helped Brent clean dishes and load the dishwasher, we all head back out to the back porch. I head over to the wine cooler and pour myself another glass of Sauvignon blanc. Brent really knows how to throw a party. I've already told Blake that we need to leave some money or go to the store while we're here to help out. He laughed embarrassingly loud, asking me if I knew how much his brother was worth.

"Gemma," I hear behind me. It's Brent. He motions for me to come over to where he and some others are sitting on the sectional outside. I sit down next to him as Hugo comes over and almost sits on top of me. There's barely any room, so Brent lifts me and sets me down on his lap. I flush, but it feels very natural. At least he's a gentleman about it.

"Rhodes travels to Georgia a lot on business," Brent says as I take a large sip of my wine. I like that Brent is a big guy, so I don't feel like I'm squishing him. He places a hand around my waist, moving us over a bit to give Hugo some more space. He's swaying back and forth unsteadily. I look behind me at Brent, and he whispers in my ear. "If the big guy goes over, I want to be able to make a quick get-away." I laugh, and he looks back over to Rhodes, who's watching us expectantly.

"I grew up in Savannah," I answer, and Rhodes nods excitedly.

"I'm there a couple times a year to golf. That had to be amazing growing up there. It's so beautiful." I tense, not knowing how to answer. My experience in Savannah wasn't ideal, but I'm not going to disclose that to anyone here. People assume when they find out I'm from Savannah that I lived on some beach front property mansion with sweeping views of the ocean. I know Brent had to feel me tense up.

"Yeah, Savannah is a pretty cool city. I didn't grow up in a very nice area, but it's a wonderful place to visit," I say nonchalantly. Blake comes over and sits on the end. This leaves Brent and I squished in between him and Hugo. I laugh a little, and Brent leans up to whisper in my ear.

"It's all fun and games until Hugo passes out or pukes. We were safe before because we had space to move. Now I'm not so sure," he chuckles. I feel like maybe I'm not safe at all here in Brent's lap. In my experience, I've always skipped from the flirty to the bedroom and then got the hell out of there. For some reason it feels like with Brent we stay in this zone. Like he knows he's in control of it. I'm not used to this. I'm used to staying in control.

Eventually some people head inside and that frees up some space around us. I move over so I'm sitting next to Brent, and I shiver, missing the heat from his body. It's getting chilly outside.

"Are you cold?" he asks, and I nod my head.

"Just a little cooler without your body heat," I answer as Brent looks down at me smiling. We know we are both extremely attracted to each other, but at the same time he has no idea what he's up against. He's also my boss so I feel like I'm playing tug-a-war. I look over at Brent and can tell he's weighing this as well.

"Do you want to go on a walk?" I look over to Blake and see he's watching Brent and I as he talks to Rhodes. He nods his head, and I'm surprised he heard Brent. Or maybe he's just nodding for me to go for it? Hugo has just fallen over on his side next to me. I scoot over and feel Brent wrap his arm around my waist, pulling me closer. "Told you," he whispers and I laugh. Blake stands up, stretches and kisses me lightly on the cheek.

"I'm calling it a night," he whispers as he walks into the house. I look from Hugo to Brent and then notice that most everyone is calling it a night.

"What time is it?" I ask. It can't possibly be that late. Normally I'm the first one to peace out.

"10:30," Brent says, looking down at his watch.

"Yeah, let's go on a walk," I answer… I follow him down the path to the beach. Thank God I brought a ponytail holder because it's windy as hell. As we start down to the beach, there's an easy silence between Brent and I. The sound of the crashing waves brings me back to my childhood. It was very rare I was allowed to go to the beach as a child. As I got older, I had more freedom as my father and I spent less time in each other's presence.

I often wonder if my mom loved the beach. I know next to nothing about her. I have one photo of her and nothing else. My father and I didn't have the kind of relationship where I could ask him about her. It breaks my heart a little to think about it, and as we walk the wind is in my eyes, making them water a little. I silently wonder if this is me tearing up or just the wind.

"Are you enjoying yourself so far?" he asks, and I nod, coming back to the here and now.

"I really am, I've enjoyed today. You were right. It's very laid back. Also, thank you for earlier. I kind of froze up when he asked me about Savannah."

"I did notice. I'm sorry," he says. "I didn't know…" I cut him off.

"How could you know?" I add, and he looks over at me with sincere concern.

"I'm here if you ever want to talk about it. I know our friendship is new, but I'd like to think that we could be the type of friends that can confide in each other. I'd like you to know that you can trust me."

"Thank you, Brent. We should probably head back." We walk back to the house making small talk. He tells me a little more about where he grew up and it's easy. Mostly because I like hearing him talk about his childhood and funny stories about Blake. I guess some things never change, and that's apparent where Blake is concerned. As we approach the house it looks like everyone just abandoned their drinks. I look over at Brent, and he rolls his eyes.

"I can clean this up. Why don't you head in and warm up?" he adds.

"Not a chance, King," I answer as I start grabbing glasses and taking them inside. We finish loading the dishwasher. It's a little after midnight now.

"Well, look at that. You didn't turn into a pumpkin after all," he jokes, referring to my statement when we were in his Manhattan apartment.

"Not yet. My fairy godmother might be in a different time zone?"

"Doubt it! If there was ever a fairy godmother it would be Blake, and he's here. You know that was his dream-job growing up, right?"

"To be a fairy godmother?" I ask, laughing.

"Yes! Growing up he would always tell every-one that his dream job was to be Cinderella's fairy godmother. My mum didn't have the heart to tell him that the movie wasn't real."

"That explains a lot, but it's also the cutest thing in the entire world. Suits him."

"It really does," he answers as we close the dishwasher. I place my hand towel by the sink and turn to head to my room.

"Did you believe in fairy tales too, growing up?" he asks, and I try to not let the smile fall from my face. My face has always been an easy read.

"I learned a long time ago that fairy tales weren't real." I answer. As I turn around to head to my room, I stop and turn back around. "Where are my manners?" he's standing there looking at me like I kicked his dog. "Thanks for tonight, Brent. I'll see you in the morning."

The next morning I'm up with the sun. I'm not at all hungover, and I think that's due to the quality of wine that Brent stocks. Blake is still snoring away, so I go to the bathroom then head out onto our bal-cony. I sit down in the chair, putting my feet up on the railing. It's a little after 8 a.m. I see someone running up the beach toward the stairs. I can tell it's him before he even gets close enough for me to see him. He walks up the stairs, removing his shoes and then heading to the pool. He's in athletic shorts slung low on his hips and no shirt. He dives into the deep end and surfaces close to the stairs in the shallow end. Sensing someone watching, he looks up at me and I smile. I'm still wearing my sleep shorts and a tee shirt. He walks to the edge of the pool, leaning on his forearms and looking up at me. My heart skips a beat as he watches me.

I head inside and into the kitchen. I grab a cup of black coffee and then pour some creamer into it. Apparently, someone was up early if there's a pot of coffee already made. I open the door leading outside and walk down to the pool. I carry my coffee and grab a towel from the cabinet near the lounge chairs. I place the towel down on the edge of the pool and sit on the edge next to Brent. I dangle my legs over the edge, and he scoots closer to me.

"Good morning," he says, smiling up at me. His voice seems a little huskier this morning. It's still pretty early.

"Good morning," I answer back with a small smile. He places a hand on my calf, and I can't help the smile that breaks through on my face. He and I are almost nose to nose, and I bite my lip trying not to embarrass myself. I'm giddy being this close to him. "I'm sorry," I whisper, placing a hand over my face. "I can't help it."

"I can't either, Gemma." He runs a hand over my leg, dripping the cool water from the pool. I feel chill bumps run all the way up my body, lingering tantalizingly where I'd love to have him touch me the most.

"You're so damn sexy," I add as he laughs and moves to stand between my legs. I take a sip of my coffee then place it down beside me.

"So are you," he answers back as he leans his forearms on either side of my thighs. "You have no idea how alluring you are, Gemma. In your sweet fitted t-shirt with no bra. Giving me a hint of how incredibly sexy you are underneath. And then," he whispers as he trails his hand down my thigh to my calf and then back up again. "There's these gorgeous legs of yours. I'd love nothing more to have them wrapped around my waist. With not a stitch of make-up on, yet you're still the most beautiful woman I've ever seen." I put my hands behind me so I don't touch him back. I'm not sure I could stop myself if I touched him right now. His athletic shorts are hanging just low enough so I can see the deep V that runs down to the very intimate place I'd love nothing more than to explore. I look back up at him, biting my lip, and he's smiling that irresistible sexy smile. "I'm glad my lower half is under the water or I might be startling some people first thing this morning," he adds as he moves back from me a little. He puts some space between us and runs his hands across the water. He's tall enough that I can tell that he's going to need a minute before he gets out of the shallow end. I smile shyly and take another sip of my coffee.

"Did you have a good run?" I ask, hoping a change of subject might cool us off a bit.

"I did. Did you sleep well?" he returns as I nod.

"I did. I slept with your brother last night," I add, and a laugh explodes from him. I feel it reverberate all over my body and see him look down at my chest. My nipples are extremely hard and somewhat visible through my tee shirt. He groans, walking back over to me. I feel his hands run up the outside of my thighs, but before he reaches the edge of my shorts, he moves his hands to either side of my hips and picks up my coffee cup. He takes a sip and then comes back to stand between my legs. When he looks up at me and our eyes lock on each other's, I feel our connection as strong as ever. I'm extremely turned on, and I can feel his attraction towards me coming off us in waves.

"Was he any good?" he asks trying not to crack a smile.

"Meh. He snores a lot," I answer as he places the cup down and floats away on his back. I hear someone approaching behind me and see it's Hugo. "Don't you dare," I warn, then I'm being launched into the air. I close my eyes as I hit the water. I'm laughing as I reemerge but stay down since I have no bra on. There's no doubt in my mind that my shirt is completely see through right now. Hugo runs toward the water, and I only have a moment to move before he cannon-balls into the pool. I feel Brent grab my arm, pulling me towards him. I move behind him, and my chest presses against his back.

"Wet t-shirt contest?" I hear Blake yell from the back deck as he approaches the stairs toward the pool. "Why didn't anyone invite me?" Brent wraps an arm protectively behind his back holding me to him. "Well, wouldn't take long to figure out who would win that contest, sugar tits. I'll say this though, Hugo launched you about 20 feet in the air. I give you a 10! However, after Hugo's cannon ball, we need to add some water back to the pool. Won't have to water the greenery around here 'til next weekend."

"Thanks, Blake," I say begrudgingly. Blake holds up a towel, and I climb out of the pool, my pajamas clinging to me like second skin.

"Jesus!" I hear Brent say under his breath from behind me, so I look back at him. I wrap the towel around me and start towards the house. "Thanks for my coffee, Gemma!" Brent yells as I follow Blake up the path to the house. SHIT, that man is delicious! I hear Brent tell Hugo to "shut the hell up," and I can only imagine what just transpired between the two of them.

I get in the bathroom and literally peel the clothes off my body. Blake tosses me a sundress and some underwear, so I throw them on. I twist my hair up into a bun and put some moisturizer on my face. We head into the kitchen and Blake starts making breakfast. I'm not a huge breakfast person, and since I didn't finish my cup of coffee earlier, I grab another cup. I head into the living room and sit down next to Blake. It's the fourth of July today, and I'm so grateful for today. For our freedom and for the country we live in. Blake turns the tv to the parade and we watch in comfortable silence. I'm sitting there drinking my coffee when a delicious Brent walks in with no shirt on. I whimper, and Blake tells me to control myself.

Brent

Later that afternoon, everyone is showered and dressed when the chef I hired for the evening arrives. He comes in with trays and platters of food and a bunch of coolers. He's making a seafood trio and bone-in rib eyes. It's always one of my favorite nights. Surf and Turf night at the beach house is always popular with my guests. I head outside after I've gotten the chef and his assistants squared away in the kitchen and grab a drink. Gemma is drinking a Jack and Coke, and, no surprise, Blake is drinking some kind of fruity cocktail. I sit down at the table next to Blake and Hugo. Gemma is sitting on the other side of Blake beside Elaine. Elaine has taken a liking to Gemma. What's not to like? I feel Gemma put her hand on my arm behind

Blake, and I look over at her.

"What's for dinner?" she asks as I push Blake up a little so I'm not talking in his ear.

"Surf and turf," I answer.

"Yum! Thanks again for all of this. Blake and I are going to do some grocery shopping tomorrow. You shouldn't have to buy everything for this weekend," she comments as she leans closer to me.

"Absolutely not," I reply as she moves her hand away to grab her drink. "You are my guest, Gemma. You don't need to be doing any shopping unless it's to buy something nice for yourself. The shops will be back open tomorrow, and you should go into town. This weekend is my treat," I reply as Blake, without missing a beat, turns to her and smiles.

"Told you," he mocks as he turns back around and continues his conversation with Rhodes.

"I appreciate it. I'm just not used to this," she adds shyly as I reach over, touching her arm gently.

"Which is exactly why you should let me treat you to a wonderful weekend," I answer, rubbing the back of my fingers gently up and down her shoulder. "You got some sun today," I say, running a finger closer to her collar bone where her tan line is. She opens her mouth but doesn't say anything. She just watches me. Whenever our eyes meet it's always so powerful. I gently squeeze her shoulder, not wanting to aggravate her sun-kissed skin. I only move my hand away to grab my own drink. I take a healthy sip, trying to regain my composure.

"Dinner's ready," the chef's assistant announces, so we all head inside. We are each served a bone-in ribeye and a lobster tail with fresh drawn citrus butter. Hugo comes around and gives me a big hug. I laugh because I already know what he's going to say.

"I could cry," he whimpers as he takes his overloaded plate back outside. We are all seated and eating our dinner when the chef comes outside to see how we like everything. Dinner is perfect. I head inside to make sure that they are squared away with the card I put on file. When I come back out Blake waves me over. He and Gemma are seated on one of the double loungers by the pool.

"Everyone's fine. Come and sit with us," Blake says, scooting over so I can sit down on the edge next to Gemma. "I love this. All my favorite people and the fireworks will start soon." The fireworks are amazing! Not as great as the show in Manhattan, but they are pretty great.

After cleaning up around the kitchen, I walk into my bedroom and take my clothes off. I walk to the bed and crawl underneath the covers, savoring how the buttery soft fabric feels against my naked skin. I roll over to turn the bedside light off and the moon takes over illuminating the room. I don't shut the blinds, I'm too tired. Tomorrow morning the sun will come through like a bitch, blinding me, but I don't care.

The next morning, I wake up and head toward the kitchen. I'm in my athletic shorts as I turn the coffee pot on. I turn around and see I have an audience. I'm not used to anyone being up this early but me. Hugo and Gemma are both staring at me, but with two very different expressions. Hugo is looking at me like I've ruined his morning, and Gemma is looking at me like I'm her last meal. I chuckle and then head over to both of them.

"Well, aren't you a sight for sore eyes!" I say to Hugo, and he grumbles. He's hung over and not in the mood.

"Are your eyes giving you trouble old man?" he asks as I lean down and give him a side hug. He hates it but still entertains me. Then I walk over to Gemma and do the same.

"Sleep well?" I ask

"That I did! Hugo was just informing me on how many times he threw up last night," she adds as I grimace.

"Well, I'm sad I'll miss this conversation, but I'm going on a run." Hugo groans in misery, and I hate it for him. "Save me a cup of coffee," I yell as I head out the door.

Gemma

"**G**od! Why is he so damn hot," I ask, looking out the window at Brent's retreating form, and Hugo laughs behind me.

"It's one of life's greatest mysteries. I've been asking myself that for a long time. You know how hard it is to attract women when one of your closest friends is the sexiest man in New York?" I laugh and so does Hugo. "How long are the two of you going to pretend like you don't want to rip each other's clothes off? I haven't seen sexual chemistry like this since Maria and Captain Von Trapp." I turn around, staring at him as he puts another huge bite of steak in his mouth. I sit down next to him with a curious expression.

"Didn't really peg you as a Sound of Music

kind of guy," I say, and he feigns offense.

"Please tell me you've seen that movie. Julie Andrews and Christopher Plummer have the best on screen chemistry. You and Brent have that same kind of thing happening this weekend!" he says, pointing his fork at me. "That, 'I shouldn't want you, but I do' vibe. The chemistry that pisses other people off. You think they're 'wasting precious time that they could have already ripped each other's clothes off and got on with it,' kind of thing?"

"I'm not sure how to respond to that, Hugo?" I reply as he booms out what I've come to know as a Hugo laugh. Pretty sure he rattled the windows.

"Next time you watch it keep that in mind. That scene where she's trying to teach one of his kids a dance and Captain Von Trapp cuts in. The way they look at each other is magical!" He says, stabbing another piece of steak. I watch him chew his steak and burst out laughing.

"Beautiful," he repeats shaking his head, and I can do nothing but laugh.

"Hugo, you are too much."

• • •

It starts raining after lunch, and most everyone goes inside to take a nap. I fall asleep and almost immediately I'm jostled awake. I was starting to have another nightmare. What is the deal? I've been having them more and more often and they kill my insides. I sit up, nauseated, and I try to clear my head. I grab my swimsuit and slip it on, walking quietly out toward the back porch. It's a plain white bathing suit with palm trees. It's stopped raining, but the sun's not out. The pool is supposedly heated so I spend my last afternoon enjoying the pool. There's no telling when I'll get to enjoy this kind of luxury again. I grab a towel from the cabinet beside the pool and put it down on a chair. I step into the water and it's deliciously warm.

I'm sitting on the tanning ledge in the deep end looking up at the sky. My head is resting comfortably on the edge of the pool. The sky is getting darker now. I think that means it's probably going to storm again. I feel a cold rain drop land on my face and it feels amazing. Brent's back yard has a lot of trees so when the wind picks up I can hear the rustling of the leaves. It's very relaxing, and I close my eyes finding some peace of mind. I place both of my arms out of the water on the outside of the pool and hear a small splash at the other end of the pool. I lift my head and see Brent sitting on the steps watching me from the other side.

"It's about to start storming, so I'm not sure how long you're going to get to stay in here." I smile at him in acknowledgement, and he smiles back at me. He steps into the water and then goes under. I can see him under the water getting closer and closer to me. I get really excited knowing I'm going to get to touch him very soon. Not necessarily in a sexual manner, but a girl can hope. I do love holding his hand. His touch is so strong, yet tender and sweet. It's not something I'm used to and nothing I've experienced before. I'm not a virgin by any stretch of the imagination, but I'm not used to this kind of intimacy either. He pops up right in front of me then joins me on the tanning ledge. The water comes up to my chest, but on Brent it's just below his ribcage. He puts his arms out of the water as well, his left arm covering my right one. He leans back and closes his eyes. We sit there for a few minutes, enjoying being in this peaceful bubble.

"Pretty amazing, right?" I say as the wind continues to rustle the leaves on the trees above us.

"I love it out here. It's one of my favorite places to be." He rubs circles with his thumb on my bicep and it only slightly tickles. It's more sensual than it should be. My nipples immediately pebble up, and I smile with my eyes closed.

"I do love it when you touch me," I whisper and hear Brent hum in acknowledgement beside me.

"Not as much as I love touching you, Gemma. Honestly, it's hard for me not to touch you. Whenever you are in the room my body comes alive, sensing you're close. It's happened all weekend. If we were alone," he whispers trailing off, and I laugh.

"We are alone."

"You know what I mean. If we were here in my house alone without the other guests, I'd be having a really hard time not devouring you right now. I like your bathing suit by the way," he adds, and I can tell he's turned his head towards me.

I look over at him and he's looking down at my chest. I know he can tell that my nipples are hard. My top's not see-through even though it's white. There's enough green of the palm branches to cover all the areas that could show through. He moves his hand from my arm, and I immediately miss the warmth of his hand. I move my arm under the water, and he takes my hand in his, our fingers intertwining. He lifts my hand, kissing it and then placing our hands back under the water. The rain has started to fall a little heavier, so I sit up a little so it's falling on the top of my head and not my face.

Brent pulls me toward him tenderly so I'm sitting in front of him, and he wraps his arms around me from behind, his warm chest against my back. I sigh, feeling like we fit together perfectly. His lips trail a soft line from my shoulder to below my ear, and I feel his teeth gently scrape the bottom of my ear. My head falls back, resting on top of his shoulder and neither of us moves. We both realize we are at a crossroads here. The rain is now pouring steadily on us. Our bodies are heating up, and honestly, I could let him take me right here in the water. I want him and I know he wants me. Something is stopping me though, and it's not just his arms holding me in my place. I turn my head and place a gentle kiss on the side of his neck. His hand gently cups the back of my head, and my breath catches in my chest.

"Gemma," he whispers as I leave my face in the crook of his neck. I feel safe here with him, and my heart begins to hurt. I close my eyes, overcome with emotion. I'm not used to this kind of intimacy or being loved this way. The way Brent just whispered my name, like we are the only two people in the world. I feel a tear slip out the corner of my eye. I open my eyes, in shock for a moment as I feel my heart fluttering with need in my chest.

This is the first tear I've shed since I was a little girl. My heart starts to race as I squeeze my eyes tightly together, willing them to stop so I can enjoy this moment. I know he can't tell because it's starting to rain harder. I want to feel this way a little longer. It's not just because of who he is. I know I'm out of my league here. It's because of who I am and who I'm not able to be for him. His hand is gently running through the wet strands of my hair, and I place my hand on top of his. We aren't even having sex, but this is the most intimate moment of my entire life. The arm around my waist pulls me even closer to him. I can feel his arousal against me. I know it's only a matter of time before he has to release me. "I don't want to let you go," he whispers, and I smile sadly as I fight my quivering lip and impending breakdown. Another tear slips out of the corner of my eye. I never cry, so I know I need to shut this down before the dam breaks. This is not the time or the place. I don't understand what's happening to me.

"You have to eventually," I whisper, and my voice breaks with emotions I can't control. I sit up but can't turn around to look at him. I gather myself as his warm hands gently release me and the coolness of the water seeps back over my body. I slowly turn around, and he looks into my eyes.

"Gemma," he whispers, and the look on his face breaks my heart. Confusion, concern, and what might look like pity from anyone else is compassion on his perfect face. I look down, knowing if I stay any longer, I'll break. I can't let that happen. I have to force whatever this is down. I feel out of my element here and out of control. I need to leave.

"I'm fine." I remain as stoic as I can, but he shakes his head.

"Just because you're fine doesn't mean you can't fall apart sometimes." He places a hand on my cheek, wiping away a stray tear as if he can tell the difference between the rain and my tears.

I look up at him, knowing that I'm close to falling apart and I can't. I simply cannot. "Gemma. You can trust me," he says.

"I know that. That's why you're not safe for me. I don't want to fall apart here. I can't." I answer, my voice barely above a whisper. He moves his hand and I move to my knees beside him. I lean over, grab his face and kiss him chastely on the cheek. "I've had a wonderful time while I've been here," I add, and he stops me before I can stand up.

"Please don't go, Gemma. Not like this. If you want to sit here in silence, we can. We don't have to talk. I don't want you to leave."

"I don't want to leave you, Brent," I answer as I look away. The damn tears are disobeying me and falling against my will. "But that's exactly why I need to go."

"Please stay. I promise you, you're safe," he says, unshed tears in his eyes. I place my hand over his on my cheek and look into his eyes. "I'm someone you can trust. I'm someone who can love you the way you deserve to be loved," he adds as I lower my head. I remember dreaming as a young girl that one day I'd hear these words that I've never heard, and my heart simply can't take it. I've never fallen apart, never let it catch up to me, never dealt with the pain and abuse from my past. It's too late for that now. I can't go there.

"I know you could," I say as I turn away from

his gaze. "I can feel it, Brent. Part of me is dying for you. The other part of me is running the other direction, but I can't fall apart here, Brent. Not now," I say as I turn my head back to him, unable to look him in the face. I can't even open my eyes. My strength and resistance are pulling me away from him, but for some reason my heart has settled on him. "My heart was shattered into a million pieces a long time ago. You don't understand what you're getting yourself into."

"You've been in survival mode your entire life, Gemma. It's time for someone to take care of you. Stop running away. Even if I'm just your friend," he says as I lift my hand and place it on his arm, willing him to stop.

"Please don't, Brent. I can't do this." My resolve strengthens just enough to drag myself out of the pool. "I'm so very sorry," I add as I walk away, grabbing my towel and disappearing into the house. My heart breaks once I walk into the bedroom. Blake sits up, looking at me alarmed and I shake my head. "Please don't, Blake. I can't right now. I just can't." I can barely even finish my sentence. I can barely breathe, and I feel like my heart is about to burst from my chest. It's agony.

I walk into the shower and turn it on. The dam breaking. I've spent my entire adult life avoiding this kind of pain. Avoiding the pain and hurt from my childhood from bubbling up and coming back to swallow me whole. I will give myself a couple minutes to cry, then I'll pull myself back together. I should probably leave too. No need in staying after I've embarrassed myself like this. I fall to my knees on the cool tile of the shower and let myself fall apart. I hear the door to the shower open and I whisper, "Not right now, Blake."

I feel someone pull me into their lap and instantly I know it's not Blake. It's Brent. I fall apart as he pulls my head against his chest. My body is wracked with sobs as I cling to him. He pulls me closer, holding me, but not saying a word. His hand runs up and down my legs then up and down my spine into my hair. I'm not even embarrassed about it at this point. What's done is done now. "I'm so sorry," I whisper, and he leans down, moving my hair away from my face.

"There's nothing to be sorry about, Gemma. You've done nothing wrong," he says, his chin resting firmly on the top of my head.

"This should be easier. Unemotional, detached, simple exchange between two people. We should be having sex right now, not you holding me in the shower as I fall apart. For some reason I can't do it that way with you."

"I think you have it all wrong. Those aren't any of the things I want from you. Unemotional, detached, simple. That's not what I want." He places his hand on my cheek, and I close my eyes again.

"I'm out of my element here too, Gemma." He turns the water off and pulls me back into his arms. "I'm going to go out on a limb here and say that you've never been intimate with anyone. Sex, yes. But true intimacy?" He lifts my chin so he can gently kiss my cheeks, my nose, and my forehead. He supports me with one arm, his other hand in my hair. I can feel his arousal against my side, and I lean into him, letting him know I feel him.

"Have you ever had this?" he whispers against my lips, pulling back so he can look deep into my eyes. I haven't and he knows it. "Neither have I. I've never felt like this before, Gemma. Have you?"

"You know I haven't," I answer, and he closes his eyes. His forehead touching mine. When he opens his they are determined but still soft.

"Stand up, Gemma," he whispers firmly to me, and I immediately pull myself to standing. He stands up, pulling his bathing suit off and tossing it into the corner of the shower. "Turn around." I turn around as he unties my bathing suit and tosses it into the corner next to his. "Is this okay?" he asks, and I nod. He crouches down, pulling my bathing suit bottoms off as I slowly step out of them and brace myself against the side of the shower.

"You know it is. I mean it's not like you haven't seen me naked in the shower before," I say as I laugh, and he does too. He turns the overhead shower on, pulling me backwards. My back against his front. I can feel HIM hard against my back, and I groan in response. He pulls us under the shower and reaches over for my shampoo. I gasp when I realize what he's doing. When his hands go into my hair, lathering the shampoo with his gentle fingers I close my eyes. He's taking care of me. He rinses my hair and then grabs the conditioner. He puts it in my hair and then grabs the body wash. He puts it in his hands then starts to rub it all over my body. I lean into his touch and then feel him pull me against his chest.

"You are so damn beautiful, Gemma. Your body is incredible," he whispers as he washes all of me. And I do mean all of me. I moan as his hands wash my breasts and in between my legs. I lean against him, placing my hands behind his neck. He leans down, kissing my shoulder but avoiding my lips. He washes the conditioner out of my hair, and then I take the shampoo and pour some in my hands. He's much taller than I am, so he turns around so I can return the favor of washing him as well. He groans and hums as my hands run all over his body. I imagined he would be large, but he's not only that, he's beautiful. His entire body wet from the shower makes me want to beg for it.

When I'm done, he turns the water off and grabs a towel from the cabinet outside of the shower. His eyes never leave mine once our gazes meet. He places his hand on the side of my face, wiping another tear away. I curse the tears for betraying me this way. We had a deal. We don't ever fall apart. Especially in front of other people. Especially in front of the man I know I'm already falling for.

"You deserve to be loved and cared for like this, Gemma. I know you don't believe it, but I'll be damned if I stand by and let you not feel it. I know you don't do relationships. Right now, I'm not asking you to be in a relationship with me. I know that's the fastest way to get you to run, and I'm okay taking it a day at a time. Don't ever apologize for falling apart, Gemma. Not with me. Every single tear that falls from your beautiful eyes means something me." He leans forward, kissing me tenderly on the forehead. "Let's get you dressed," he says as he grabs another towel and wraps it around his waist.

He follows me out, and when we get into the bedroom Blake and Elaine are sitting on the bed. Blake takes one look at me and grabs Elaine's hand, pulling her out of the room. Blake knows I don't fall apart. Brent grabs some lotion from the top of the chest of drawers and starts to rub it into my skin. He pulls the towel completely off of me and finishes moisturizing my entire body. He hands me some sleep shorts and a tank top from the drawers, and I pull them on. He wraps me in his arms with his hand tenderly on the back on my head. His heart is beating so incredibly fast when I place my hand over his heart. I look up at him, and he has unshed tears in his eyes.

"Don't," he says as I open my mouth to speak. I'm horrified that I've done this to him. "Don't tell me not to cry for you. I won't hear it." He takes my hand. "I have a couple things," he says, clearing his throat and looking down. I can see his arousal is still prevalent and I smile knowingly as I look up at him. "A couple things I need to take care of. Why don't we have a movie night? It's still raining out and for some damn reason Hugo wants to watch 'The Sound of Music'." I laugh out loud, and he pulls me close to him again, smiling adoringly at me. "I love that sound!"

"The Sound of Music?" I ask as he shakes his head at me.

"No, smartass, the sound of you laughing. I'll see you out there in a bit," he adds as he leans down again, kissing me gently on the cheek then turning to leave the room. I wait to hear the laughter and teasing from everyone in the living area, but I don't hear a thing from them. Maybe they aren't out there? Or maybe they know this isn't the time? Either way I sit on the edge of the bed and look at myself in the mirror. I look drained and exhausted. Blake comes in a couple minutes later and grabs my hand.

"Let's get your hair dried, Gem."

After Blake dries my hair, I give him a replay

of everything from the time Brent joined me in the pool until he left to go to his room. Blake cries, of course. I tear up, but now that Brent is gone, I'm able to hold it together. For some reason I sense that I'm only going to fall apart when Brent is around. Which is still a puzzle to me?

"He's right, Gemma. You deserve to know what it feels like to be loved by someone, to be intimate with someone. You and I both know that you don't do intimacy. I think Brent's offering you something that you've never had before. Here's the catch, it will cost you nothing and everything at the same time. Maybe the cost is that your body and soul know that you need it, and he's the only one who can give it to you. You are still in survivor mode. He's absolutely right about that. I've never been prouder of him in my entire life. I'm proud of you as well for letting him comfort and love you like that. How do you feel?"

"A little embarrassed now, but not when he's around. What happened between us felt so… natural. I feel completely drained," I answer as he pulls out the straightener from my bag and plugs it in.

"That's normal. When was the last time you cried like that?" he asks, even though we both know what the answer to his question is. "I know not in front of me. I've never seen you cry."

"Never. At least not since I was a little girl," I whisper hoarsely, thinking back on all the times

I've cried.

"Gemma," he says tenderly as I look up into his brotherly eyes. I never have to question whether he feels the same about me as I do about him. He's the sibling I never had but always wanted. A big brother to protect me.

"What if I've ruined everything?" I ask, worried, and he shakes his head.

"Or what if everything is falling into place," he interjects, and I look at my reflection in the mirror. "You and I both know that you aren't done falling apart. That was only a sliver of what needs to come out of you. You know it, I know it, and Brent knows it. You've got a lot of pain and hurt to sift through. This was a good start, but I think it might be time for you to talk to someone. Other than us. I know you don't believe in that kind of stuff. You know I'm happy to be your sounding board, but it's time for you to heal so you can give your heart to someone who can take care of it." I don't respond. He knows I'm not into counseling or therapy, whatever you want to call it. I have more walls to break through, but for now I'm going to sit here and let him straighten my hair.

"Thanks, Blake," I whisper, and he leans down to kiss my cheek. I haven't said I love you to too many people in my life. It's just not how I'm wired, and I'm not sure I understand what that means for my future.

"I know. I love you too!" he says, and I feel so grateful to have him in my life.

We head into the other room, and I'm laughing because Blake trips over the table outside of our bedroom, almost falling flat on his face. Brent's ordered pizzas and they're sitting out on the kitchen island along with a bunch of snacks. Man, when he puts something together he really does it full out. There are gummy bears, Sour Patch Kids, Blow Pops. All kinds of candy and savory snacks.

"Will you guys hurry the hell up," Hugo asks Blake and I. I grab a plate of pizza and sit down next to Brent on the couch as Blake sits on the other side of me. "You do know this movie is like three hours long?"

"What movie are we watching?" Blake asks, and Hugo smiles at me.

"The Sound of Music!" he answers as I sit back laughing. I'm kind of excited about this.

Brent

The movie starts, and she leans against my arm. I take a bite of my pizza and so does she. I find I'm watching her more than I'm watching the movie. I've seen it before, although that was a long time ago. Apparently it's some sort of inside joke between Hugo and Gemma. I love that my friends like her. At first, I thought I was going to have to beat them off with a stick. Now they all laugh and throw things at each other. My heart is so full. My heart broke into a million pieces earlier. Every time I think about it, I feel my emotions getting the best of me and I'm not normally an overly emotional guy.

She finishes her pizza and puts her plate on the table in front of her. I'm already done with mine so my hands are empty. I pull her so she's lying beside me. She rests her head on my chest, and I feel like I'm on top of the world. After the events of today I feel closer to her than I have ever felt with anyone before. Having her this close to me is the best feeling, but having her trust me enough to be held by me is something I don't take lightly. Her feet are in Blake's lap, and I pull a blanket from behind me to drape over her. She cuddles up against me, and I pull her into my arms, leaning down to kiss the top of her head. We get to the party scene and Hugo throws a pillow at Gemma, hitting us both.

"Seriously, Hugo?" I say, annoyed, as Gemma laughs.

"She knows what I'm talking about," he adds as the party scene unfolds.

I look down at Gemma, who's watching the TV with awe and wonder. I'm not sure what their inside joke is regarding this movie, but I grin. I watch as Maria and Captain Von Trapp dance, and the way they look at each other does make me feel something. Something more than I thought I'd get watching The Sound of Music.

I do feel like something's changed between us since this afternoon. What exactly, I'm not sure. It seems like I've broken through a couple barriers with her. I have a feeling that once we're back in Manhattan and not in the same house, the odds of her walls staying down are low. We watch as Maria runs away from the house and the intermission starts. I pray that it's not foreshadowing of what's to come. Blake sits up, and stretches and jumps when Hugo yells.

"Go to the bathroom, get some snacks, and then come straight back. Everyone is watching the whole damn movie."

"Geez, you guys run a tight ship around here," Gemma whispers sleepily, looking up at me, smiling. Her smile could light up an entire room.

"No kidding," I whisper back as she sits up and steps over me to get a snack. She winks at me, and I wink back. I look over at Hugo who is making fun of me with Rhodes making kissy faces. I laugh, and Blake hits my leg. I could give two shits what those two jackoffs think of me anyway.

"You're a good guy," Blake says, and I nod at him in understanding. I don't necessarily feel like a good guy. I still have my faults for sure. I haven't always been a good guy. The difference now is that I want to be a good guy for Gemma. She deserves that kind of man. I want to be the kind of man she needs. Not by changing who I am, but by loving her the way she needs. She throws a bag of chips at Blake, and he thanks her. She comes back with a cup of candy and another piece of pizza.

"Thatta girl," Hugo says as he starts the movie again.

Once she finishes her pizza, she lays back down

half beside me and half on top of me, her leg resting over mine. She places her hand under my shirt, and I place my hand on top of hers. I pull her up so her head is resting on top of my shoulder. I kiss her head, squeezing her tightly to me. God, I love the feeling of her in my arms. I want this forever, I think, and then immediately have a moment of realization. I'm not normally one to want these "forever things." But I do. I want this. I want this more than I've ever wanted anything in my entire life. I know earlier something broke within Gemma, but something broke inside me too. I'm scared to lose her. I know that's a silly thing to be scared of, especially when she isn't mine to lose. I want her however I can have her. Friends, lovers, or more. I want her. I feel her body slacken a bit and know that she's fallen asleep. I close my eyes, joining her in sleep.

When I wake up, it's just Gemma and I on the sofa. I look over at the clock on the wall. It's after midnight. I don't want to wake her, but I know that we'd both be more comfortable in bed. I pick her up, and she sits up for a moment in my lap.

"I think I fell asleep," she says, lifting her head and wrapping her arms around my neck.

"I think we both fell asleep. Hey, you still haven't turned into a pumpkin," I whisper, leaning over and kissing her lips lightly. "Sleep with me tonight, Cinderella?" I ask, and she smiles at me.

"I mean literally sleep, baby," I laugh and so does she.

"Please," she says, leaning over and kissing me softly on the lips. She places a hand behind my head, pulling our mouths together. Her lips are so soft, and the feeling of our first kiss blows my mind. My heart beats against my chest like it's never held a woman before. Never been kissed before. This is something different. I groan against her mouth and give in to my desire for her. She's so soft in my arms and I'm having a hard time telling myself any reason I should stop. I pull her so she's straddling me on the sofa. I sit up, wrapping my arms around her and pulling her ass toward me so she can feel how much I want her. She places her hands on either side of my face as she deepens the kiss even more. She grinds into me, and I swear I could lose it right here when she whimpers against our open mouths. I've never in my life been this turned on by a make-out session, but I'll be damned if it's me that stops this. When I press myself against her harder, we both moan, and I know we're on the cusp of something neither of us is truly ready for. She has a part of herself that she's hiding from, and I won't give her a reason not to trust me. I want this. Hell, I've never wanted anything so much in my life, but I can't. This is not the time, nor the place to have her, and as much as my body wants to I won't. I pull back ever so slightly and gently press our heads together as we catch our breath. I plant small kisses on her cheeks, her lips and down her neck as we slow down our pace. I'm almost dizzy from my need for her. The way she's looking at me and I at her, I know that what we're feeling is more than just a one-night stand. More than just a "friends with benefits." This goes so much deeper than either of us are ready to say out loud.

My heart flips in my chest as I pick her up and carry her into my room. I turn the lights off and then pull the covers back with one arm sliding us into bed. She rests her head on the pillow next to mine as I rest my head on mine. I cover us up and pull her gently against me, my arm resting around her waist. "Thank you," she whispers as I kiss the top of her head.

"Always," I whisper back as we fall back asleep.

The next morning most everyone leaves early. For the most part, everyone was fairly sober last night in preparation for leaving today. Elaine and Joseph left at sunrise, and I was able to give them a hug before my morning run. Hugo and the boys left soon after so they could beat the traffic back into the city. Gemma and sleeping beauty Blake are the only ones left. I head back into my bedroom and see that Gemma is still sleeping. I'm glad we stopped when we did last night. It's not something I would have regretted. Little chance of that, but

I'm glad we took a step back. I want to gain her trust, and I have a feeling she hasn't had many men in her life that she feels like she can.

I head out to the kitchen as Blake strolls out of the "Queen's room" as he calls it. He's wearing Jackie O shades and a wide brimmed hat. I want to laugh, but at the same time I love him so much. He's everything to me and I'm blessed as hell to have him as a brother and a partner in business. I'll also never be able to repay him for bringing Gemma into my life. The more I'm around her, the less I worry about her working for me. She's someone worth fighting for, and I hope one day she will let me prove it to her.

"Tell Gemma I'll see her at work on Monday!" he says as he walks past me like I'm his assistant. "Also, try not to screw it up while you're at it!" he adds in parting, and I nod as I open the door and let him out of the house. I chuckle as I head back into the kitchen to start to clean-up. I have the cleaning service coming to clean bedrooms, sheets, etc. but I always like to make sure I've done everything I can.

When I come back inside from picking up around the yard, Gemma is standing in the doorway to my bedroom. I smile when I see her, and she bites her lip. I reach out my hand for her to take, and she bypasses it and wraps her arms around me. As she leans her head against my chest, I lean down and give her a chaste kiss.

"Where is everyone?" she asks, a little hoarse from sleep. I fill her in on when everyone left. "Well alrighty, then! I guess I need to pack up my things as well.

"Take your time. We don't have to rush." She heads into her bedroom, and I go into mine to pack. I don't have to pack much because I have stuff that I keep here. Most of the time when people come to use the house, the master bedroom stays unoccupied. I don't have to worry about anyone getting into my stuff. I head out of my bedroom and see Gemma standing in front of the floor to ceiling windows. I want to take a picture of her like this so I never forget this moment, but I won't. I wish she knew how special she is. One way or another I will show her so she knows. It looks like it might rain, and I have to say I'd rather stay here in bed cuddling with Gemma but after that kiss last night, it's probably wise if we get on the road.

"Is there a house you own that doesn't have amazing views?" she asks as I come behind her and wrap my arms around her.

"No!" I answer, and she leans back against me.

"Do all your houses have amazing sheets?" she asks with a small giggle.

"Yes, and I look forward to you enjoying all of them!"

•••

We grab a quick bite to eat and then head back into the city. The drive home goes by so quickly that I'm shocked we are back so soon. She peppers me with a million and one questions about Scotland and my childhood. I think it's easy because we are talking about me. Whenever we talk about Gemma the vibes in the car change. She tightens up a little, and I reassure her that we have all the time in the world to get to know each other. She doesn't have to talk about anything she's not ready to. I want to get to know her, of course, but these things take time. Luckily, time is something we both have.

I get a call as we are pulling up to her apartment. I missed Sunday night dinner with the family, so Da always calls me afterwards if I'm not there. I answer the phone and tell him to hold on a second. I come around to open Gemma's door and help her get her bag. She doesn't pack like the women I'm used to. One weekender is all she brought. She's something else, that's for sure. I help her to her door and then lean down, giving her a gentle kiss on the lips. We've exchanged numbers, and I hope she will feel comfortable enough to call. I don't want to push her, but I hope after this weekend together she does. After she's inside, I slide back into my car and head for home.

"Da, you still there?"

"Of course I am, son. I'm sad you missed tonight, but I'm glad that you've found someone so special. Blake came tonight. You boys deserve to have good people around you. Seems like Gemma is one of those from what Blake's told us. He didn't go into details, but he said that she's special. Has some work to do, like the rest of us, but that you were there for her. Son, I'm proud of you for that. That's what truly separates the men from the boys. If you don't take care of your woman, someone else eventually will come along and do it for you. I know you two are just friends at this point, but I'm happy for you son. She sounds like one of the good ones."

He can't see me, but I'm beaming from ear to ear. I pull back onto the road and tell Da about the weekend. For the most part, my Da and I have no secrets. I don't tell him everything, but I give him an idea of how everything went. I pull into my garage and put the car in park. We say our goodbyes, and I say hello to security as I head to the elevators. Shadow comes out of my bedroom when I step off the elevator, and I kneel to give him some love. He's the best dog. I unpack my bags and check the fridge to make sure I'm stocked for the week. As I'm getting myself prepared for the week, I can't help but smile. This weekend was amazing. This was the first time that I've ever really enjoyed having someone in my bed. I got to hold Gemma, smell her hair and kiss her beautiful face. I head to bed a little after 10:00 and do it with a big smile on my face.

• • •

Monday morning, I'm still floating from the weekend. My first assistant, Layla puts her two weeks in because she and her husband are moving. I should be frazzled by this, but I'm not. I call HR, as well as a few of the executives, to give them a heads up. Everyone I've spoken to has brought Gemma up as a great candidate to replace her. They don't know that she and I spent an amazing weekend getting to know each other, but at this point it's none of their business. Gemma would be an incredible candidate. Hell, she would be deserving of this promotion moving from second assistant to first. It's not against the rules to date an employee. However, would she want to work for me? That would be weird right? She'd be professional about it for sure, but my GOD! I place my head on my desk and then my phone rings. It's Blake.

"Are you kidding me right now?" Blake growls, and I sit up.

"What?" I ask.

"Trying to steal Gemma from me! Hell, she spends one weekend with you and all of a sudden you want her all to yourself," he says, and I start laughing. Damn, that was fast.

I give him the run-down of Layla leaving the company, and he backs off. He knows Gemma is deserving of this promotion, he even says so himself. We talk about different options, but we always end up right where we began with candidates. I have so many changes I want to implement, and I'm not sure I want to bring anyone brand new in until I have a plan laid out.

That night Blake and I get together for dinner. Brett joins us about midway through and tells us he's excited to start at the company here in a few weeks. I'm completely stoked to have all my brothers at the same company. This is exactly what Da has always wanted. I have to say, it makes us unstoppable in the industry. I ask about Gemma, and Blake tells me that she is doing well. I haven't spoken to her since I dropped her off, but we aren't dating. We are just getting to know each other. I think we both want more, but what does "more" mean for the two of us? Did I dream the whole damn thing?

Wednesday, a few buddies ask if I want to go out. I meet the guys for drinks first at Perrone's, and then we have plans to go out to a new club after that. I'm not the normal "clubbing" kind of guy. That desire expired a long time ago for me, but I'm game to tag along. There's always a new club popping up where an old one used to be. It's the new thing I guess, but as we leave Perrone's that evening I take one last look around, hoping I'll run into Gemma.

Gemma

'm already tipsy by the time we arrive at Snog. It's a British bar and I've been here a few times with Blake and his friends, and tonight I reluctantly agreed to come, even though I'm not really in the mood. I've been questioning all week whether I've made up this "thing" in my head between Brent and I. Deep down I know it was real. I get that we are back in the real world, but I haven't heard from him. Blake told me to get over it and send him a dirty picture. I told him I'd rather die. He laughed and said, "He's already seen you naked. What could it hurt?" LOL, it could hurt a lot to send my boss a dirty picture.

We sit at an oversized booth with the most gorgeous red velvet seats. Everything is red, white and blue here, but not for America. This place is like a Spice Girls Party on crack! I tell Blake I'm going to the bathroom and leave to get some air. Blake attracts some of the most interesting people and for the most part I love it. Tonight, I'm just not feeling it. I want to dance, eat some French fries and then go home. I'm over it already.

As I'm leaving the bathroom, I almost run into a girl waiting for me to exit. She gives me a nasty look, and I laugh. Get over it already, honey! It's a club and bathrooms are the worst with a bunch of drunk girls. I am trying to think of how I know the girl that ran into me when I realize she was the girl whose ear Brent was whispering in the other night at Perrone's. I turn back around, and she's already gone. I shrug my shoulders and head up to the bar. I look over at Blake's table, and it's a who's who of New York celebrities and socialites. I don't care about that crowd, but Blake is in his element.

I lean over the bar and make eye contact with one of the bartenders. He comes over after a few minutes, and I ask for a Manhattan. He nods and then starts on my drink as two guys move on either side of me. This is my biggest pet peeve. Guys that need a posse to talk to women make me want to gag. I don't care about your stupid joke or the fact that you went to some elitist school. I'm not that kind of girl. The guy to my left starts talking over me to the guy on my right, and I roll my eyes. I need to go home.

"You're hot!" one of them says as the bartender hands me my drink. I give him a $20 and tell him to keep the change. He nods at me and then attends to someone else.

"Not interested!" I answer as I back away. I'm wearing a black cocktail dress with my chunky gold lamé platforms. You have to be shoe smart in New York. Your feet will be the first thing to take you down if you don't wear something you can run in. I start back towards the table when the girl from the bathroom catches my eye. She's wearing a red cocktail dress and the man dancing with her is none other Brent King. The. Brent. King. The same guy I've been waiting on to call me. The way he moves is not only seductive but sexual. I don't understand how it makes me feel, but I see RED. If Blake is right about the way his brother's dancing translates into the bedroom, then I could vomit with jealousy right now.

I'm not one to ever get jealous. I don't think I've ever felt this way. I take a deep breath, and I'm not sure if I'm mad, sad or relieved. I don't feel like putting up with Blake's antics so I walk to a cocktail table and place my drink down for a minute. I take a large sip of my Manhattan and then pull my phone out. I find Brent's phone number and go to delete it, but I stop. Why? Just delete the damn number. But I can't. I place my phone down and look up. I think I'm sad. What the hell? I take another sip and then pick my phone up again. I take a picture of him and the chick in the red dress dancing.

Real nice, Brent! Glad I've been waiting for you to call.

Won't ever make that mistake again!

As I turn around, I almost run into the two idiots from the bar. One stands in front of me like a bouncer. The other stands next to him like he's some kind of mobster boss. I have no time for this nonsense. I start to walk around them, and then big dude tries to block me. There is one thing that annoys me more than anything and that's dumb-ass men. Tonight is not the night to fuck with me.

"Please move. I'm not in the mood!"

"I'll make this quick. I think you are into me. I think the way you stuck out your chest when I approached the bar earlier tells me you know exactly what you do to me." The little mob boss says, and I start laughing. This is unbelievable. I was with Brent King in his Hamptons mansion this weekend and now I'm stuck dealing with these two bumbling idiots.

"I think you need to move before I embarrass the both of you! I'm leaning towards drunk, and I have zero patience for lowlifes like the two of you tonight!"

"Oh, she has claws. If I get you really angry,

will you make me pay for it like I'm going make you pay for insulting me," the little guy says as I rear back and punch him square in the jaw.

"Gemma!" It's Brent. He's beside me, looking down at the mob boss, and he starts to laugh. "Damn!"

"Go away, Brent! As you can see, I can take care of myself!" I retort, and the big guy starts laughing at Brent. We both look over at him, and he stops laughing immediately.

"You're gonna pay for that, little girl!" the big guy says, and I roll my eyes.

"She's not paying for shit!" Brent says as he gets in the big guy's face. I don't have time for this shit. As I start toward the door, I hear Blake calling my name. GEEZUS! I can hear the guys behind me getting into it, and when I turn around, I see it's turned into a circus. Brent's buddies have joined in, and I walk away thinking that it's exactly what they all deserve.

As I'm getting ready to hail a cab, I hear Blake yell my name again. DAMMIT!

"Gemma, wait!" he yells, and I turn around.

"What?" I yell as I turn around, and he looks taken aback. I soften, knowing this isn't on him. "I'm sorry, Blake. I shouldn't have come out tonight. I'm going home."

"What the hell happened back there?" he says as he takes my hand.

"I don't know! I'm just done!" I say as I feel myself tear up! "What is happening to me?"

"Babe!" Blake says as he squeezes my hand.

"Gemma!" I hear Brent say behind us. I don't turn around though. My hand kills, and I just want to go home. I don't care how much it'll cost. I was supposed to stay at Blake's, but I knew the minute he invited me out that I'd end up back in Brooklyn. Could this night get any worse? Blake sees Brent, and he knows that's why I'm upset and goes off on him. As they're getting into it, I start to head up the street. I'll hail a cab away from this mess. I hear Brent behind me calling my name, and I feel so childish running off like this. I start to walk a little, but I know he'll eventually catch up with me. As I'm getting ready to cross the street, I feel Brent grab my hand and I yelp like a dog that's been kicked. Brent takes a step back, and I grab my injured hand. GEEZUS that hurts.

"Gemma, are you okay? What the hell happened?" he asks, and I roll my eyes.

"I'm tired, Brent. Okay? Let's just call it what it is. You aren't really that interested in me, and I should've known better!" I say as I get ready to turn around again. He deflates, and I almost feel sorry for him.

"Please, tell me you are kidding. I'm not into you since when?" he asks, and I stare at him in awe. "I saw your text."

"Brent, please let's not do this here!" I say, defeated. I'm trying hard not to cry, and I think he can see it.

"Okay. Come with me," he asks as he puts his hand out for me. I just stare at his hand. "Please?" he asks sincerely, and I give him my hand. "Maybe your other hand," he jokes, motioning to my already swollen hand. "We need to get some ice on that." I groan, knowing he's right, and give him my uninjured hand. He pulls me closer to him, and for some reason I can't help myself. I'm more than willing to go with him. Maybe it's the alcohol or maybe it's the fact that I do like him more than I'm allowing myself to admit, but damn him, I still go with him. He hands the valet his ticket, and I can't even look up at him. He puts his arm around my waist, and I don't know whether to pull away or wrap my legs around him. Maybe both?

The valet pulls up with Brent's Aston Martin, and everyone around us oooh's and ahh's like the Batmobile just pulled up. I shake my head and hear Brent laugh as he opens my door. I sit down, and when I look out of my window, the girl in the red dress is standing at the door of the club with her hands on her hips. She gives me a nasty look, and I flip her off! It's my injured hand so as we pull away from the curb I cry out in pain. Brent heads a few blocks away and then stops in front of a building. I'm not paying attention, but I feel like I've been here before. I groan as he gets out. I don't want to make any more stops. I just want to go to bed! He walks around to my side and takes my elbow to help me out of the car.

"Can't we just go home?" I ask, and he shakes his head.

"We need to get some ice on that hand, and my GPS says there's a wreck on the bridge. We can either sit in traffic for a hell of a time trying to get back to Brooklyn and talk, or we can go inside now. So, I can either carry you into the building or you can walk?"

"Lord Jesus, Brent. I'm not a child!" I say as I walk past him… I press the button for the elevator and then wince. I keep forgetting I've injured my-self. I look down at my already bruised and swollen wrist and want to cry. WHY? Why does this shit feel like it only happens to me? The doors open, and when I walk in Brent walks behind me. There are a few other people in the elevator with us, so I move to the corner. Brent moves to stand in front of me, and I'm so tired that I place my forehead on his back. I don't care that I'm pissed at him. He's still a soft place to rest my head. He wraps his arm behind him pulling me closer to him. His touch arouses me and comforts me at the same time. However, I'm still pissed as hell!

We step off the elevator, and I follow Brent into the mostly empty apartment. I've been here before, so I walk over to the couch and sit down. I place my bag beside me and sigh. I hear Brent in the kitchen, but I can't do anything but stare out the floor to ceiling windows. Brent walks in front of me and then drops to his knees. He takes my hand and moves it under the light of the side table. I wince as he runs a finger over my knuckles up to my wrist. He takes a bag of ice and places it on my hand. As he reaches down for my shoe, I don't stop him even though I know what he's going to do. He looks up at me, but I don't react. I can't. I don't know if I'm going to scream, cry or laugh.

"May I?" he asks, and I nod my head. He takes off my shoes and it's the sweetest and sexiest thing at the same time. He runs his hand from my ankle to my knee and then stands up. "Can you let me explain about tonight?" he asks, and I sigh.

"We don't have to do this, Brent."

"I think we do," he replies as he sits down next to me on the couch.

"Whatever."

"I'm sorry if I hurt you, Gemma. If I honestly thought that dancing with another woman would hurt you, I wouldn't have done it. Well, that's not entirely true. If I'm honest, I've been kind of put off that you haven't contacted me since the Hamptons."

"WHAT!" I say as I sit up too quickly and immediately regret it. I place my hand on my forehead and Brent has the gall to laugh at me. "You've got to be kidding me. You were upset that I didn't contact you! You had my number too, Brent!"

"You had mine as well, Gemma!" he comes back at me, and I open my mouth to reply but I can think of nothing. He's right. Well, he's not wrong. "I went out tonight because I was a little pissed off I hadn't heard from you this week. My God, what are the odds that we'd end up the same damn place. I got your text while I was dancing with Mindy and immediately went to look for you. I don't want anyone else but you. When I spotted you with those guys, I went to intervene, but you obviously didn't need my help. I went outside to find you…" I stand up ready to go to war, and Brent's eyes tell me he's not going anywhere.

"I've been fighting for myself, by myself, since I was a little girl, Brent. I have to take care of myself. There's no one else to do it for me. You aren't the only one pissed off here. You think I wanted to watch you grind on the chick in the red dress? Your brother was right. You are something else on the dance floor, and honestly after the weekend we had in the Hampton's together I wanted to vomit seeing the two of you. How would you feel if you saw me dancing like that with some dude?" I ask, and he groans. "Like I thought."

"I would have been pissed, and there's a good chance I might have knocked someone out. I know

I have a very professional demeanor, Gemma, but I haven't always been the good guy. I think it's ironic that the two of us have been pissed off at each other for the same reason. I should have texted you, and I'm sorry I didn't, but you could have texted me too. I feel like I'm in university again. I don't know what to do with myself. I like you, a hell of a lot, but I'm also your boss. I'd like to be your friend, but I feel more than friendly towards you. I'd like you to trust me, but it feels like it's going to be one step forward one step back with us. I know you have some things in your past that make it hard for you to trust people. I'm not asking you to tell me anything. Not if you aren't ready, but I just don't know how to progress this between us. I mean, I do. I just, I like you a lot more than I probably should at this point and the thought of not being with you again shattered my week."

"You don't think my week was shattered? I felt like I'd been played like a used guitar. Dammit, Brent." I say as tears start form in my eyes. "You think I know how to make this work? I'm over my head here. I've never done this before! You're the guy. Aren't you supposed to take the lead?" I ask and he smiles at me. "Why are you smiling like that?"

"I don't know. I guess I just thought we'd take it slow. Become friends, get to know each other first. Then, worry about who takes the lead and where

we go from here. I feel lost in this too. I'm not try-
ing to sound cocky, but I've never done it like this.
This isn't how my usual relationships would have
happened. I was trying to blow off some steam.
You're not the only one feeling vulnerable here,
Gemma. It's no excuse for hurting you tonight, but
I swear that wasn't my intention."

"Tonight sucked! Can you just understand how
hard it was to see you dance like that with another
woman? You kissed me this past weekend like no
one ever has. I've never been jealous of another
woman. EVER! I didn't hear from you all week
and I kept asking myself why. I'm sorry, Brent, but
you have to understand that I'm way out of my element here. I don't do relationships, and I don't
do this," I say, motioning between the two of us.
"I don't even know how to fight with someone. I
don't know how to do this!"

"Okay," he answers as he takes my uninjured
hand. I'm still tipsy, but I can tell he means it. "I'm
not going push you to do or be anything you aren't
ready for, but you're going to have to communicate
with me."

"If I hadn't sent you that text, would you have
slept with her?" I ask, and he grimaces.

"No. It's Mindy. She and I have been intimate
before, but not in a long time. She's a flirt but that's
it."

"You don't mind if I call your bullshit on that,

do you? The way she looks at you, the way she looked at me tonight, tells me she wants more than just dirty dancing with you! And I can't say you didn't look like you were having the time of your life!"

"It was only dancing for me, Gemma. I promise you. A very bad decision in hindsight, and I'm sorry that you had to see it. I'd be mad, too!"

"Can we just go to bed? Dammit!" I want to cry. "I don't have any other clothes. I lost my damn watch! We have work tomorrow. It's only Wednesday!" Brent laughs, and I look at him like I could rip his arm off and beat him with it. "I'm so tired, Brent."

"I know! We'll sleep this off, and then in the morning we can worry about clothes and watches?"

"So that I can do the walk of shame in your fancy lobby?" I add, and he laughs even harder.

"Gemma. I will go out and buy you something to wear for work tomorrow before you even get up," he says as he stands up and takes my hand. He heads into the master bathroom, and I have to squint it's so bright. He places me on top of the counter like I weight nothing. He reaches into the cabinet and grabs a jar of arnica cream. He rubs the cream on my knuckles and hand and then places it back in the cabinet. He grabs a packet of something behind me and smiles at me.

"It's make-up remover. It might be a little dry

because it's old, but I'm sure it will still work." I roll my eyes and get to removing my make-up. Lord knows who it belonged to. Brent leaves and comes back with a large t-shirt. He's already seen me naked, but I'm grateful when he closes the bathroom door behind him to give me privacy. I change out of my clothes and pull the t-shirt over my head. It smells like him and even as pissed off as I am, I have to say it's still comforting. I run my hands through my hair and I'm grateful that I don't look like a deranged animal after tonight. I walk out of the bathroom and head into the master bedroom. Brent comes out of the closet wearing nothing but some athletic shorts, and I have to smile. He's stunning. I walk over to the bed and crawl in. He comes around to my side and sits on the edge of the bed.

"I'm going to go clean up in the other room. You should take this tonight," he hands me two tablets of something, and I look down at it before I look back up at him. "It will help your hand feel better and will help with swelling. I'm not trying to drug you, Gemma. Well, I'm not up to any funny business. It will help. Trust me."

"You said you used to not be a good guy, Brent."

"I used to be a brawler in my younger years, until I found boxing. I have arnica cream and some anti-inflammatory and pain medication at all of my homes. I box during the week, and they both help when I've overdone it. I'd say you overdid it tonight, and tomorrow you'll be sore enough as it is."

"Didn't know if this was the moment you told me you were into Christian Grey kind of shit," I say, laughing and then yawning. He hands me a glass of water, and I take a sip as I swallow them down. I go to place the glass down, and he puts it back up to my lips.

"You're going to want to drink the entire glass, Rocky!" he says, and I remember his accent. I notice it's stronger when he's tired or had a drink or two. Or maybe it's when I'm tired and had a drink or two. Regardless, his voice is a comforting sound. "You alright?" he asks, and I lay my head down after I finish the glass. "I'll grab another glass of water just in case you need it later tonight."

"What time is it?" I ask.

"11:30," he answers. "We will get you another watch, pumpkin!"

"We are such losers!" I say as I lean my head back onto the pillow. "We didn't even make it to midnight!" I close my eyes as I feel him kiss my forehead. The lights are turned off, and then I'm out like a light as well.

Brent

I should be mad, but I'm not. If anything, fight-ing with Gemma is better than making love with anyone else. We are going to figure this out as we go. At least I hope that's the plan. I head back out into the living area and clean up a little. Her shoes are lying next to the couch with her handbag. I head over to it and pull her phone out, plugging it in next to mine in the kitchen. I set my alarm for five so I can get up to run. Then I'll need to figure out clothes for tomorrow. I could call in sick, but I'm pretty sure that's not the right call. I have a lot of work to catch up on, and we have a big event coming up. If my sources are correct, there is a good chance that Gemma will be busy as well, since Layla seems to be leaving at a very inopportune time. I head back into the bedroom and crawl into bed with Gemma. We're lucky Brett hasn't moved in yet and that I've kept this place stocked. This is where we normally send business associates and their spouses or significant others if they're visiting from a different location. I close my eyes and feel Gemma move her hand out like she's trying to find me in her sleep. I pull her hand to my lips and kiss it gently. We are in over our heads, and I pray that we can keep whatever this is above water.

The next morning after my run, I head down the street to a Target and grab a few things. I know from her dress from last night about what size she is, so I pick her up a few things and some shoes just in case. It's not the first time that I've gone shopping for a woman. When I get back to the apartment it's still dark inside, even though the sun is already up. New York, the city that never sleeps, is always alive. However, something feels different this morning. She'll be working in the downtown office today, and I'd like her to enjoy herself.

I start some coffee, and by the time I get out of the shower, Gemma is up too. I wrap my towel around my waist as I step out of the shower. She looks me up and down, and I pull her into my arms. I really like this. Maybe more than I should this soon, but I do. She moves around me and starts to undress, and I have to say this is the best way to wake up. Maybe not the most productive. If she was my girlfriend, we probably wouldn't make it into the office on time, but we are still "learning" each other. Friends first, I tell myself, then laugh because we are way past the friends stage.

We make it into the office on time, and I think we are both grateful for that. I don't think anyone noticed that we arrived together. If they did, they didn't make a stink about it. Gemma walks over to the reception area and starts talking to someone else. I walk straight back to my office and get to work. By the time lunch arrives, I have three missed calls from Blake. When I call him back, he starts going off on me about everything I've ever done wrong. I don't have time for his nonsense today. Then he tells me to check my email. He's sent me an article written by a well-known New York gossip columnist. Apparently, someone got me on video telling off the two guys from last night. Luckily, Gemma had already made her getaway outside, but I wasn't so lucky. All it says under the photo of me with my finger in the big guy's face is *Is New York's favorite Bad Boy back on the scene? If so, where do I sign up? Come to Momma!* I call our publicist, who advises me to just ignore it. "It's gossip, and if anything, you look great in the photo." Most onlookers said I was just sticking up for an unknown blonde.

I work straight through lunch. By the end of

the day, I'm exhausted. Gemma knocks on my door, and I motion for her to come in. She whispers something, but I can't hear it over the commotion out in the hall.

"I can't hear you," I say as she comes inside my office and closes the door.

"I said, I'm so sorry!" she states, and the look on her face makes me want to pull her in my arms. She looks sad. I stand up and walk around my desk, sitting on the edge of it.

"Why are you sorry?"

"Everyone is talking about the photo of you last night. I'm appalled that this is falling on your shoulders." I take her hand, and she takes a seat in the chair in front of my desk.

"Gemma, it's not a big deal. There's nothing for you to be sorry about. For one, I did this to my-self. Two, I would have punched the guy's lights out if you hadn't already. I will never feel guilty about standing up for my friends." She seems to re-lax, and I give her a small smile. "How's that hand feeling, Rocky?" I ask. Her knuckles look better, but the bruise on her hand is hard to miss.

"Sore. Thanks to you I'm sure it looks better than it would have. Thank you," she says as she stands up and heads for the door.

"Hey!" I add as she's almost out the door. She turns, and I give her a small smile as I sit down in my chair. "I'd really like to kiss you right now!"

She blushes and bites her lip.

"I know!" she says as she exits and shuts the door to my office.

At the end of the day, I run into Hayden in the staff kitchen, and he gives me a look that tells me he's not one to be fooled. With his background this is no surprise.

"What?" I ask as I pour myself yet another cup of coffee.

"Nothing, just wondering if you want us to think we are all as stupid as you apparently think we are?" he asks, and I can't help laughing. He's always been incredibly in-tune with every situation. I appreciate that about him because he's amazing at reading people and situations. However, I never thought I'd be on the end of one of his readings. "Ah, so you *do* think we are stupid. I'll say this -- I like the two of you together! Great article, though. There was a story there that they missed out on. Plus, I love a good office romance!" Jeremy, one of the other executives, walks in and looks at the two of us.

"Who's together? Did I miss some good office drama? Dammit, I miss all the good stuff. Guess that's what I get for being so good at my job," he adds sarcastically. Hayden rolls his eyes, giving me a knowing look and then walks back out. "I bet it's Joan and Markus in finance. They always look like they're up to something!" I nod knowingly and then take my cup back to my office. Some people are just more aware than others, I guess.

As I walk back to my desk, I turn the corner and see Gemma talking to our office Casanova. Gerald is a nice guy, but also a womanizer. To him Gemma is fresh meat. The girls around the office are always droning on about him like he's God's gift to women or something. Gemma laughs at something he says, and I admit I wish she was laughing with me and not Gerald. When I make it back to my desk, I see that my mail has been delivered. I sit down, going through the pile, and see a name and address that I recognize.

I open the invitation and see it's for a gallery opening this weekend. A dear friend of mine's fiancée is opening her first of what I assume will be many galleries in the future. I feel honored to be invited to it. I pick up my phone and send Gemma a text.

Hey Rocky! Any Plans this weekend?

Nope! Are you feeling like you are in the need of some company in the boxing ring?

I am not. I was wondering if you wanted to join me for an art gallery opening for a friend of mine's fiancée Saturday.

I've never been to an art gallery opening. I'd love to go with you!

Wonderful. It's Saturday at 8pm.

You think you can stay up that late?

Can you?

I guess we will find out. Tell your fairy godmother I need you until at least midnight. Eastern Time!

I'll let him know! No promises!

Sounds perfect!

I look up from my desk and see Gemma and Layla working on something at Layla's desk. The way Gemma is bent over looking at Layla's screen gives me a direct line of sight to her cleavage. She's so incredible. Alluring and yet innocent in a way. She tucks a strand of hair behind her ear, and when she smiles at Layla, it feels like my heart flips inside of my chest. She's distracting in the best way, and I have to say if she came to work in our down-town office, I'd definitely have more incentive to come to work.

My phone rings and it's another executive with some questions about an account. I get up to close my door, and when I do Layla and Gemma both look up at me. Layla looks away after seeing I don't need them. When she does, I wink at Gemma, and she sweetly blushes. I feel seven feet tall at her reaction to me. As I'm about to close the door, I see Gerald checking her ass out from his office. He looks up at me and then looks away. As I close the door, I feel like I did back in my early 20's. The testosterone in the air is palpable and I'd love nothing more to scare other men away, but that's not the way I roll anymore.

• • •

Saturday night, I pick Gemma up from her apartment. She's wearing a baby blue silk slip dress. The slit up the side gives me a view of her gorgeous, toned legs. Her nude strappy heels make me want them wrapped around my waist. She's perfect! Her blonde hair is down and barely brushes her shoulders. She has an overnight bag with her, and she laughs when she sees my reaction to it.

"Don't get too excited. Your brother invited me to stay over tonight after the opening. We will see if it works out or not. Most of the time he's out until dawn, and I can't wait that long to sleep." I laugh and nod in agreement. I take her hand as we walk to my car. She's so exquisite. I open the car door for her, but before she can get in, I pull her back to me and kiss her. She seems a little surprised at first but then sinks into my embrace. I finally relent and let her into the car.

"I've been wanting to kiss you again since we left for work Thursday morning," I say as I pull into traffic heading into Manhattan.

"I'm not going to lie, I enjoyed that very much. But if you kiss me like that again I don't think we will make it to the gallery opening," she jokes, and I'm seriously tempted to try it. The attraction and chemistry between us isn't letting up at all. In fact, I think it's growing stronger by the day. I've never been this attracted or connected to anyone in my entire life.

"Let's at least control ourselves long enough to stay for cocktail hour," I joke. As we head into the city, I tell her about my friendship with Scott and his fiancée. We met when we were both interning in the city and have stayed in touch through the years. He ended up going a different direction in business, but we still meet up occasionally.

When we arrive, I pull up to the valet and come around to let Gemma out. She's stunning, and I don't want to let go of her hand. However, we can't stay connected all night. A few people take our photos as we enter the gallery, and Gemma handles it like a champ. I'm sure the photo of us will make the gossip columns tomorrow. Through the years I've learned how to handle the press. I'm guessing Gemma will need to get used to it as well as she's just filmed her first movie.

I introduce Gemma to a few people, specifically Scott and his fiancé, Amber. Gemma recognizes someone she knows and excuses herself as I stay and speak with Scott.

"She's lovely," Amber says of Gemma, who is speaking to an older woman on the other side of the gallery. "The two of you make a stunning couple."

"Thank you. It's new and we are still getting to know each other. She's incredible."

"She's different than the women I'm used to seeing you with," Scott adds, and I look over and laugh. "In the best way possible."

"You have no idea. It's been years since I've dated anyone and honestly, I wasn't interested in dating anyone until I met Gemma. She's a remarkable woman. Beautiful, of course, but also kind and genuine," I answer back, and he nods in agreement.

Gemma rejoins us a few minutes later, and we excuse ourselves to look around the gallery. As we are moving through the rooms, I spot my ex, Brandy. She's here with my ex-best friend, Gene. It's always uncomfortable when I run into the two of them. New York is a big place, but it can also feel like a small world when you have mutual friends. Brandy looks up and sees me, and I have about 15 seconds to give Gemma a heads-up. She's studying a painting, so I lean down and whisper in her ear.

"Do you remember me telling you reason I ended up going in alone on the Hamptons House?" I ask, and she nods. "My ex-girlfriend, Brandy and my old acquaintance, Gene are here. I just wanted to give you a heads up. If they come over to speak, I want you to be prepared. They're very petty people, but I don't want to make a scene." I say as I brush the hair away from her shoulder. "I'd be happy to walk in a different direction, but they'd take it as a challenge. Gemma takes my hand and gives it a knowing squeeze. We keep looking at a few paintings, and then I know they're close when I can smell the overwhelming scent of Brandy's lavender perfume.

"Brent," Brandy announces as we turn toward them. "I thought that was you. I was just telling Gene how disappointing it's been that we haven't run into in a while. Carmen and I had drinks the other day, and she said it had been a while since the two of you had slept together. We should all get together and catch up," she adds, not acknowledging Gemma at all. I sigh and then look over at Gene. He's looking down at Brandy like he's hung the moon by having her on his arm. I wish someone would tell him that she'll do the same thing to him that she did to me.

"Brandy, Gene. This Gemma," I say. Gene acknowledges Gemma, but Brandy never takes her eyes off me.

"You know! The last time we were all together, Brent gave Gene a black eye and broke his nose. It was really unbecoming. I'm sure he didn't tell you about that," Brandy mocks as she finally looks down at Gemma. Brandy is almost a foot taller than Gemma, but Gemma doesn't take the bait. In fact, she does the opposite of what Brandy wants and laughs.

"Gene, Brandy. I wish I could say it was nice to meet you, but unlike the two of you I'm not full of shit. Also, Brandy, I'd say Gene deserved it. Wouldn't you?" Gemma adds as she looks up at Gene. Brandy's mouth drops open. Gene looks impressed, and I have to say it's refreshing. I cackle a little as Gemma takes my hand.

"Well, this has been a waste of our time," I say as I lift Gemma's hand to my lips so I can kiss it. "Do enjoy the rest of your night." We start to walk away, and I hear Brandy cursing at Gene. I'm so glad I avoided that train wreck years ago. I'm not sure what I was thinking at the time. More than likely, I wasn't.

I study Gemma's face to see if we're good after that run-in. I will gladly explain the situation if it makes her feel more comfortable, but I don't want to rehash old news if it won't help. She takes a deep breath as we walk away, smiles at me and says, "Where to next?" I can hardly believe my luck having her by my side.

"I know a place," I say, taking her hand.

After we say our goodbyes, we head a few blocks down to a rooftop bar. It's a beautiful night, and I want to spend it with Gemma. We are seated in the corner, and we order appetizers and drinks. I'm driving tonight, so I'm going to babysit my drink a little. Gemma is turning more than a just few heads tonight, and I smile as she scoots her chair closer to mine. I'm glad she's with me. The night is amazing. There's a breeze, and when a strand of hair falls in her face, I take the opportunity to move it behind her ear.

"Gemma, you look beautiful. You always do, but tonight there's just something so carefree about you. I'm glad, all things considering, that you came out with me tonight. Other than the run in with my ex, did you enjoy yourself?"

"I did, and I am. I'm not even thinking about your ex. Although, I am thinking about how I'd like to rid you of some of those clothes you're wearing." I burst out laughing as the waiter brings out our food and drinks.

"I think you might be on to something there. Did you have a good week? I feel like I didn't get to speak to you much about being in our office. I enjoyed you being there, but did you?"

"I did. Mostly everyone is kind. There's a lot of work to be done, but I don't mind the hard work. Makes the week go by faster. How about you? Why'd you enjoy me being there so much?" I reach over and run a finger over her still bruised hand. It's turning a yellowish color now, so I know it's healing properly.

"You remind me of what I've been fighting for all these years. Why 10 years ago I bought a warehouse in Brooklyn so I could remove myself from the "New York Elitist" crowd that I used to run with. You remind me of why I've not been in a relationship in years. In the hopes that one day I'd find something special. Some*one* special." She sighs as she leans forward, kissing me like we're the only ones in the room.

I drop her off at Blake's apartment, and before getting out of the car, she leans over and kisses me passionately. I pull her so she's sitting sideways across my lap and kiss her back with the same fervor. She tugs on my hair, and my hand slips up to rest against the inside of her thigh. She moans against my mouth, wanting more. As much as I'd like to take this further, I know if I do, we won't be going anywhere but the closest place, and that's my old bachelor pad. I'll be damned if we do that at my old place. When we pull back, she's looking at me with question in her eyes. I run the back of my fingers down the side of her face.

"Don't look at me like that. You know how I feel about you. It's more than obvious, but I don't want to go any further in my car and I sure as hell don't want to take you to my old place. I want something different with you, Gemma. Stay with me next Friday," I ask, and she closes her eyes as she smiles. "I want you, Gemma, but not like this. Spend next weekend with me."

"Okay!" she answers as she leans down, kissing me tenderly. I place my forehead against hers as we catch our breath. I move the strap of her dress back in place and then kiss her shoulder. Eventually, we get out of the car, and I walk her to the entrance of Blake's apartment. I look down at my watch and see it's almost midnight! Which reminds me of something I want to get for Gemma.

"Got you home just in time, Cinderella!" I joke as she laughs and wraps her arms around my neck. I lift her off the ground so we are face to face.

"Does that make you my Prince Charming?" she asks jokingly, as her beautiful blue eyes stare back at me. I kiss her gently before pulling back and smiling at her.

"I sure as hell hope so!"

• • •

Monday morning, I get a call from Blake, who tells me to check my email. He's sent me an article from the gallery opening this weekend and there we are. Gemma and I entering the gallery. Under the photo of Gemma holding my hand as we enter the gallery it says,

Brent King, pictured above with an unknown blonde. Onlookers say the PDA between the pair was more than PG-13. Brent is also pictured below with Gallery owner Amber Arnold and her fiancé, Scott Harold. It's been a while since we've seen the Scottish heartthrob out about town with anyone. We hope the New York billionaire is as lucky in love as he has been in business. Can he have both? Only time will tell.

DAMMIT!

Gemma

Dammit! I think as I close the email that Blake has sent to Brent and I and wonder if anyone else has seen this. God, I hope not. I hope they don't think I've been receiving any preferential treatment from Blake and his brother. This is not what I wanted, but here we are. Blake is out at a lunch meeting, and I didn't have plans to get out of the office today, but I feel like I need to. I need to process this. I get a text from Brent that asks if we can talk, and I close my eyes. It was all going so well. I bet he's upset or going to try to end things. I knew people had taken our photos, but I didn't know it would end up in a freaking magazine article. Not to mention a reputable one. Gossip is one thing; glossy New York City magazine is another.

I shut down my computer and head toward the elevators. It said unknown blonde, so they don't have my name, but it will only be a matter of time before they figure out not only my identity, but that I work for his company. This cannot be good.

I cross the street and walk down to my favorite sushi place. It's fairly empty as it's only just now 11. I grab a table at the back of the restaurant and sit down. I give them my order and pull my phone out to respond.

> Hey! Sorry for the delay in response.

> I stepped out the office for lunch.

> No problem. I'm guessing you saw the article Blake emailed us. You ok?

> Am I okay? Is it okay? Are you upset?

> Where are you?

> At Sushi Soul.

> Be there in 5.

I look up and then back down at my phone. He doesn't work five minutes from here so I'm confused. Five minutes later he's walking in the door. He looks around the restaurant and spots me in the back. I stand up, unsure of what I'm walking into, but he pulls me in his arms. I didn't know I needed this, but once I'm in his arms I relax.

"No, Rocky, I'm not upset. Everything is going to be okay! I promise!"

"Are you sure?" I ask, and he gives me a smile I can only describe as a Playboy grin. If I didn't know any better, I'd think he's happy about this. "I didn't know if this would change things between us."

"No, it changes nothing for me! I was nervous because I don't want anyone prying into our personal lives. No one at work is going to care. It's not against any rules to date someone at work. The longer I sit with it, the only concern I have is how you are feeling. That's why I rushed up here. I don't want you to feel alone in this. It's just a picture, but if I'm being honest, I love that I have a photo out with you. The picture of you is stunning."

The waitress stops by, but Brent doesn't order anything. "You're not eating lunch?"

"I have a lunch meeting downtown in an hour. I just wanted to see you, make sure you're okay. By the way, I love how we look together," he adds.

"Thank for you coming to check on me. I started to panic that you'd be upset. I guess I was looking at it differently. I don't want people to think that I'm getting preferential treatment from you or your brother. Most people know I've worked for Blake for a while now. I want people to respect me, but some will talk and have their own ideas regardless. I just didn't want it like this. I've worked really hard to get where I am. As I know you have, too. I don't want someone to think I'm sleeping with the boss to get ahead," I add as he takes my hand across the table.

"That's not going to happen. If they don't know you yet, they know me, and they know that's not who I am or how I do business. If I thought you were using me to try and get ahead I wouldn't be with you. That's not how this unfolded. I didn't even know you worked for the company until after we met. But even if I did, that wouldn't have changed anything for me. I felt something the moment you showed up at my table at Perrone's."

"I know. I guess I just don't want to be a joke."

"You aren't. You could never be a joke," he reaffirms as the waitress brings me my roll of sushi. "I'll let you eat, but I wanted to check on you."

"Thank you, Brent. You didn't have to come all this way just to check on me, but I'm grateful you did."

"Yes, I did!" he says as he leans down, kissing me passionately before pulling back. He places a hand on my cheek. "I'm excited about Friday!"

•••

I'm so nervous! Why am I so nervous? I've slept with men before. Hell, I've had plenty of "dates." If that's what you want to call them. I think I'm more nervous because there's a part of me that needs this to go well. I know this isn't just a one-night stand. Since he picked me up at my apartment, I haven't been able to focus on anything other than I can't believe this is happening. I've slept in the same bed with him before, but this feels bigger than that.

We pull up to his warehouse and my god, I've forgotten how big this place is. We pull into his garage, and I see five other vehicles. I'm not sure what they are. I recognize the Range Rover and I see an Audi and a Tesla. Other than that, I don't ask any questions or delve further into the car situation. He's a billionaire. Of course he has more than one luxury vehicle. There's space for more, but who am I kidding, my Corolla would look out of place in here. I'd have to park my car around the corner as to not offend the others. Plus, my Corolla would probably feel bad about herself in here. I realize I've gone on a mental tangent and laugh to myself as Brent comes around to open my door.

"Do I want to know?" he asks, and I shake my head.

"Probably not, but I'll tell you anyway. I was thinking how out of place my car would feel in here," I say as he laughs.

"Don't be ridiculous, Gemma! Besides, your clown car belongs in the circus and not in a garage," I gasp and slap his arm. We both laugh as he takes my hand, grabbing my bag, and walking over to an elevator. He introduces me to Paul in the security office next to elevator and then presses the button. He pushes the button for the second floor once we are inside the elevator, and we are there quicker than I feel ready for. Shadow comes out to greet us, and I get down on the floor to give him a big hug.

"You smell better than the last time I saw you," I say as Shadow wags his tail in response.

"I hope you are referring to the dog and not me," Brent jokes as he drops my stuff in the kitchen. There's an entire cake sitting out on the kitchen counter. "The cake is for later," he says, winking at me as I place my hand in his. "This floor is the kitchen, half bath, my study, dining room, living room and master," he says as he shows me around the second floor. "You've spent some time in my bathroom, so you probably don't need to see it again," he adds as we both laugh. I don't think I'll ever live that down. We don't walk completely in each room, but I at least get the gist of where everything is. Up the main staircase to the third floor are the four guest rooms each with a full bathroom. The fourth floor is his gym and an unfinished bonus room. The fifth floor is the roof access. There's a plunge pool, al fresco dining area and a small garden. It's beautiful up here. I can't imagine having all of this at my disposal. The lifestyles of the rich and famous is beyond comprehension.

"Are you kidding me?" I ask, and he shakes his head.

"You're welcome to look around while I put the steaks and veggies on the grill. Make sure you're down in about 10-15 minutes to watch the sunset over Manhattan from the living area. It's one of my favorite things about this place. The view is spectacular. It's a little too warm right now to eat outside or we'd eat up here tonight." He turns around to walk back inside but stops. "I told you that the view was better here."

I wander around, first heading to where we came in. There's a full study and a library with floor to ceiling windows. The view is incredible in here as well. I head into the formal dining area, then into the kitchen where I want to run by and lick some of the frosting off the cake. Maybe I'll lick some off of Brent later. I head into the master bedroom and stop to take it all in. It feels different walking in here this time. I head into the bathroom and there's that huge walk-in shower I've already enjoyed. Situated in front of the floor to ceiling window is the beautiful clawfoot tub. I walk over and running my hand across the cool, smooth surface before turning around and heading back into the main living area.

Brent has moved up to the roof to grill the food for tonight. I head up the grand staircase to the third floor and see that all the bedrooms are pretty much the same. I climb up to the roof, not bothering with the elevator and I see Brent taking the steaks off the grill. His smile makes my heart flutter in my chest. I'm not sure which is more beautiful -- the view from the roof or Brent? There is an unobstructed view of Manhattan, and I can only imagine how incredible it is to come home to this every night. The view outside of my apartment window is of another building, so this is quite spectacular for me. The little herb and veggie garden up here is so cute, and the patio furniture being strategically laid out gives it a quaint feeling. Like something you'd see in little Italy with the twinkling lights hanging from above. His place is magnificent. It's a hot afternoon, but hopefully it'll cool off as the night progresses. I take his hand, and we head down to the second floor. I walk into the kitchen with Brent, and he pulls some kind of mashed potatoes out of the oven.

"Family recipe," he says. He plates our meals, hands me one and then takes my hand. "Dinner is served."

"Why, thank you," I reply as we sit down to eat.

The food is delicious. Better than I expected for a home cooked meal. He really is over the top. The potatoes, the veggies, the steak, everything is cooked to perfection. As we eat, we watch the sun set over Manhattan. He takes my hand, and I look over at him.

"Dessert?" he asks, and I grin. "I'll take that as a yes. I'll be right back." He gets up, taking our plates and then comes back with one big slice of cake. It looks like strawberry. He moves his chair so he's sitting closer to me and slices into the cake. He lifts it up to my mouth, and I take a bite. The flavors explode in my mouth, and I groan.

"That's amazing. Don't tell me you made this!" I ask as he laughs, shaking his head.

"No. A friend of mine has a bakery not far from the office. She made the cake for tonight." I take a bite, and after I've swallowed my piece, he leans over to kiss me. I kiss him back, and he pulls me onto his lap. I wrap my hands behind him as he gently runs his hand through my hair. "God, you're just as sweet as I remember," he adds, and I smile but roll my eyes.

"I think it's the cake that's so sweet," I answer as he moves a piece of hair away from my face. "No, darling. It's definitely not the cake. What would you like to do now, Gemma?" he asks, and I lift my eyebrows. He laughs, bringing my hand up to his lips. He kisses the inside of my wrist, and then places it back on the table. "Do you want to finish the cake and head upstairs to have a drink outside? Do you want to stay here? We can watch a movie? We can go to a movie? What do you want to do?" I give him a small smile. I just want to be with him.

"You. I want you," I whisper, and he leans down, kissing me again. This time a little bit more passionately.

"I'm yours, Gemma. I think you know that by now, but we have time."

"Let's go outside then." He nods, standing up and pulling me to my feet. We stand by the wet bar trying to figure out what we want to drink, and of course we both want whisky. I follow him into the elevator, and he leans against the wall watching me.

"You look beautiful tonight, Gemma." I blush. "If I haven't said that already, please forgive me."

"So do you, Brent," I reply as I take all of him in. He's in a dark green button down with his sleeves rolled up to just below his elbows, showing off his toned forearms. He's wearing jeans, brown loafers, and even his watch is attractive. Which reminds me I need to start saving up for a new one.

"If you keep looking at me like that, Gemma, this night is going to be over faster than either of wants it to be."

"I'm not so sure that's possible," I answer, and he hums knowingly.

"You are dead set on rushing this, Gemma. You shouldn't. I want to take my time with you. I want to savor tonight just like I want to savor you. Nothing has to happen tonight."

I follow him out onto the rooftop area. He pulls me so I'm beside him on the double lounger. It's truly amazing up here. Manhattan is all lit up, and I'm overwhelmed by her beauty. I take a small sip of my drink and roll over closer to Brent and let him hold me. God, I hate to admit it, but I miss being in his arms when he's not around. You'd think with time I'd gain more perspective, maybe come to my senses a little, but I feel like it's done the exact opposite. It's given me a hunger for something and someone I know I can't have. Especially long term. I snuggle deeper into him, trying to cement this moment into my memory. I would love for this to work out, but I'm a realist. As much as I'd like to be a dreamer, life has conditioned me to know that nothing like this is truly for me. Plus, like I told him in the Hamptons, I don't believe in fairy tales. I don't understand why I can't just enjoy where I am. I think it's because I know how heartbreaking this will be for me when it does end. He's a man's man. Someone who can take care of himself and the people he loves. I should be thinking about how lucky I am. All I can think about right now is how much I don't deserve this and how much I know I'll miss him when this is all over.

"I'll be up front and tell you I don't really know how to do this." I say, breaking the silence.

"Do what?" he asks, and I sigh.

"You know I don't have much experience with relationships. I've never been romanced. I don't know how to transition into the stuff I do know."

"You mean into sex?" he asks, and I can tell he's smiling, but not making fun of me. I look up at him, and he runs a hand through my hair. "I don't have any expectations of you, Gemma. I think that's the difference between what you're used to and what I'm offering you. In a way this is new for me too. I've never been with anyone who wanted to lie here with me. The women I've been with just wanted something from me. Whether it was materialistic or what circle I could introduce them to. You haven't asked me for anything. So, I'm a little out of my comfort zone as well. I'm glad you're here with me now. I wouldn't want to be lying here with anyone else."

"See," I groan, rolling onto my stomach and playing with the buttons of his shirt. "Normal guys. They don't say those kind of things to girls like me. You're so open and honest. Kind and romantic. I feel out of my league here. I'm not used to going with the flow. I'm a 'get in and get the hell out' kind of girl. In the past it hasn't been a pack a bag and stick around for the weekend."

"Exactly, Gemma. In your past," he says as he plays with a strand of my hair. "But we're moving into new territory here. I'm not saying we have to make any lasting promises to each other. All I'm saying is that maybe the way it used to be… you need to forget. Let tonight be the start of something new. Something better. Give me the opportunity to show you what it could be like. For both of us. I've never romanced anyone like this because I haven't wanted to. I don't do all of this for everyone. That doesn't mean I was an asshole, but this is new for me too. I'm enjoying myself just like we have been this entire time. Even when you were angry with me, I'd rather be arguing with you than anywhere else, with anyone else. Let's see where it goes. If we fall asleep, then we fall asleep. If something happens, wonderful. Hell, we both know we want it to, but that doesn't mean it has to. Just give it a chance, Gemma. I promise to be open and honest with you, and I hope you'll do the same. You have so far," he jokes as he pulls me up on top of him. He places his hands on my ass, pressing me into him, kissing me harder than he has all night, and I reciprocate. I moan into his mouth. "I know it will be amazing, Gemma. I promise I'll take care of you. You're safe here with me. Always."

I can't even answer as I lean my chin on top of his chest. He rolls us over so we're laying face to face on our sides. He's looking into my eyes like he can see through me. I feel like I'm getting ready to panic. I want to believe everything he says. I know I should be able to but I can't. I just can't. There's a wall that even I can't break down and it makes me want to run.

"Why don't we walk down by the waterfront?" he suggests, and I nod my head in agreement. I'd love nothing more than to explore Brooklyn with Brent.

As he cleans the kitchen, I freshen up a bit in the bathroom. When I come out, he's leaning against the back of the sofa. I stop dead in my tracks. His stare is lethal, and I'm curious what he has in mind.

"Come here, Gemma," he requests, and I go to him. "You good to do some walking in those shoes?" he asks, looking down at my tan stilettos.

"You'd be surprised what all I can do in heels," I answer as he groans, leaning down to kiss my bare shoulder. "Take me for a walk, Brent!" We head out of the garage door, and he types a code in.

"If for some reason you need to get in or out of the garage, type in this code. 72685263. It spells out Scotland." I laugh because that's so fitting of him. We walk around to the waterfront and hold hands, enjoying the evening as it begins to cool off. At least it feels cooler with the breeze off of the water. We head down to a grassy area with some benches and sit down. Brent pulls my legs into his lap, rubbing my calves. "How are your feet?" he asks.

"They're good. I've still got a couple miles to go," I answer, and his laugh reverberates through my body.

"Glad to hear! How was dinner tonight? Did you enjoy it?"

"I did. Everything was perfect. The cake was amazing too," I stand up and sit in his lap, taking his phone. He unlocks it and pulls up his camera. I lean back against him, and we take a picture. "Give me a kiss, Gemma," he asks, and I laugh, leaning over and kissing him passionately. The next thing I know, is he's no longer holding his phone but has his arms wrapped around me with his hands in my hair. I sit back after a long minute, and when I finally open my eyes, his grin is bigger than I've ever seen it.

"Let's head back." No argument here.

When we get back to his garage, he tells me to enter the code. I type in Scotland with the numbers and the door unlocks. I walk in first, and even though the lights came on it takes me a second to orient myself to my surroundings. His garage is huge. I turn around as Brent hits the up button on the elevator, and I follow him inside. We make it to the main floor, and Brent heads over to the cake.

"More cake?" I ask as I remove my heels and head over to him.

"Yes ma'am," he answers as he takes a plate out and puts a slice on the plate. "But I have an idea as well," he says.

"Ok. What's your idea?" I ask as he brings me the slice of cake. "Are you not eating this? The cake I mean," I add as I stumble over my words. I really didn't mean it how it sounded.

"Your double meaning isn't lost on me, and I haven't ruled either out tonight," he answers as he tucks a piece of hair behind my ear. "If I wasn't here and you were by yourself. What would you do?"

"Umm…I'm confused," I answer swallowing a piece of cake. "Why wouldn't you be here, and why am I alone? You mean like would I steal something?" He burst out laughing, taking the plate from me and placing it on the counter.

"No, Rocky. I mean, let's say this was your house, and you were alone. What would you do? I think I know, but I want to hear it from your lips."

"Kinky!" I look around and then remember the clawfoot tub in the bathroom. "Take a bath in the clawfoot tub," I answer, and he smiles.

"Come on," he says as I stare at him in disbelief until he's about 10 steps ahead of me. He walks through the bedroom and into the bathroom. I stop in the doorway, watching as he turns the faucet on and pours something that smells incredible into the bathtub. I lean against the doorframe watching him.

He walks over to me and smiles. "Do you want to pull your hair up?" He asks, and I nod.

I grab a hair tie from my bag in the bedroom and pull my hair up, and when I turn around he's traded places with me. Now he's standing in the doorway of the bathroom watching me. I walk over and kiss him affectionately, looking up at him as he takes the straps of my dress and pushes them off my shoulders. My dress falls to the ground, and I'm standing in front of him in my designer bra and underwear. I tried to be smart about my lingerie for tonight. I figured we would have had sex earlier in the night, and I'd be home by now. I should have known better. I chose my white, sheer bralette and matching thong. It has light blue appliqué flowers and it's one of my favorites. He takes a step back, looking me up and down, then into my eyes.

"I shouldn't be surprised but Jesus, Gemma," he expresses as he runs his hands down my shoulders and around my waist, pulling me to him. His hands move down from my waist to cup my ass, and he lifts me up. I wrap my legs around his waist and my arms around his neck. He kisses me gently at first and then our kisses intensify to the point where I have to remind him about the water.

He walks back into the bathroom, turns off the faucet, and then comes back into the bedroom. He lays me down at the end of the bed, then sits up to look at me. His eyes are on fire for me. The way he looks at me is overwhelming. He stands up, leaning over me as he kisses my lips and then moves down my neck to my collar bone. He kisses in between my breasts and then pulls one of my nipples into his mouth. My body moves closer to his mouth with every lick. I want him everywhere, and lucky for me he's everywhere I want him to be. His hand roams down my stomach, under my panties and caresses me gently across my sex. I whimper as he inserts his finger into me and takes my other breast into his mouth. I groan at his administrations, and he hums, encouraged by my sounds. I buck off the bed and into his hand as he inserts another finger inside me, stretching me in the most delicious fashion. He whispers my name as he continues his kisses down my stomach, across my ribs and then places a gentle kiss on each hip bone. He pulls my panties down my legs, and I lift my head to watch him. I'm panting as he places kisses on the inside on my ankle and licks up my leg. I lower my head back to the bed and stare up at the ceiling. He bypasses my sex and goes down the other leg until he reaches my other ankle. He pushes me up the bed and moves the bench at the end of the bed so he can kneel in front. I take a deep breath, anticipating his mouth where I want him the most. He spreads my legs further apart and then puts each a leg over each shoulder.

"I've been imagining for a while now how

sweet you'd be," he states as I lift my head up to look at him. I groan when he leans down, running his tongue up my sex. I have to lower my head back to the bed before I pass out. "Breathe, baby," he whispers before he starts to absolutely devour me. I'm whimpering and yelling his name as his hand comes up, grabbing my hand. His other hand moves to play with my breast, and I know it will be no time at all before I'm falling over the edge. My hips start to move of their own accord, and Brent grabs my ass, pressing me harder against his mouth. I fall deliciously over the edge, yelling his name as I go. I know I didn't pass out, but I feel like I could have when I finally come to. I feel him pressing gentle kisses against my sex, my hips and my stomach. He crawls up the bed, wiping me from him mouth and leaning down to give me the most incredible kiss. "You were better than I could have ever dreamed, Gemma," he whispers as I lift my head up, grabbing his neck and pulling him back to me. "Sweeter than strawberry cake!"

"That was… incredible!" I whisper against his lips as he pulls me up to a sitting position, then picks me up. He carries me to the bathroom, and I can tell the bath is still hot. He places a hand in the water, then lowers me carefully. My body and mind are still reeling with what just took place. I've never in my life had a sexual encounter like that. It was mind-blowing and we haven't even had sex. I mean, my god, I don't know what to do with myself. Now I'm sitting in a bath that he's run for me, and he's left to give me a couple minutes to myself. I didn't even get the opportunity to ask him if I could reciprocate. I lean my head against the back of the tub and give myself a second. I hear him come back in the bathroom, and I look up at him. He's still dressed, and I roll to the side to face him. He's leaning against the counter watching me, smiling. I smile shyly at him, and he looks up to the ceiling, as if pulling strength from above.

"How do you feel?" he asks as he crosses his arms. I look him up and down and notice he removed his shoes. When I reach his face, I notice he's watching at me with a contented expression.

"Sated," I state as I put an arm over the bathtub. "I'm tired and really relaxed. You?" I ask as he uncrosses his arms and puts his hands behind him on the counter.

"I feel really good. That was amazing, Gemma. I've never felt so connected to someone in my entire life." I watch him for a few seconds and then look down at the ground. I kind of understand how he feels, but I'm not sure I can say it out loud. I want to, but I can't. I can't tell him that my heart feels connected to him more than I care to admit. I look up at him and feel like he can read my thoughts. He nods knowingly, giving me a small smile. "I could do that a million times and still want to do it again.

I think I'm hooked on you. Now that I've touched you and tasted you, I'm not sure I'll ever be able to stop. You are addicting, Gemma. In the best way!"

"I'm glad to hear that," I answer, my voice laced with humor. "So, I'm hearing that I'm not the only one who enjoyed it."

"More than I could ever express to you, Gemma. I'm happy to prove it if you'd like," he mutters as he pushes his sleeves up a bit. My heart flips in my chest and I press my mouth against the side of the tub hiding my expression. "Stay with me tonight." I look up into his eyes and know I'm going to stay. I knew it as soon as he picked me up that I'd stay. As soon as he wrapped his arms around me, I knew there wasn't any place I'd rather be but here with him. I nod my head, but he raises his eyebrows like he's waiting for my answer.

"I'll stay with you," I answer, and he beams in my direction.

"Take your time in here, Gemma. I mean it. I'll be out in the den whenever you're done." He leans over, kissing me chastely on the lips, and then walks out of the bathroom. I lean back again, closing my eyes and enjoying the heat of the bath all over my body. I've never had anyone love my body like he just did. I open my eyes, needing to redirect my thoughts. I look beside me and see a towel waiting for me. I climb out of the bath, letting the water out and drying off my body. The oil and moisturizer in the water feels amazing on my skin. There's a hint of rose petals, jasmine and a bit of spice. I hang my towel up on a hook and walk into his bedroom. I packed pajamas, but I see his green button down and jeans lying on a chair in the corner of his room. I pull on his button-down and take my hair down. I walk out to the living area and see him sitting on the sofa with the TV on. When he sees me, his head falls back onto the back of the sofa as he groans.

"This okay?" I ask, and he nods.

"Of course. God, I could get used to seeing this! Come here, you sexy little vixen," he asks as I walk around the sofa and he pulls me onto his lap. "Do you want to try and watch a movie? It's after 11, but I'm good to try and stay up if you want to watch something."

"Are you tired?" I ask, and he nods.

"A little. Why? What did you have in mind?" he asks, and I shrug my shoulders.

"I'm good to stay up!" He laughs and then turns me so I'm sitting sideways on his lap.

"Let me get to know you a little better. I know you aren't too keen on personal questions, but I guess this is a date."

"Ok," I answer a little hesitantly and he runs a hand under the shirt I'm wearing placing his hand against my back.

"How about you ask me three questions and I

ask you three questions? You can go first," he says, and I nod, a little relieved.

"That sounds good." I think for a second of what I want to know, and I figure I might as well just ask random questions. "How many women have slept over at your place?" I ask and he smiles.

"This place? Three, including you," he answers, and I look at him, stunned.

"Three? That's it?" I ask, and he laughs.

"You asked how many women have slept over here. My arrangements with other women weren't necessarily that they'd stay over after sex. When I lived in the city, I had women stay over there more often. That was a long time ago. I'm not the same guy I was back then. This place is a little different. Well, at least to me it is. I don't let just anyone stay over here. This is my home and you're the 3rd woman to sleep over since I've lived here. I know you aren't going to believe this, but a lot of the women I was with didn't want to come out to Brooklyn. It was beneath them, or at least that's how they acted. Catarina, my last girlfriend, never stayed out here. She would come by if I was having a party or people over to make an appearance, but she never spent the night. You're also the first person to use my bathtub," he adds, and I open my eyes in shock.

"WHAT?" I say, and he nods.

"I could tell by the way you looked at the tub

earlier that you were into it. Ok my turn," he says, and I whine. I like asking him questions better, but I'm going to play fair. "Anything I ask that you don't want to answer you don't have to. I just want to get to know you better. I think there's a lot more to you than you allow people to see." I look over at him, and he presses a finger to his lips, shushing me before I can respond. "It'll be our little secret," he adds with a sexy wink. "You just finished your first film. Do you think you'll continue down that road of doing more films?"

"I really enjoyed filming the Sinatra biopic, but I didn't enjoy the sex scenes. Not because I'm a prude or it was uncomfortable, but because it didn't feel natural to me even though Dalton made me feel comfortable. He was really understanding and easy to work with," I add, and when I look up at him, he's watching me like he gives a shit what my response is.

"If that's not something you want to do, Gemma, you know you don't have to do it. You can add that to your contract. I'd be happy to look over any script that comes your way if you'd like. I know Blake said he handled your last one."

"I appreciate that. It's not that I don't want to do it. It's just that it was my least favorite part, but again I enjoyed the process of filming a movie. Plus, it would be hard to film a Lana Turner biopic without talking about her sex life. She was remarkable in that sense. Ahead of her time if you will. I'm not sure if that's something I'll continue to pursue. It was great money. I was able to pay off almost all my student loans and credit card debt. I put a couple thousand dollars aside for Blake to help me invest, but we still haven't been able to get around to that. If I did another movie, I could pay off all my NYU debt. Luckily, I met Blake when I was still in college, and he was able to help me land this incredible internship that actually paid well. You probably haven't heard of them. There a small potatoes firm," I add sarcastically. "King Brothers & Associates. Ring any bells?" He laughs, pinching my leg, and I giggle. "Does that satisfy your question?" I ask as he leans in, kissing me gently. He sits back, taking me with him. I melt into him and enjoy the fact that's he's only wearing his boxer briefs. His chest is so warm and comforting.

"For now. I do have other questions surrounding the finance bit, but we can talk about that later. Your turn!"

"What's your favorite color?"

"Green. What's yours?" he asks, and I smile.

"Blue. What's your favorite food?" I ask as he runs his hands between my legs, and I giggle. "Seriously!" I slap him across the chest, and he laughs.

"I'm a carnivore so steak is my favorite," he answers and then nods for me to answer.

"Any seafood," I answer, and he looks surprised. "I grew up near the coast where seafood is fresh. Expensive, but fresh. I didn't get to eat it much growing up, but it's something I really enjoy now."

"Want to keep on going?" he asks, and I nod. "I know you lost your mom when you were little. When was the last time you talked to your father?" he asks as I deflate a little inside. It's a fair question. I'm not offended he asked, it's just not a fun topic for me.

"My high school graduation. He showed up, drunk as usual. He stayed for the ceremony. Then in front of some friends he stated loudly that he had fulfilled his role and that he was done with me. I haven't seen or talked to him since. Since moving to New York after high school, I haven't been back to Savannah. In case you're wondering, I don't plan on going back for a very long time. There's nothing for me there." I look into Brent's eyes, and he looks incensed. I touch the side of his face, and he shakes his head. "It's okay, Brent. I mean, I know it's not okay what happened to me. The things he said and how I was raised. I just meant I'm going to be okay. I appreciate your anger on my account, but it doesn't solve anything. Believe me, if it had, I'd be in a better place with all of it."

"Your turn," he says, his voice barely above a whisper. "Please ask me something." I run my hands through his beautiful hair and love seeing the dark auburn sprinkled through his dark mane. He runs my hands down the side of his face and over his chest. He closes his eyes as I lean down, kissing his chest. I scoot off the sofa and in between his legs. I look up at him, and he's watching me with fire in his eyes. "Gemma, you don't have to do what I think you're about to do," he whispers. I reach up, trailing my hands down his chest and over his stomach. I place my hands on the waist band of his underwear, and he doesn't move.

"Please," I ask. He reaches down, placing a hand on my cheek.

"Do you feel like you are supposed to reciprocate from earlier or do you actually want to do this?" he asks as I grab the waist band of his underwear and smile.

"What makes you think I don't want this? I've been trying to have sex with you since I got here tonight. Yes, I'm used to a mutual exchange, but I want this, Brent. I want you." He lifts his hips, and then leans down, kissing me hard. I push his chest back down on the sofa and he lays back willingly. He places a hand over mine, squeezing gently. I start kissing down his stomach, the defined V of his hips and then the tip of HIM gently. He groans as I wrap my hand around his hard shaft. I slowly pump my hand up and down a couple times, and then look him in the eye. I know with everything inside me that I want this man more than I've ever wanted anyone. I take him in my mouth and give him the same intense treatment that he gave me earlier. He groans and his hips start to move slowly. After a few minutes, he starts to grow harder in my mouth, and I know he's close. I feel him reach down, pulling me up from under my arms so I'm on top of him. He kisses me hard, and I shake my head in disbelief at him.

"Sixty-nine with me baby," he groans as I spin around. He devours me again as I take him in my mouth. It takes absolutely no time at all for both of us to climax together. I can feel HIM pulsating beneath me as I lay my head on his leg. He kisses me gently across my sex as the aftershocks of our encounter subside. A wave of exhaustion takes over, so I shift off him and lay down beside him on the sofa. He carries me into his bedroom and places me gently on the bed. "I'll let you clean up while I shut everything down out here. I'll be right back. I promise," he whispers as he leans over, kissing me tenderly before walking out.

I head into the bathroom and look in the mirror. I look the same, but I feel something I've never felt before. At least something I haven't felt since I was a tiny girl. When my mother was still alive, and life made sense. I feel loved. I feel the emotions of it all start to bubble to the surface, but I shove it down hard. Why the hell does this beautiful man make me so emotional? I close my eyes, willing myself to hold it together. I need to go to bed so I can re-group. I open the bathroom door, and Brent is closing the floor to ceiling blinds in front of the bed.

"If I don't, it'll blind us in the morning. Better if we keep it dark in here," he states. I notice he hasn't put his underwear back on, and I smile. He walks over, kissing me gently. He grins down at me as I wrap my arms around his neck, smiling up at him. "Also, you're not a natural blonde," he adds, and I laugh. "I like your hair a lot. I imagine you were a stunning brunette as well." He starts to unbutton my shirt, or *his* shirt that I'm wearing. Once he undoes the last button, he pushes the shirt off my shoulders, looking down at me. "It's like unwrapping my very own present each time." He goes down to his knees but throws his green button-down shirt on the chair in the corner by his jeans. "You want to go again?" he asks, smiling as he looks up at me.

"I think you've been on your knees enough tonight," I reply as he picks me up and carries me to the bed. He does have the same mattress and bedding at all of his places. I snuggle into the buttery-soft sheets and sigh.

"Told you," he adds as he turns the lights off and moves closer to me. He wraps an arm around my waist and kisses the back of my head. "Thank you for everything, Gemma. I won't forget this night for a very long time." I turn around, bringing my hand to rest on his cheek. I kiss him gently in the dark and feel my heart explode. This man loves me, I can feel it. It scares the hell out of me. Not because he's loving me like no one has ever loved me, which is accurate. But because I feel the same damn way about him. I'm falling in love with him. I close my eyes and try to fight the feeling that I need to run. Run back to what I know. What's un-complicated.

"NO! I DON'T WANT TO GO BACK!" I scream as I wake up in my childhood bedroom. I try to open my bedroom door to escape, but it's locked. I run to the window, and it's sealed shut. I push as hard as I can, but it doesn't budge. I start to cry, knowing I'm stuck here forever. No one will ever come to check on me.

I walk to the mirror above my chest of drawers and see the faint bruises on my neck and cheek. The blood is dried at the corner of my mouth, but the red stain on my peter pan collar is still wet to the touch. I look down and see the faint red splotches of blood on my new shirt. When I look back at my reflection, I don't recognize myself.

Then I hear him, screaming and wailing for me. He's drunk, and he sounds belligerent. I hear him hollering my name and the crashing of glass and metal. He screams that he is finally going to kill me. How much he hates me and how I belong in the ground with my dead mother. His voice is getting louder, and I know he's outside of my door. "NO, DADDY PLEASE DON'T!" I scream. I back up against the window and panic. I don't know how to get away from him. He's going to finally kill me. I scream, and then hear a voice whisper my name. I don't recognize the voice, but I know it's an angel.

I sit up, coughing like I've been choking. I touch my cheeks and find I have tears running down them. I look around, trying to reorient myself with where I am. It's dark, but I know I'm not in my childhood bed anymore. The sheets are too soft, and it doesn't smell like cigarettes and stale beer. I place my hand over my heart and try to breathe in and out. I think I'm going to pass out.

"You okay, baby?" I hear Brent ask. His voice is hoarse, so I know he's been asleep for a while. DAMMIT! Why are these nightmares happening more and more often?

"Yes, sorry to wake you." He places a hand over my hip when I lay back down. I try to fall back asleep, but I can't. I wait until Brent's back asleep to quietly crawl out of bed. I head into the kitchen to his built-in bar and take a glass out. I pour two fingers of Jack Daniels and toss it back. It burns like hell going down, but it is what it is. I pour another two fingers and sit down on the bar stool. The coolness of the leather seat feels amazing on my burning skin.

"May I join you?" he asks, and I laugh.

"How could I say no?" I answer, and he leans forward, kissing my bare shoulder. We are both naked and sitting in the dark. The only light illuminating the two of us is the moon. I can see Brent perfectly, and I know he can see me. In more ways than one.

"I'm not going to ask if you want to talk about it. I'm only going to say I'm here if you do," he says as he pours some Jack Daniels in his own glass. He takes a sip and then places his glass next to mine. I look at our glasses sitting next to each other, and it makes me sad. Brent and I fit perfectly together. We may be from different parts of the world and different tax brackets, but I feel so at ease with him. Somehow, I managed to cross paths with this beautiful man that I know I don't deserve. Even so, I still want him.

"I don't know what to say other than I've been having nightmares more and more often. Flashbacks at times and sometimes just nightmares. They used to happen maybe once or twice a year. Now they happen regularly, and I don't know what's triggering them. I want so badly to forget, but I don't seem to be able to." Brent grabs hold of my bar stool and pulls me so I'm sitting closer to him.

"If I could take away your pain and these nightmares I would," he says a hoarsely. He takes another sip of his whisky and places his glass back down. "I don't know what else to say or do, but I'm fucking pissed as hell that you've been dealing with this shit alone since you were a little girl. I'm not a homicidal man, Gemma, but I would kill that man in an instant and be happy to spend the rest of my life behind bars if it meant you never having to think about that bastard again." I hiccup as I break down from his words. That's all I have ever really wanted. Someone to protect me. He pulls me onto his lap, and I rest my head against his shoulder and let the tears come.

"You know growing up all I wanted was someone, anyone, to protect me from him. I used to pretend that I had an older brother that would come in and save me from my father's wrath. In my head, at least, that's what would happen. I've never told anyone that."

"I'm sorry there wasn't anyone to protect you or save you from him. You have no idea how sorry I am," he whispers, and I feel his cheek wet against my neck as he breaths me in. He's crying for me, and it's a pain that's hard to take but also feels so safe and beautiful. He's acknowledging what I went through, and I feel justified in my pain and anger for the first time ever.

"I'm ready to go back to bed if you are?" I whimper. He picks me up, carrying me back into his bedroom. This time he holds me tightly to him, and I fall asleep tucked safely under his arm. I fall asleep quickly and peacefully, knowing I'm safe in his strong arms.

Brent

I wake up and feel Gemma still asleep beside me. I look over at the clock and it's almost 9 a.m. This is the latest I've slept since I can remember. I feel Gemma's naked body against mine and smile at the soft feel of her. Last night was eye-opening. Little by little she's letting me in, but I still feel like she'll run. If it was up to, Gemma she would have screwed me and then run back to her apartment before dinner. I don't want that for us. I know she can tell that I want to savor this weekend and my time with her. Even if we do have sex this weekend, I can't imagine that being enough for either of us. I know she's used to her sexual experiences being an exchange and then cutting out and cutting ties. I can understand that. I've had similar experiences and arrangements in the past.

However, I know I've never felt about anyone the way I feel about her. I thank God I've met her and have the opportunity to love and treat her well. She deserves that. I have wanted so badly to tell her exactly how I feel. Her words and tears after her nightmare last night absolutely slayed me. I want nothing more than to shield her from any more pain and suffering, but I know that's not how it works. She has shit she needs to deal with, and all I can do is be there for her when she's ready to share. Last night when she left the bed and went to pour a drink, I was worried. Not about her leaving, but that she would bottle all of it up and shove it down deep.

I know she can look into my eyes and see that I'm falling for her. She's holding back, but I'm going to give her the time she needs. It's time I have to give, and it's not a sacrifice for me. I know she's worth fighting for. No one seems to have ever fought for her. I wrap my arms around her, pulling her closer to me and fall back asleep.

Saturday morning, we explore the Saturday Market and walk around the waterfront. We stop for a late lunch at an Italian restaurant. Gemma and I laugh as we people watch. We have a couple of cocktails, and by the time we leave it is already late afternoon. We walk back hand in hand to my apartment, and when we get there Gemma enters the code to get in. This shouldn't excite me as much as it does. I've never given a woman access like this to any of my places.

I push the button for the roof, and she looks over at me confused. I put a finger to my mouth, and she laughs. We walk out into the bright afternoon sun and into the heat again. I take all my clothes off and step into the plunge pool completely naked. She takes her clothes off as well, and I take her hand as she joins me in the pool. I guide her so that she's sitting next to me. Her nipples are barely breaching the water. I want nothing more than to lean down and take one in my mouth. I look into her eyes and can tell she's happy. She's so damn sweet.

"This is incredible," she says as she looks around us. "I can't believe this is my life right now!" I want to tell her this could be her life forever, but I don't want to scare her off. I smile at her as I link my fingers with hers under the water.

"What do you want to do tonight, Gemma?" I ask.

"You really want me to stay another night?" she asks, as if the answer isn't already clear. Life really has made her feel so disposable and replaceable.

"What do you want, Gemma?" I ask as I reach between her legs and gently caress her. She's wet for me, and I groan as my fingers slip easily inside of her. She leans her head back as I plant sweet, chaste kisses up her neck. I stand in front of her, and she looks down at my arousal. I shake my head as she licks her lips, then I move backward, and she pouts. "This is about you, not me, Gem."

I pick her up, placing her on the side of the pool. I pull her legs up to the ledge above the water. I hold her hands as she lays back and devour her like I did yesterday. She's incredibly sweet, and I enjoy myself immensely. I pull myself out of the water after she's climaxed and lay my head on her stomach. She places her hands in my hair and we sit there for a couple minutes as we come down from our high.

"You are so good at that," she states as I lift my head to look at her. I stand back and go under the water. It's hot today, and after the dessert I had, a la Gemma, I need to cool off. When I come back up, she's in the water walking towards me.

"Why are you so far away right now?" she asks as I lean on the other side of the pool.

"Because I'm trying to avoid the direction that you and I both want to take this," I add, and she tilts her head in confusion.

"You don't want to have sex with me?" she asks, and I shake my head.

"Not out here. I want you, don't ever doubt that for a second. The next natural thing to happen would be for me to take you on the side of this pool," I reply as she wraps her arms around me. I lean down, kissing her gently. "I want to slip inside of you so bad, Gemma. But I don't want our first time to be in a pool. I'm not saying that it wouldn't happen at some point. However, this is not where I want us to share our first time together."

"Our FIRST time together?" I nod, watching her reaction cautiously. "Like there will be more?"

"I sure fucking hope so! Yes, Gemma! Many, many, more. I hope." I don't apologize or try to pull away. I watch to see how she reacts. "If it's anything like the experiences we've had so far, I imagine I'll be pretty addicted to you." I can see the love in her eyes and feel it in her touch. She needs to know this isn't a one and done thing for me. "What we have between us is very strong and I really, really like it. That's about as strong of words as I'm ready to say to you and you're ready to hear. Let's head downstairs. You like sushi, right?" I ask, and she smiles like a kid on Christmas.

"I LOVE sushi!"

"Good. There's an amazing place close by. We can pick it up and eat here, maybe watch the sunset but this time from up here."

When we get back with the sushi, Gemma throws on a bathing suit, the white one with palm leaves from the Hamptons. We grab some waters and take the sushi up to the roof. We sit under the umbrella until the sun starts to go down. The sky turns different shades of pink, orange and purple. It's an absolutely gorgeous sunset. Gemma and I clean up and then move to the lounger to lie in each other's arms as we watch the sun disappear behind lower Manhattan. I know this is my last night with Gemma, but I don't want it to be. I sigh, and Gemma turns to look at me, confused. She looks at my expression and places her hand on my chest. I place a hand over hers as she rests her chin against my chest.

The skyscrapers start to light up one by one in lower Manhattan, and it's one of my favorite things to see. The city that never sleeps is pretty accurate. I want to ask Gemma to join me for dinner at my parents, but I'll wait to see how she's feeling tomorrow. She might need to get ready for the work week. I know if I had things my way, she would stay the week as well. Gemma leans up, kissing me, and I wonder how long I've been lost in my own head.

"Sorry," I apologize, looking down at her.

"Not a problem. I was asking if you were getting tired?" she repeats as I lift her hand to my lips, kissing it gently.

"I'm not that tired, actually. How are you feeling?"

"Honestly," she replies, and I laugh.

"No, lie to me."

"Promise you won't hold it against me!" She turns to look up at me.

"I promise."

"I feel like I don't want this moment to end. Like I could stay here forever with you. But…"

"No buts," I add as she laughs. "I mean I love your arse, Gemma. But no buts. I feel the same way. I didn't say it because I'm terrified of scaring you off or pushing you too hard."

"I know, but I need more time," she whispers as I lean down, kissing her head.

"I can do that, Gemma. Let's head downstairs. Maybe we can find a movie or something. I can never find anything to watch, but maybe you'll have better luck!"

We head downstairs, and I motion for her come over to me. She walks around the counter to stand in front of me. She's still in her bathing suit, so I untie the back and then the tie around her neck. It falls to the floor, and I lean down, taking a nipple into my mouth. I take my time, kissing every inch of her chest. By the time I reach her lips, she's got her hand in my shorts. I groan when she wraps her hand around ME. I stand, lifting her up so she can wrap her legs around my waist. I know this is a pivotal moment for us. I take her into the bedroom, dimming the lights. I pull the comforter back and place her on the bed. I lie on top of her, and she nods her head. She wants this as much as I do. I pull my shorts off then drag her bathing suit bottoms down her legs, my lips trailing hotly behind them. I throw them to the side and lean down, kissing her gently across her stomach.

"Tell me what you want, baby," I ask, my voice hoarse.

"You," she answers as I gently slide a finger inside her.

"That's not good enough. You already have me. What do you want me to do, Gemma? Tell me," I repeat as I insert another finger.

"You! I want you inside of me. Now," she gasps as she closes her eyes and her hips buck up against my hand. I lean down, taking her mouth. "I'm clean Brent, and I've been on birth control since I was in high school." I kiss her gently again and move the hair away from her face. "Please," she whimpers as I push her further up the bed.

"I'm clean as well, Gemma. You can trust me," I add as our eyes meet. I gently push myself inside her, fitting perfectly. I stop to give myself a second, and she lifts up to kiss me. I start to move, and we both groan in unison. Sweet Jesus, I've never experienced anything like this. I lean down, kissing her as I begin to move faster. She closes her eyes as I lean down, licking and sucking at her breast. She lifts her head, and I pull her up to me, my hand holding up her head. I'm deep now. I know I am. "Are you okay?" I ask, and she whispers yes.

I continue at this pace for a while until know she's getting close. Hell, I know I'm not that far from getting off either, especially when I watch her expression closely like this. I pull her leg up around my hip and reach down to gently caress her. I continue, and she opens her eyes. The love I see there is what sends me over the edge. She screams my name, and I swallow her whimpers as I lean down, kissing her as we both come down from climaxing together.

I lay down next to her and pull her close to me. She leans into my arms as I kiss her forehead. We are both breathless, and my heart is so incredibly full in this moment. I'm completely overwhelmed. There's no doubt in my mind that I love this woman more than I'll ever love anyone in this entire world. I lift her chin so I can kiss her and feel a tear escape from behind her closed eyes. I wipe it away.

"My beautiful Gemma," I whisper as she snuggles deeper into my side. I want to give her a moment. I only know the surface of what she's been through in life. I can only imagine, and even that is devastating to me. This is all new to her. Shit, this kind of intimacy is new to me too. She runs her hand up my chest and I grab it. I bring her sweet hand to my lips as I ask, "Are you alright, darling?"

"I think so. I'm a little overwhelmed if I'm being honest. I knew I would be, but I wasn't expecting this. I didn't know it could be like this," she whispers as I pull her tighter to me. If I could take her pain away I would. I know she has a long and difficult journey ahead of her to find healing. It doesn't change the fact that I want to save her from any more pain. I love her. I know I'd do anything for her. "I'm going to clean up a bit," she says, and I nod. I probably should too, but I don't want to move. I grab her hand and pull her down so I can kiss her again. She's a little tense at first, but then she melts into me. I release her after a moment, and she heads into the bathroom.

Gemma

What the hell was that!? I think to myself as I pull my hair up and hop in the shower. I let the hot steam wash over my body. That wasn't just sex. That was him making love to me. I'm out of my element here. I don't know what to do with myself. I knew I was falling for Brent before we even had sex, but what I'm feel for him now is on a completely different level. I wash off quickly and then head to the sink to brush my teeth. Something just happened in there that I wasn't prepared for. I don't understand it. I finish brushing my teeth and then let my hair down again. I run the brush through my hair. This is too much. I can't stay. But how do I leave? How can I leave now, after that?

I hear my father's words echoing in my head. That I'm nothing, that I'll never be anything to anyone. How I ruin everything. How worthless I am, just like my mother. That's all I can hear as I look in the mirror. The only picture I have of her is in the top drawer beside my bed and all I want to do is hear her say it's not true. That it's not our fault. We didn't make him this way. He was always this mean and cruel. I place the brush down and my hand begins to shake.

I want to do is smash the shit out of the mirror in front of me. I want this, but I don't deserve it. Brent will find out soon enough, and he won't want me anymore. I will only be left with the shreds I deserve. I knew better and I know I can't stay. Brent sees something in me that I can't, something that's probably not even there. How can I be honest with him when I can't even be honest with myself!

I gather myself and try to focus on what I have- this moment, the only one before reality hits me in the face again. I walk out of the bathroom and get back into bed. I climb in beside Brent, and he gently grabs my hand. I lift it up to my lips and kiss his hand gently. He's been so good to me, more kind than I could ever deserve. But that's just it. I don't feel like I deserve to be loved like this. He has to know that the woman I am right now can't return the kind of love that he needs, that he deserves. That's not fair, not to him. I know that now.

No one will ever love me like Brent loved me this weekend. I can't even tell him how I feel. I know he loves me in the purest sense, and I can't return it. That kind of love isn't inside me. I have to end this now.

Brent falls asleep holding me, and I let him. I know that this is the end. Knowing I can't give him what he wants, what he needs. I feel the tears come and I mourn for the love I know I'll never have. He won't want me once I leave, when my past starts to creep up on me and I can't do anything but run. That's not the life I want for him. He's promised me more time, but if I'm honest I don't know how much time I need.

I quietly slip out of bed and head back into the bathroom, grabbing my things. I pull on my pajamas and grab my phone from my purse. It's almost dead. I haven't bothered with my phone almost all weekend. I call an Uber and then walk over to the rest of my bags, making sure I have all my things. I slip into my flip flops and realize I left my bathing suit but it's not worth it. I walk out into the living area and try to keep my focus on getting outside.

I hate the feeling of sneaking out, but I couldn't live with myself if I saw his face. It's going to be hard enough to see him at work during the week. He'll loathe me at first, which is fine. I loathe myself enough for the both of us. I get a notification that my Uber is here, and I press the button for the garage. I walk past the security office and nod at Paul. He stands up to ask me if I need something, and I shake my head.

"I have an Uber waiting!" I whisper, and he notices my tearstained face. He nods and presses a button by the door to open it for me. My eyes fill with tears, and I have a moment where I want to run back upstairs and crawl back into bed. Pretend like I was never going to leave. That I want to try and make it work, but my head feels all jumbled and panicked. I put my hand on the door of the Uber and close my eyes. Tears fall down my face as I take a deep soothing breath. I'm not even strong enough to turn around and watch his home fade into the background. I can't. I'm that much of a coward.

We pull up to my apartment, and I'm so damn grateful that my roommates aren't here. I put my bags down in my room and climb into bed. I don't even bother to plug my phone in. Brent will know what happened. He's not an idiot. He knows I'm a runner. I normally leave to make it less awkward. This time I fell in love before I could get out of it. Before I fall asleep, I send a text to Blake.

I need to see you tomorrow. I made a big uh-oh.

My phone's about to die but I

need to go to bed.

I get a text back immediately.

> Expected as much. You lasted longer than I thought you would. Plug your damn phone in and meet me at Perrone's at 10 AM for brunch.

I roll over, reluctantly plugging in my phone. Blake knows me well. I look down and notice that I have another text. It's from yesterday. God, I haven't checked my phone in a while. Brent must have sent it a while ago. It's the pictures of us on the waterfront. One of me sitting in his lap and the other is us kissing.

My sheets don't feel anything like the ones I've slept on this weekend. I cry harder than I've cried in sometime, and this time I know I deserve this pain. Just like these scratchy cheap-ass sheets. I deserve this pain and it feels like home. Just like I remember it. I'm reminded of why I've spent my entire life avoiding this kind of feeling.

Brent

I wake up and roll over to look at the clock. It's a little past seven. I place my hand on the other side of the bed and it's cold. I sit up, orienting myself and realizing that her stuff is gone. Her bags aren't in here anymore. Maybe she's just packed her stuff and is waiting for me to get up so she can say goodbye. Like yesterday, maybe she's sitting on the couch with a cup of coffee. I sit up, walking into the bathroom and see her hair tie sitting beside the sink. I release the breath, knowing that she's still here with me. I smile and head out into the living area but there's no one there. The lights are out, and I feel my heart shatter. Not just for me, but for her. I sit on the edge of the sofa and look around. Just yesterday I was having the time of my life. I'm not an idiot. I knew there was a strong chance that she'd get spooked and run. I thought we'd agreed I'd give her time. Hell, I'll give her all the space in the world if that's what she wants.

This isn't over, I tell myself as I walk over to the coffee pot and hit the start button. I walk back into the bedroom, picking up my phone. No texts. I look at the last text I sent, and it was to Gemma. The photo is from our walk to the waterfront the first night. I place both of my hands on the counter and lean my head on the cool surface of the marble. Why? Why did she have to leave? Why didn't she just wake me up? We could have talked this through. Hell, I would have taken her back to her apartment myself. Did she call a cab or an Uber in the middle of the night? Does she not understand how dangerous that could have been? I roll my neck around as I feel my anger start to rise. I push it down and head into the bathroom, turning on the shower. I stand in the stream of scalding water, letting it beat into my skin.

I'm not giving up on her. Not yet. She's going to have to try a lot harder than this to push me away. It's too damn late for that. I sadly wash the remaining scent of Gemma off my body and then turn the water off. I look at myself in the mirror and hear my Da's words. He's always taught us to ask ourselves this question when we are at a crossroad. *What kind of man do you want to be Brent?*

She's so used to people giving up on her. Abandoning her. I won't do it. She expects me to get angry. To scream, shout and prove to her that I'm just like everyone else she's ever known. Like her good for nothing father. Well, I'm not. I know what I want, and I'll do whatever it takes to show her. Love always finds a way. I reach over, picking up her black ponytail holder and slip it on my wrist. I head to the roof to enjoy my coffee.

I'm assuming she's at her apartment, probably still asleep. When she wakes up, I pray she feels peace. I hope she at least doesn't feel alone. If she does, I pray to GOD she misses me. I pray she dreams about me. When she thinks she's run far enough away to shove her feelings down like she's used to, I pray that she sees my face. I pray she remembers what it felt like to be loved by me. I pray when she touches herself that she can only see my face and remember what it felt like to be loved by me. This is what she was avoiding, and I know she's beating herself up about it. I finish my cup of coffee and the coolness of the morning is wearing off. Inside the elevator, I press the button for the main living area. As the doors close, I smile to myself. The Manhattan skyline disappears as the doors shut tightly. My heart will always find Gemma's. I just pray that Gemma's heart can find its way back to mine.

I didn't sleep at all. I think I closed my eyes and started to drift off, but all I could see was Brent. This is the worst kind of torture. At seven, I got up and went running. ME. I don't run. Hell, if you see me running, you should run too and ask questions later. I head back to the apartment and take another shower. I still smell like Brent. I smell his shampoo and body wash. The oils from the bath he ran me the first night I stayed over. GOD, this is torture. I look down at my phone and see I have a missed text. I click on the message icon as Blake's name pops up.

See you at 10 Gem. Perrone's.

See you then. Thanks Blake!

I text him back and see that only an hour has gone by since I went on my run. I'm running out of distractions. I decide to get dressed and head into the city early. Maybe I can just park and walk around. I park my car in a garage near the restaurant. I don't have the kind of car you want to valet. I walk down the street, seeing I still have 30 minutes to kill. I walk down a couple blocks and then cross the street, walking back up the other side. I'm still a couple minutes early, but I head inside anyway. Blake's already there, and when he sees me, he stands up and heads toward me.

"You look like shit, Gemma," he jokes, and I laugh for the first time since yesterday.

"I'm aware. It's nothing compared to how I feel. I've made a pretty big uh-oh Blake."

"Like I said earlier. I expected that. How big of an uh oh? What did he say when you told him you were leaving?" Blake asks, and I look down at my menu. "Gemma?"

"I left early this morning or late last night while he was sleeping," I answer, not completely sure, and purposely not looking at him. The waiter comes by, and Blake tells him we're going to need a minute.

"Ah! The other famous romantic movie. Except from the horror film version of 'While you were

Sleeping.' You just left. Did you at least text him?"

"No. I went home, texted you and then laid in bed the rest of the night staring at the ceiling. I got up this morning and went on a run." He places his hand on top of mine looking shocked.

"You went running?" he gasps, and I nod, looking down at my menu. He takes the menu from my hands and places it on top of his. He lifts his hand, and the waiter comes over. "We're going to do the bottomless mimosas and the Belgian waffles with everything on them. Bacon, biscuits and lots of honey butter," Blake says as the waiter walks away. "Gemma. What the hell? Has he texted you? Is he freaking the fuck out?"

"No. He hasn't been in contact, AND I don't expect him to." I answer, looking into Blake's eyes, and realize what I fear the most. Maybe Brent doesn't care? Maybe it was all my imagination? I mean he is Brent King.

"Oh," Blake says nonchalantly, sitting back and taking a sip of his water.

"He's probably fine. Like you said, he probably expected it as well. He's more than likely going to lick his wounds the rest of the day and tomorrow when I see him at work, he'll be fine."

"Uh huh," Blake responds. He takes a sip of his Mimosa, "Oh, these are always so good. You still planning on going into the downtown office tomorrow?"

"I'm a professional, Blake. It's my job to go into work. That's kind of what you guys pay me to do. Plus, with Layla leaving I need to oversee the interns that were working alongside her on the Mid-Summer's Night Eve Event. It's in two weeks. I've got to go over the menu with the caterer, make sure that the seating arrangement is done and then check in with the venue to make sure we've got everything finalized. The red carpet still needs to be staffed, and I don't really know all the interns. For the most part they're set up in the downtown office. I have a lot of work to do, and I don't have time to be nervous about seeing Brent. I'm sure I'll barely see him. Why are you looking at me like that?" I ask as he smiles at me.

"Yes, you have a lot to oversee. It'll be a good distraction for you. What are you going to do when all the distractions are gone and you're stuck with your feelings?" he asks, emphasizing the word FEELINGS. "You know, the ones you're currently stuffing down. I think deep down you don't feel like you deserve him, but you're so damn used to running that this just feels like a normal Sunday to you. What are you going to do when you finally have to stop metaphorically running and all the shit catches up to you? Huh?" he asks as I pick up my mimosa and take a sip. "You can't keep running, Gemma. It's way past time to stop. Turn around and face this shit. I know my brother, and he's the kind of man who won't give up without a fight. You aren't used to that. So, things are about to get a lot damn harder for you. He doesn't fall in love easily, but I know he loves you. You know it too, and that's what scares the hell out of you this time. Finally, a prince was able to get past the walls you've built up. He jumped over all the damn hurdles you've set up to keep people away. He got close to catching you, and you liked it. In fact, you loved it. It scared you, as it should. Anyone would be scared to feel that way for the first time. You're used to people abandoning you, but this time you left the prince in the castle while he was slaying all those dragons to come and save you. While you ran the other way."

"But this isn't a fairy tale, Blake, and I'm sure as hell not a princess. I don't need saving. For all I know I could be the damn dragon," I whisper, and Blake puts his hand over mine.

"I think we're going to need something stronger," he says when the waiter comes by.

"Maybe I am the dragon?" I say as I stare down at my hands. "Maybe that's my problem. I look like a princess, but on the inside I'm just a fire-breathing dragon."

We finish our waffles, and while it did help to emotionally eat, I still feel like shit. Now I'm not just emotionally feeling bad, but physically I feel like shit too. Most everyone that is coming in is dressed in their Sunday best, which makes me think of Brent. I wonder if he went to church this morning. If he thanked God for me or if he cursed me. Blake and I have been drinking our bottomless mimosas for… I don't know, I think it's been an hour or two.

I excuse myself to go to the bathroom, and when I come back there are two people standing at our table. Their backs are facing me. One is a brunette woman who looks very familiar, and the other looks like Brent from behind. I get closer to the table and can tell for sure that it's him. My purse is still sitting next to my seat, so I know there's no escaping. Might as well go ahead and face this. I just hope he doesn't make a scene. The older woman standing next to him turns to me, and I recognize her. It's Greta, the woman from the event hall we've rented. She smiles when she sees me, and I give her a small smile until Brent turns around. I look up at him, and when our eyes meet his face breaks into a huge grin. My heart stops beating, and I stop way before I get to them. I remember myself and walk over to say hello to Greta.

"Gemma, it's so nice to see you. I almost didn't recognize you," she says, and I smile. Same, I don't recognize myself this morning either. I know she's referring to my hair, since the last time I saw her, I was a brunette.

"I sometimes don't recognize myself," I reply

as she smiles kindly at me.

"I'm looking forward to working closely with you for the event in a couple weeks. Layla said she was going to give you my contact information. I was just telling Mr. King that we are good to go on our end. We still have to finalize the menu and as soon as I get the final seating chart, we can start running with everything. Layla said you have gorgeous penmanship. That you'd probably be taking care of the name cards for the guests. I know you have a team of interns, but if you need help on anything please do reach out to our office."

"Yes. That does sound like something Layla would say. We are going to miss her terribly. I'll be in touch," I say with a sarcastic but polite undertone as I start to sidestep her. I feel Brent's hand on my back.

"I was just telling Greta that you have it all handled and that she shouldn't worry. You'll be in touch with her if you need anything. There's plenty of time and many hands around the table to help if you guys need it," Brent adds, and I feel myself flush.

"Yes," I choke out, feeling his hand press familiarly on my back. "I don't plan on sleeping the next couple of weeks until the event is over." She laughs, and I giggle sadly to myself. At this rate I'll be done with everything for the event in December. Freaking Layla. There are over 500 people attending the event this year. I feel sick to my stomach, and I sidestep Brent to sit down. I feel like I'm going to pass out. Brent tells Greta to go ahead and have a seat and they'll be right there. He comes to crouch next to my chair, careful not to touch me again. I take a sip of water and notice my hand is shaking. I look up at Blake who's been watching the last five minutes transpire like a tennis match. He looks into my eyes and whatever he sees there tells him now is not the time. The waiter comes by, and I ask for the check. My voice comes out barely a whisper. I'm starting to tense up and know I need to get out of here. What are the damn odds that Brent would end up here? I look up at Blake, and I can tell he's sorry. He must have told Brent we were here.

"Why?" Brent says beside me. I close my eyes for a moment, and when I open them, I turn to face him. What I see are his beautiful eyes blazing with love but also with unanswered questions. "Why do you keep running, darling?" he whispers. He places his hand on top of mine, and it's my undoing. I close my eyes as tears escape from the corners of my eyes. I hear Blake gasp. I reach into my purse, grabbing some cash and throwing it on the table. I stand up, almost bumping into the woman behind me as I head out the door. I start walking toward my car, and I know Brent is following me. I hear him call my name, but I keep walking towards the parking garage. Maybe I can just take a nap in my backseat. I've had too much to drink and I can't drive. I didn't freaking think this thing through.

As soon as the walk sign comes on, I speed walk across to the other side. Seeing Brent was harder than I thought. However, seeing Brent with love still in his eyes for me was devastating. I'm almost to the parking garage when I feel him gently take my arm. He pulls me to the side of the parking garage, out of everyone's way and wraps his arms around me. I crumble into him and lose it. He rocks me back and forth. Part of me feels overwhelmed with love and part of me wants to scream. When I finally settle down, he places his hands on my shoulders, steadying me. I can't look into his eyes yet, so I keep my head down.

"I have to go," I whisper, and he squeezes my shoulders tenderly.

"Do you see how easy that was, Gemma? That's all you would have had to say. I wouldn't have stopped you. Hell, I would have driven you back to your damn apartment and tucked you into bed myself. I'm not out to destroy you. I love you," he whispers, his voice breaking. I look up at him and see unshed tears in his eyes. "Do you know how hard it is to watch you keep running from all of this? To watch, whatever it is you are running from, continually try to destroy you. It controls every single aspect of your life, Gemma. I'm no longer afraid to scare you off. I'm going to continue to love you until you realize how much you love me too. I'm not a freaking psychopath, Gemma. I know what's between us. You can't fake this. I also know what's keeping us apart, and it's not me. This isn't about me. It's about you. You have to decide what's more important. Running, or staying and fighting. I can't do that for you. No one can. But I'm going to love you through it. You want space? Fine, you have it. You want time? I have all the time in the world for you. You want to run? I'll watch you go, and I'll try my damnedest to keep up, but I can't outrun your demons any more than you can. You want to stay and fight? I'll fight right beside you, but YOU have to decide. I'll say it again in case you missed it before."

He places his hand on the side of my face, running his thumb across my cheek bone. He wipes away a tear, and I think he's going to kiss me. He doesn't. He just looks deep into my eyes. A tear runs down his cheek, and I close my eyes. I can't watch it. It's too painful to see him sad or hurt. He waits until I open my eyes again and he gives me a small, sad smile.

"I. Love. You," he says steadily, and I lean back against the concrete wall of the parking garage, the sound of the busy city continues around us. He steps forward, placing a hand above my head, and leaning down until his forehead is resting on top of mine. "You can't drive home, Gemma. Let me take you home," he whispers, and I agree.

"What about Greta?" I ask.

"Greta's meeting with Blake now. It's about time he took on his share of this damn event. Hell, it was his idea to have it in the first place. He can suffer through a meeting with Greta. We were both supposed to be meeting with Greta at noon at Perrone's. Hate to say it, Gemma, but Blake set you up," he adds, laughing as I move away from the wall.

"I can see that now," I say, my voice emotionless.

"He means well. You'll see that one day."

"Was it his plan to get me drunk too so you could drive me home?" I ask, and he smiles.

"I think you guys did that all on your own. He texted me on his way here this morning to tell me that he was having an emergency brunch with you. Blake only brunches at one place. I was in church, or I would have come earlier. I needed some church this morning. I mean this with love, but you can be one infuriating woman. Where's your car?" he asks, and I nod towards the parking garage. "Keys," he says as I reach into my bag and hand them to him. He walks beside me up the ramp to my car and of course opens the passenger side door for me first. I get in and sit down, pulling my seat belt on. Brent gets in the driver's side, and it takes a good 30 seconds for my seat to move all the way back for his tall body to fit in. I laugh, and he looks over at me, smiling. "If that's what it takes to get you to smile, I'll fill my garage and storage units with your little clown cars."

"I think they'd feel out of place," I whisper as he heads out of the parking garage. We head toward Brooklyn, and I turn my head so I'm looking out the window. He doesn't hold my hand or even speak, and I think that's for the best. I fall asleep hearing him cursing about "little clown cars" and something about "the circus." When I wake up, Brent is crouching beside me with the car door open.

"Come on, Gemma," he whispers as I grab my bag. He walks with me to my door, and I stumble up the steps. He grabs my arm before I faceplant, so I thank him.

"I'm sorry. I think I'm a little tired," I add, and when I right myself he opens the door to the ground level of my apartment complex. I stand inside of the elevator and realize he doesn't know what floor I live on. "And maybe a little drunk."

"Gemma," he says as I push the button for the 3rd floor. When the elevator door opens, I walk over to my apartment door, and he unlocks it for me, letting me in first. My apartment is the size of Brent's master bedroom and three people live here. I walk into my bedroom and put my purse on the floor beside my bed. I crawl into bed too tired and drunk to care what he thinks. He's standing in the doorway of my bedroom, and he looks so out of place here. He's too tall and too beautiful for my bedroom. For my apartment in general. Maybe even for me.

"You're too beautiful and perfect to be here, Brent." I whisper as my eyes close. I know I'm not far from drifting off to sleep. I feel him lean over me, kissing my forehead and running a hand through my hair. Or at least that's what I imagined so that I can make this moment last. I can't keep myself from drifting off, so I crash.

Brent

I walk back to Gemma's car and climb in. Literally climb in. I can't believe a normal size human can fit into this car. I head back towards the city and call Blake. I ask him to meet me at the office in my car when he's done with Greta. He lives walking distance from the restaurant, so I know he didn't bring a car, and I left mine in valet. He's had an hour or more to sober up so he should be fine. I park in the garage under our building and head up to my office. Instead of heading home, I get some work done since I'm already here.

Later that evening, I pull into my apartment and pick up my phone once I'm parked. I shoot out a text to Gemma and hit send.

> Wanted to let you know that I'll pick you up from your apartment tomorrow at 7. Your car is already in the parking garage at work. If you need anything let me know. Hope you are feeling ok. Love you!

It's around 5:00 in the afternoon before I hear back from her.

> Thank you, Brent. See you at 7:00

The next morning, I pick up some coffee from a nearby coffee shop and head over to pick up Gemma. She's waiting at the curb in a black fitted shift dress and red heels. I'm not sure my heart can handle it, but here we go. I pull up to the curb, and she immediately reaches for the door. I roll down the window as she bends down, giving me a nice view of the top of her breasts. Even though when she's standing up her dress is fairly conservative. Her door is locked, and I smile.

"Seriously, Gemma? Did you think I'd let you open your own door?" I say as I roll her window up. She steps back, rolling her eyes, but I can see a small smile on her face trying to break through. I get out of the car and walk around to let her in. She has to squeeze by me, and I enjoy the feel of her body against mine. I hand her a coffee and her returning smile tells me she is grateful.

The ride to work was short, but still we didn't speak. I wanted to give her some space. She seems lost in her own thoughts. Gemma puts her hand on my arm, and I look over at her. "Thank you for my coffee and for yesterday," she says, stopping and swallowing. I turn my body to face her, and she moves her hand.

"Gemma," I start to say, and she squeezes my arm to stop me.

"Please, Brent. Listen, the next couple of weeks are going to be difficult for me. I have a lot on my plate and a lot on my mind. Work specifically, is already going to be a lot with the event coming up. On top of that, things with you," she says, trailing off, and I give her time to finish her thought. "I'm asking you for time. I can't promise you anything, Brent. I know how you feel, and that makes things a little harder for me. It also makes some things easier. I can't say more without having a breakdown. Last night I thought a lot about the last couple of weeks. I'm telling you this, but I haven't said anything to Blake yet. So please let me tell him. I'm going to start going to therapy. My first appointment is the Saturday after the event. I'm letting myself have this time to prepare for my first appointment, but also the time to ensure the event goes well. Therapy is something Blake mentioned to me a while ago. I've never been a fan of the idea of going but I'm going to try. I know it's going to be hard. I just want you to know. I'm not making any promises, Brent. I can't make any promises." My heart explodes at her bravery, but also breaks for the journey ahead of her. That I know with all my heart, but I will be there for her when she needs me.

"I promised you I would be here. That isn't going change. You shouldn't make any promises to anyone but yourself at this point, Gemma. I'm only going to tell you that I'll be here if you need me. Otherwise," I say as I open my door, "let's get to work!"

It's 2 p.m. before I have time to take a break. I'd love to say that I've enjoyed having Gemma in our office, but I haven't seen her much today. Gemma comes to my office toward the end of day. We go over the plans for the gala, and she's right, we are behind. I ask her if I can go with her to the meeting at the event site tomorrow to meet with the caterer and to tie up any loose strings. While we are meeting, I feel like I should tell her some of my plans for the office I've been dreaming up. I'm still trying to work it out in my head, but as I lay it all out, I look up and she's staring at me with awe. It makes me feel like I'm on top of the world. She not only believes I can make the new plans for the company work, but she wants to help me with my proposal. We've been in my office for over an hour. Time flies when you're with the woman you love!

Gemma

The next afternoon I'm so damn tired. It's almost time for Brent and I to head to our meeting with the caterer, and I can barely keep my eyes open. Yesterday when I got home, I put a proposal together for Brent. Mainly because I couldn't stop thinking about it. I couldn't turn my brain off even though I was so tired. I sent it to him last night, and he immediately emailed back saying that he was putting one together at the moment as well. He ended up merging the two proposals together since he loved what I sent.

Brent's still in his meeting about the new structure, and I hope it goes well for him. It would be sad for it to die in its infancy since it's such a stellar idea. We need to leave by three for our meeting. Blake is in the meeting as well, and he has to be uptown by 3:30 for his meeting with a couple of new clients. Blake and Brent come out of the conference room smiling and ribbing each other. I love seeing the two of them together. They both look my direction, and Blake gives me a thumbs up as the other associates disperse. Brent walks by me into his office, shutting his computer down. Blake gives me a hug and picks me up. I'm wearing a red pantsuit with a cream fitted body suit underneath it. I'm glad I chose a pantsuit today since Blake is flinging me around.

"You're brilliant, Gemma," he whispers as he puts me down. I fix my body suit and roll my eyes at him. "And you look hot as shit today. Everyone loved your proposal."

"Oh, it wasn't my proposal. I just helped," I add, and he winks knowingly.

"I know, but I could hear your voice all over that proposal. I'm proud of you, sugar tits! As always, I think you're great!"

"And I think you're about to be late," I interject as I look down at where my watch normally sits. Damn, I really need to get a new watch. It's just not in the budget right now. Brent comes out with his bags, and I smile at him. He looks like he's on cloud nine, and I can't wait to hear how it went. Blake looks down at his phone and screeches.

"Yikes! I'll talk to you guys later." He jogs to

the elevator as I laugh at him. Always fashionably late.

"You ready?" Brent asks, and I nod.

"Let me grab my stuff. We're going to the event site. So, I probably won't come back here afterwards."

"You want to drive separately?" he asks, and I shrug.

"I mean we don't have to. Do you want to ride with me?" I ask.

"In your clown car?" he jokes as I giggle. I look up and a couple people are watching us. Most of them either look back down or smile kindly at me. Most everyone else is kind and I get the feeling they want to continue to see their boss happy.

"You're right. You'd probably be more comfortable in a coffin," I joke as he shakes his head, but his returning smile makes my day.

"How about I drive? Then I can drop you off back here. Unless you want to drive, and I can follow you. I know how much you love to drive in Manhattan," he ribs me as I sit on my desk, resigned. It's the perfect angle for him to look down at me and he does with admiration. From his vantage point and his closeness, I know he can see down the front of my body suit. "I'm looking into your eyes, Gemma," he says reassuringly, more for himself than for me. I shake my head and stay silent. "What?"

"This is becoming difficult. We can't even decide on who's driving." He looks heavenward and then back at me. He looks deep into my eyes and smiles. "What?"

"Come on!" he says, annoyed, but I see a smirk pop through. As we head past reception, he presses the button for the garage. Normally I look more put together, but when Brent is around my body does devious things. I look up at him, and he's staring at me like he wants to hit the stop button and take me right here in the elevator. The elevator dings, and I button my jacket as we walk out into the parking garage. "This way, Gemma," he says, his voice a little hoarse. Walking over to his car and hitting the key fob, he turns to me and releases a deep breath.

"With the little holdup we had upstairs, we are going to need to hustle to be on time, Mr. King," I say as he takes my bags and puts them in the trunk. I grab my computer bag since it's all I'll need for our meeting. Brent walks over to my side, and I don't even protest. We're going to be late. I get in and put my seatbelt on as Brent comes around to his side and gets in. We make great time and arrive with five minutes to spare.

"I made great time," he adds as he comes around to my side.

"Yes, due to my impeccable directions and navigational skills," I retort. He laughs, and I smile as we walk near Battery Park.

The new event space was only recently finished, and we're the first people to get to utilize the space. Brent is impressed with it, and I give him a short run-through of where everything will be set up. He looks down at me and grins. Luckily the caterer is running behind, so Greta lets us wander around until they show up. Greta is very taken with Brent. I personally think it's his accent. She's about 20 years older than he is, but still a very attractive woman. I smile to myself as Brent is stopped by Greta. I'm finally getting to walk through the finished space for the first time. I take a couple of pictures, and when I take a step back to get a shot of the full space, I back into Brent.

"Thanks for saving me back there," he whispers sarcastically, and I don't move. I enjoy the feeling of his warm, tall body against mine. If there's one thing I miss, it's being this close to him. Not being able to touch him is harder than I could have ever imagined now that I know what it feels like to be touched by him. He doesn't move either, and I try and enjoy this for just a moment. I don't want to torture him, but I need this.

"Sorry I'm late!" Glen, the caterer says, snapping me out of my daze. I hand out my proposal for food, appetizers, layout and how many wait-staff we will need to pull everything off. Everyone seems to be on the same page. Glen makes a couple of suggestions, and I take notes. We work through the final layout and menu.

"I think that's going to make everything perfect, Glen. Thank you," I say, and he beams.

"You know, Gemma, you're one of the most prepared clients our team has ever worked with. If you ever think of getting into event management, let me know. I think you have a real eye for events at this magnitude. Not many people have that kind of caliber."

"Thank you, Glen. I appreciate that." I say, not wanting to go down that path. I can't get sidetracked right now. I look down at my wrist, and again, no watch. I take my phone out and ask Glen if wants to look at the space now since we have more time. We walk into the Great Hall, and I give him the rundown on how I feel everything should go. I take a couple notes and so does his assistant. Greta joins us a little later, but I notice Brent doesn't. He was here for the meeting, and this last part is just the extras. I shake Glen's hand, then Greta takes him back to the catering kitchen.

Brent is sitting in a chair outside of the Great Hall. He has his forearms on his knees, and he's watching me closely. The light filtering in through the glass behind him looks like he could be on the cover of any fashion magazine. He's a gorgeous man. I lean against the doorframe, and he looks down at the floor shaking his head. I walk over and stand in front of him. He takes my hand and looks up at me. I sigh and nod my head. I get it. I feel the same way about him. But I need this time. I need to spend some time on my own, and I need to put the work into getting healthy. I'm walking a very narrow line with him. This has nothing to do with Brent. It has to do with me getting a hold on the demons and monsters that haunt me. He drops my hand, and we walk silently back to his car.

•••

The Wednesday before the event, a bunch of us go to Perrone's after work. We finally wrapped the planning and prepping portion for Friday night, and we are all collectively relieved. Helen, Blake, Brianna, and a couple of interns are enjoying appetizers and drinks when Brent walks in with a couple of associates from work. I wink at him and then turn my attention back to our table. He's taking them to a different table, so I'm kind of relieved. I've done a pretty good job of avoiding Brent this week. I wanted to put some space between us so I could finish everything. We had a small party for Layla before she left. I saw him for a little while there, and then left a little early.

We're still in the interview process for a bunch of different positions. With Brent's new layout, we have options moving forward which is exciting. We have a couple interviews set up for Friday morning, and then the entire office is shutting down early before the Mid Summer's event that evening. I catch both Brent and Hayden looking over at our table, but when I look up they both look away. I'm blushing but trying hard not to feel Brent's stares. He's being so obvious. I lean my head on Blake's shoulder, and he rests his head on top of mine. I told Blake on the way over here about my therapy appointment on Saturday. I've never seen him so proud of me.

Most of the interns have left for the evening. The rest of us are sitting around when Hayden and Brent come over to join us at our table. I've never noticed it before because I haven't spent a lot of time in the downtown office, but Hayden is attractive. He's not my type. Very militant and macho, but I'm thinking he'd be quite the catch for someone. He's also nice and down to Earth. Blake's said on numerous occasions that he finds him to be quite sexy. Sadly for Blake, he's also told me that Hayden is strictly into women. I laughed, but Blake did not! Poor Blakey.

We're sitting around talking when Blake asks everyone what they're wearing Friday. I gasp, and everyone looks at me. I release my breath and put my hands over my face.

"SHIT!" I murmur and lower my forehead to the table.

"Gemma?" Brent says, and I feel Brianna's

hand on my back.

"Are you okay?" Brianna asks as I lift my head up, not moving my hands from my face.

"Do not tell me you forgot about getting a dress," Blake asks, his hand going to his mouth. "You have like tomorrow to find something. There's no way to even get one altered in time," Blake says dramatically, his voice rising higher as he works himself into a frenzy. I just shake my head.

"It's okay. I can wear the dress from last year," I answer as Blake and Briana gasp in horror. THE HORROR!

"Your dress last year was black. The color this year for the women is champagne. This was your idea. You cannot be the only one in black, Gemma. The interns aren't even wearing black. I can maybe make some phone calls, or we can try off the rack," he says with disgust, barely getting it out as I put my hands down on the table.

"It's okay. It's not about me, Blake. I'll be behind the scenes the entire night anyway."

"OH NO YOU WON'T! That's why we trained the interns. We have a walk through with them Friday morning. No ma'am. I refuse!" Blake protests as I look over at Brent, who's on his phone. He puts a finger up at us, and I frown.

"Is he talking to us?" I ask Blake, and he looks confused as well.

"Okay. Perfect. We'll be there in about fifteen

minutes," Brent says. "Come on, Gemma," he says as he throws some cash on the table. "We have to hurry." I stand up, not understanding what's happening, and Blake looks surprised too. Brent looks over at Blake. "Opal Hills!" Brent mutters to Blake as he sits back in his chair with a satisfied smile. I still don't understand and hold my hands up.

"Is that supposed to mean something to me? What is happening?" I ask, and Blake shoos me away with Brent.

"Hurry. Opal Hills," he says like that means something to me. I follow Brent out, and the valet heads to get his car. Brent opens my door and runs around to the driver's side. I hop in and the valet closes my door quickly, sensing our hurry. We are off before I can finish putting my seat belt on. I look over at Brent, and he's maneuvering like a race car driver. I don't ask questions; I just trust that he has a plan. I still don't know what Opal Hills is, but it sounds somewhat familiar. Before I can ask a question, we're pulling up to a storefront that says **Opal Hills** in cursive letters on the marquee. Brent comes around and opens my door, and I hop out, walking under the overhang that leads into the store. We walk in, and a petite blonde comes out from behind a table where she's working on a computer.

"Brent!" she says as she walks over, and he wraps her into a big hug. To say I'm a little jealous is an understatement. She's stunning and apparently close to Brent. "You must be Gemma. My emergency," she says, looking at me up and down, yet genuinely being kind about it. "I know exactly what we're going to do. Champagne color scheme, correct?" she asks Brent, and he nods. I'm still confused. She leads me to a section of champagne-colored dresses and pulls three off the rack. "Did Brent tell you who I am, or did he just throw you in the trunk of the car?" she jokes, and I laugh.

"I'm so sorry. I have no idea what's going on. I was so focused on making sure the event was perfect that I completely forgot about a dress for myself," I interject, and she smiles, looking over my shoulder at Brent.

"I love her already," she states, and I hear Brent murmur something to himself. I can only imagine. "Have a seat, Brent. This won't take long. not with her body." He groans again, and she laughs. "I'm Maggie. I'm the owner and designer of Opal Hills. I met Brent through a friend when he first moved to the city. Don't worry, we've never dated. He's not my type," she whispers in my direction, and I smile. "I know, hard to imagine that Brent isn't everyone's type." She says sarcastically, and I smile to myself. He's looking quickly through magazines trying to ignore us, but when he looks up at me, he shakes his head. "Brent and I have only ever been friends, and we will only ever be friends.

Okay, let's get down to business," she adds as she walks me over to the dressing room. Just outside of the dressing rooms is a platform in the center with a spotlight above. I walk around it to get into the dressing room. She follows me in, and I shrug my shoulders. Time is of the essence. We study all three of the dresses, both pausing at the one in the center at the same time. We hum in agreement as she smiles at me. "Exactly what I'm thinking!" I change out of my shift dress and kick my shoes off. "There's a built-in bodice to this dress. Mainly because I want women to feel good about themselves, so take the bra off."

"Are you guys kidding me in there?" I hear Brent yell, and we both laugh. She helps me into the dress and zips me up. It's a little long, but for the most part it fits. It has a fitted bodice until it reaches the upper thighs and then it flows out. It's not quite a mermaid style dress, but that's the feel of it. It is a perfect champagne color and has the most beautiful beading on the bodice. Then the beading lessens the longer the dress gets. Think Marilyn Monroe's "Happy Birthday, Mr. President" dress. Except it's a thicker material and the skirt has a lot more flow to it. I look at her, and she grins mischievously.

She opens the door to the dressing room and helps me up onto the platform in the center of the room. There are mirrors surrounding the platform and pretty great lighting for a store. I also love that I can walk in this dress. With most mermaid-style dresses you have to waddle. They look great in photos but aren't very functional. She turns on the lights surrounding the mirrors, and I feel Brent's eyes on me. JESUS, I hear him say.

"What size shoe do you wear?" she asks, and I tell her six and a half. "Okay, so you need a size seven. Your feet might sweat a little, but also swell with being on your feet all night. So, let's stick with a seven to be safe. "Brent, be a dear and grab me a size 37 in the boxes behind the counter. Also, a size 37 behind where my computer is." He stands up, and I watch him go over to the boxes pulling the sizes out she's asked for. "Okay, slip these on first." I do, and she starts to murmur to herself. "I think you're going to barely need any off the bottom, and I only need to alter the sides of the dress. You have amazing breasts, Gemma," she states as Brent walks over, giving us a dirty look.

"You guys are killing me. KILLING ME," he replies as he walks around me. He looks me up and down as I smile at him.

"Exactly the reaction we're looking for," Maggie adds as she walks back towards a desk in the corner and grabs some clips. "No matter how you wear your hair, Gemma, this dress is meant for you. It's one of my favorites. These are normally wedding dresses, but I do a lot of big events as well," she adds as Brent and I stare into each other's eyes. I look away first, checking in the mirror. Maggie comes over, clipping the dress and making some marks. She's right, the dress is perfect. "You're absolutely glowing in this dress. It's perfect," she states proudly as she sits back on her heels. "These shoes are perfect as well. Just the right amount of height, and the shoe is neutral so you can wear them again. Louboutin's go with everything!" I look skyward, trying to mentally calculate how much this is going to set me back on my credit card. I try to use it only for emergencies, but I guess this qualifies as one. I'll just use my Christmas bonus this year to pay it off. That's only like, six months away, I think to myself as I cringe on the inside. I look back in the mirror, and Brent is standing next to me watching my reaction. Sometimes I feel like he can read my mind.

"Maggie, can you ring us up for this and add the champagne clutch that's behind the counter to it as well?" Brent never takes his eyes off me as he talks to Maggie. I open my mouth to say something, but he looks at me with a warning glare that tells me to shut it. I make eye contact with Maggie in the mirror, and she winks knowingly at me. She goes to her computer, and I look back to Brent. "Gemma, I see you trying to mentally calculate how much this is going to cost you. You can stop because this will cost you nothing," he whispers, and I open my mouth again to speak. "Gemma," he warns, and I give him the look back which makes him snicker.

"The company isn't going to pay for this," I state as he nods his head in agreement.

"You're right. The company isn't going to pay for this. I am," he whispers. I lean over toward him while still on the platform, and he looks down at my lips.

"You are the company, Brent. If you pay for it it's like the company's paying for it. I can put it on my credit card."

"But you're not going to! This may come as a shock to you, Gemma, but I have money that has nothing to do with my business or the company. Don't fight me on this or I will make a scene," he whispers, and I lean back knowing he's absolutely serious. Part of me wants to push him, but I look in his eyes and can feel the seriousness coming off him in waves. "Oh Gemma, please try me. You'll make my night."

"Okay you two. The sexual tension between the two of you is going to make my fabrics wilt. Let's keep it PG-13. Shall we?" She walks over to us, and Brent hands her a card. I grimace, and he puts a finger under my chin.

"Please let me do this for you. Let me come in and save the day. Just this once," he whispers, and I give him a small smile. I feel like I've taken so much from him. As much as this hurts my pride,

I can do this. However, in my defense, I did warn him that I was stubborn. I close my eyes, and he leans in, kissing me on the forehead. "Thank you!"

Maggie clears her throat, and we both look over at her. She hands Brent his credit card and receipt back. He shakes his head at needing the receipt, and I roll my eyes. I can't imagine having so much money that you don't even need a receipt for a purchase like this. I imagine this set him back at least a couple grand. I look over at Maggie, and she helps me out of my shoes and back into the dressing room.

"He's in love with you," she whispers, and I look up at her sadly. "Oh honey!" She places a hand on my shoulder as I pull my other dress up. "It's difficult. Relationships and real life. I'm rooting for you guys though. I want pictures, Gemma. Red carpet pictures," she says. I put my other shoes on and then walk out as she takes my dress to the back. "Okay, Gemma. Come back on Friday around 3:00. I'll be ready for you. I can make any last-minute alterations then if we need to. Go ahead and take your shoes and clutch with you though. Come and change here and I'll make sure my friend Liz Beth is here to double check make-up, and Kennedy can come do your hair. What time do you have to be at the venue?"

"4:30. It starts at 7:00, the carpet opens at 6:15."

"Oh, that's a perfect amount of time. Brent, can

you have a car bring Gemma here at 3:00 on Friday? Then we can make sure you have a ride to the venue at 4:30."

"Sure thing. Gemma, why don't I pick you up from here on my way to the venue. I have a town car for the evening." I nod my head, looking up at him as Maggie gives me a big hug.

"I'm so excited," she adds, and I grab her hand.

"Thank you, Maggie. You have no idea how much you are saving me."

"I'd do almost anything for Brent. He's helped me out with some big legal battles a long time ago. And now, I'd do anything for you. See you Friday!" she says as we turn and walk out the door. Brent takes my bags and pops them in the trunk. He opens the door for me, and I slide into the car. I have yet to get more than four hours of sleep at night, but I'm sure tonight I'm going to sleep so much better. Now that everything is taken care of, I feel good to go.

We head back towards Perrone's since my car is still in the parking garage. I look over at Brent as he parks close to my car. He puts the car in park and stares straight ahead.

"Buyer's remorse?" I ask, laughing.

"Never. Not where you're concerned." The way he's looking at me makes me want to peel the clothes off his body. He's been so great, and I want nothing more to show him how I feel.

"If I kiss you right now, I don't know if I'd be able to stop. I think I need to get out of the car," I whisper as he looks down at my lips and then back up at me. He nods as I bring my fingers to my lips and kiss them. "Why does this have to be so difficult? When I know it's not," I whisper, and he nods.

"I understand, Gemma. You have some things you need to take care of. Until then I'll be here until you're ready to jump. I'm not in a hurry. I want to be with you long term, Gemma. I mean I am with you. Look at us. Many would give up because the past is too hard to face. You're facing it head on, and I know it's going to be hard. It's going to hurt like hell but know that I'm here for you when you need me. Can you get home safely? I know you've been really wiped lately. If you're too tired, I can take you home."

"No, I'm fine. My God, it's like every time I park in this garage, I end up not driving myself home," I joke, and he smiles.

"You have your laptop. Work from home tomorrow," he adds. "I need you Friday morning to help interview a couple candidates, but tomorrow I'm giving you a comp day. Sleep in. Spend some time in your pajamas and work from bed. If we need you, we will let you know. Otherwise, just rest up. Friday is going to be a long night and then you have Saturday morning."

"Thank you, Brent," I reply as I lean over and chastely kiss him on the cheek before pulling back. "See you Friday!"

•••

Thursday, I stay in bed all day working from my laptop. I catch up on a lot of work and Blake sends me funny memes all day long. Blake and I decide to meet for brunch again Sunday morning. I figure I'll be completely wiped Saturday after my therapy session. The first one is three hours long. I talked to my new therapist a little over the phone about what I wanted to achieve through therapy and a little of my history with my father. I told her I was ready to jump into the deep end, and she seemed to be supportive of my plan. I figure I'll grab something to eat afterwards and then go home to sleep. I'm sure I won't be getting home until Saturday morning anyway from the event tomorrow night.

•••

Friday morning I'm in the office early. Brent greets me when I arrive. "I'm so excited about tonight," I say.

"Me too, Gemma. Look I need you to help with a couple interviews this morning. Around lunch time you're welcome to head out to get ready for tonight. A car will pick you up at 2:30 from your apartment to head to Maggie's. She still wants you there at 3:00. I'll pick you up from there, and we will head to the venue together. You good with that?" he asks, and I nod. I can't wait to see Brent up close and personal in a tux.

"I'm excited about these interviews. I was looking over some of their resumes yesterday. I know it's hard to tell on paper, but I really like…I think her name was Lucy?" I say as I look back through the resumes in my portfolio. "She's my last interview of the day."

"I just finished interviewing her," he whispers, smiling at me. "I thought the same thing. I think you'll like her a lot. She's from Charleston, South Carolina. She's got an event management background, not to mention her administrative assistant history. She's interviewing with Paolo in HR right now."

"Yay," I say as I clap my hands together. "Your dream is coming true," I add as he smiles gratefully down at me.

"You have no idea," he whispers, and I hold back my smile and turn around to get my desk set up. I have a couple interviews before her, so I head to the conference room. Helen and I are interviewing the candidates together, so I'm excited to see how these interviews go.

Just before lunch time Helen's starting to get a headache, and we're laughing about some of the crazy things we've heard today. There's a knock on the door, and a sweet, smiling brunette pops her head around the corner. She has beautiful greenish-blue eyes and shoulder length brown hair. She's dressed smartly in a maroon shift dress and tan heels. I stand up, shaking her hand.

"I'm Lucy Lane. I'm sorry if I seem a little wide eyed. I just finished my 12th interview of the day. I promise you I'm excited to interview with you guys, but I'm a little overwhelmed. Everyone has been so nice. Honestly, I wasn't prepared for that. The culture here feels real homey," she says with a subtle twang. She sits down after shaking Helen's hand. I LOVE HER, I communicate with my eyes, and Helen winks back as we all sit down.

I know she's been interviewed by so many different people today. She's answered the same questions over and over again. I smile at her, and she smiles gratefully back at me. Half of my interviews today have seemed robotic by the time they got to us, so I know we simply need to get to know her. Her resume speaks for itself, but there's something to say about being a good human, too. She interviews very well. This next "get to know you" section is where we lost a lot of the other candidates.

"Okay. So, let's get down to real questions," I say, and she leans in. "What's your biggest weakness?" she laughs, and I laugh too. I like that she has a sense of humor.

"Chocolate. Specifically, white chocolate and peppermint," Helen grins.

"What's your biggest pet peeve?"

"Two-faced people and women that gossip at other's expenses," she answers, and I sit back. "Sorry. I'm sure you were looking for just one. However, those kind of go together."

"Smart. Last question," I state, and she sits back, crossing her incredibly toned and tanned legs. Someone opens the door and walks in laughing. It's Brent and Hayden. I look up at Brent, and he apologizes. Hayden, however, is staring at Lucy like she's his last meal, and Lucy is staring back. I see him look down at her crossed legs and then he clears his throat as he looks over to Brent, to me and then back at Lucy. Brent saw it too. "Lucy, this is Hayden, one of our top executives. He's been an associate here for a long time," I state, and he looks away from her to me, apparently snapping out of whatever that was.

"I haven't been here that long. I'm not that old," he corrects as Brent laughs, pushing him out of the way. "Also, I know there were a bunch of us in there, but I was in your third interview this morning. You did great!"

"I'm Brent King," Brent interrupts as he pushes Hayden further into the room so he can address

Lucy as well. "I was your first interview this morning," he adds, shaking her hand. "Thanks again for coming in, Lucy. We appreciate it. I've already said it, but I think you would be a great addition to our team." She nods, smiling at both. Her eyes move back to Hayden, and then she turns back in her chair toward me. The guys say goodbye and then head back out of the conference room. Lucy watches them leave, seeming to forget where she is. I put my hand over hers and she recomposes herself.

"It's okay. The interview was over a while ago. You can speak plainly."

"Oh my gosh! Hayden?" she whispers.

"Yes, Hayden," I smile, and she bites her lip.

"I'm so sorry. That was so unprofessional of me. I just couldn't help my reaction. I'm normally more put together than this. I've met a lot of celebrities and whatnot in my career. That felt, different," she says, a little confused and I smile at her. "Anyway, moving on!"

"You're good, and just between us I think you nailed the interviews today. I imagine you'll be receiving an offer letter next week. We have a big event tonight, but by Monday we should be back to normal. When are you able to start?" I ask, and she smiles.

"I would need to give my current employer,

who knows I'm here today by the way, about a two-week notice. I'd say at the latest end of August. Maybe the first week in September?"

"That's perfect. Lucy, I can't wait to get to know you better," I add, and she smiles genuinely. LOVE HER! After she leaves, Helen looks at me as if she's trying to figure something out. "What is it?"

"I can't place her. I know I've seen her. It's like she's a Disney Princess." I nod and laugh.

"Yes, but which one?" I add as we sit thinking for a minute.

"Rapunzel!" we both say at the same time, and then start laughing.

"Except after Flynn Rider chops off her hair," Helen adds, and I have catch my breath I'm laughing so hard.

"But with a better hair cut!" I say as I wipe the tears from my eyes. Brent sees us in the hallway, and he smiles before he shakes his head and closes his door.

That afternoon the town car drops me off at Maggie's store right on time. Maggie gives me a hug as I enter. We sit and talk for a while, getting to know each other and then she looks over at the clock. We try the dress on and everything fits perfectly.

"Hey! If I call a photographer friend of mine, would you let him take a couple pictures of you in this dress? I'd love to put it on the website or frame it for the studio. I don't ever make the same exact dress. Every single dress of mine is a one of a kind." She helps me out of the dress and hangs it up.

"Do it." She hands me a robe, and I slip into it. It's the most beautiful fabric. So soft against my skin. "Can I buy this from you?" I ask, and she shakes her head.

"It's yours," she answers as she types on her computer.

"It's not mine. I love it though."

"No. I mean, it's yours. Brent called me today to put a card on file. For anything and everything that you might need for this evening while getting ready. My robes have been flying off the shelf, and he said to pick out one that I thought would be perfect for you. This is one of my favorite fabrics."

"Why does that not surprise me?" I giggle like a schoolgirl and take in the moment of being absolutely spoiled. We're still talking about Brent when her friends start showing up. She introduces me to everyone, and I like them immediately.

"This is Liz Beth. She's an incredible make-up artist." I stand up, shaking her hand. She's so adorable. She's short with long blonde hair and funky clothes. She's very hippie-chic but like the designer version. "This is Kennedy. She'll be doing all things hair." Kennedy is medium height, originally from Hawaii with the most gorgeous black, silky hair. Her complexion is to die for. She's wearing jeans and a teeshirt, and I love how diverse Maggie's friends are. "This is Morrey. He's a high-end lingerie photographer. He does a lot of fashion shoots. You've more than likely seen his work if you pick up any reputable magazine." He's a stunningly beautiful black man with gorgeous warm brown eyes. His head is shaved on the sides and his hair is graying naturally at the top. He's got about a weeks-worth of scruff on his face, and I smile at him as he reaches for my hand. "Also, he's mine," Maggie whispers as I look over at her. "I know, I have amazing taste," she jokes. "Wait until you see what the four of us can do when we work together."

"I can't wait!"

Liz Beth and Kennedy take me over to an antique desk surrounded by mirrors that Maggie has in the back. While they apply my make-up and fix my hair, Morrey comes in and starts taking photos of us. Luckily, I was able to do my nails yesterday while I was at home. I painted them a pale pink and I'm glad I chose that color. I don't have a spray tan, but I still have some color from the Hamptons trip. Morrey shows Maggie a photo and she grins. He winks at her, which makes her blush, and I look away, letting them have their moment.

"These are going to be amazing," Maggie adds as she sits down and starts working on a dress. We are all sitting around talking when Liz Beth and Kennedy step back to study their work.

"AMAZING!" Kennedy says as she fluffs my hair. "Eventually, I want to see what's under all this color though," she comes behind me spraying my hair. "This chignon isn't going anywhere but just know when you take it down tonight your hair is going to have some funky curls."

"Let's get this dress on!" Maggie yells. Morrey is used to naked women, so I take my clothes off and pull on a nude thong. I step into my shoes and Morrey tells them to hold on. Maggie nods to me, and I tell myself to just go for it. I'm only wearing a nude thong and my nude Christian Louboutins. He has me stand in front of the concrete wall and asks Maggie to dim the lights. At first, I cover my chest with my arms. Maggie is looking at the photos as they come across the iMac screen. As I get a little more comfortable, I uncover myself. Morrey brings over a pale pink chaise lounge and I lay on my back and then turn on my stomach. "You're a natural. I love your curves," Maggie says as she comes over, instructing me on what to do with my arms. Maggie watches Morrey work and she smiles proudly at him. He sits back, looking through some of the photos and nods to Maggie. "Okay, let's try this again." I step into my dress as she looks everything over. I'm in absolute awe of what this team has managed to do.

"You've got to be kidding me," Liz Beth says with a smile on her face as Morrey continues to snap away and the pictures pop up on the screen. "I'm so glad you called him. These are going to be amazing, Mags."

"Do you want any outside?" I ask, and she lifts her eyebrows in shock.

"You'd be okay with that?" she asks.

"Why wouldn't I be? I want to make sure you get the photos that you want. I mean I could always come back, but we're all here now. Who am I to care if people see me out like this. This is about as put together as you'll ever get me," I add, laughing as we all head outside. Kennedy and Liz Beth stand by with their hair and make-up kits as Maggie holds a reflector for Morrey.

The most fun shot was of me crossing the street with regular pedestrians, but I'm in a gown. Everyone acts as if it's just a normal Friday. Another great one is me holding balloons as I walk. We do a few close ups with a fish net veil over my face from Maggie's shop. We eventually walk down a few blocks to Bowling Green Park and that's when the pictures really start to excite everyone. Morrey shows us a couple of the photos and I feel completely humbled.

"Maggie, please hear me say this and get it in writing if you feel the need – use these pictures however you want."

"I love you," she yells, and we all laugh. As we start to walk back, Maggie's phone buzzes and she answers it.

"Everything okay, darling?" Morrey asks, and she nods.

"Gemma, you've got a visitor back at the store!" She smiles sweetly, and I get butterflies in my stomach. For some reason I feel like it's my wedding day. I have no plans to ever get married, but this I feel deep down. We turn a corner, and I see him leaning against the town car. He looks up, and when he sees me he stands up straight. His mouth falls open, then his hand goes over his heart. Maggie slaps Morrey in the arm, and he picks up his camera. I ignore them and walk up to Brent. He looks absolutely delicious. He's wearing a black tuxedo with a white shirt underneath and a bow tie. He smells amazing, and I smile deviously up at him.

"Jesus, Gemma," he whispers as he looks me up and down. I reach up, straightening his bow tie and he smiles down at me. He looks up to the sky like it might give him extra strength, which makes me tilt my head back and laugh. "I thought already seeing you in this dress would help me make it through the evening. I don't know what to say, Gem," he says as he spreads his arms out in front of me. "You can have me. I'm yours!"

I tell him to hold on a second so I can grab my

stuff from inside, but he grabs my hand and follows me inside. A couple of people shopping in the store do a double take at the two of us. One takes out a camera and takes a photo. I keep walking, and Brent does the same. I put my stuff in my bag and as we're walking out, Brent sees the collage of photos Maggie is downloading from today on the screen. Some are in bright color, and some are black and white.

"What…" he chokes out as his breath leaves him. I walk up to him, putting on more deodorant, and he laughs. He sits down in Maggie's office chair and pulls me into his lap. Morrey shows him the photos from today, and when we get to the ones of me only in my underwear and heels, he presses his lips against the top of my shoulder. I laugh because I find his reaction comical. Maggie slaps him in the arm, and he gives her some serious side eye. When he stands back up, again he pulls me into his arms.

"Ready to go?" I ask, and he shakes his head.

"Need a minute?" Maggie jokes. Liz Beth hands me some of the lip gloss we used today for my clutch, and I thank them for everything. "You're a good man, Brent. Celebrate big tonight. Tomorrow is the first day of the rest of our girl's life." Maggie hugs me, and the other girls join her. I feel like I've found some more of my people today. "Call me when you need to. I put my card in your clutch."

Brent grabs my hand as we approach the event venue, rubbing a thumb across the top of my hand. He pulls something from his suit pocket, and I look at him in shock.

"It's not an engagement ring, Gemma. Take a deep breath," he says as he holds the box in his hands. "If you don't like it, it's not a big deal. I was waiting for it to be engraved. I wanted to give it to you earlier this week, but I ran out of time." I take the box from his hands and lean over, kissing his cheek.

"I'm sure I'll love it!" I say as I open the box and gasp. I close the box and look back over at Brent. "If you ruin my make up before we get there Maggie will kill you! Is this real?" I ask, and he chuckles.

"You think I'd buy you a fake?" he jokes as he takes the rose gold, diamond encrusted Rolex out of the box. I give him my left arm, and he goes to fasten it around my wrist.

"Wait! You said it was engraved." I flip it over and it says, *"To spending every midnight with you."*

I look over at him as I tear up, and he has to look outside the window for a moment. When he looks back at me, he has tears in his eyes. I lean over, kissing him gently on the lips and when I pull back, he hands me a handkerchief from his pocket. I notice it has his initials monogrammed on the corner. I dab under my eyes and take a deep breath as I hand him my left wrist again. He fastens the watch and kisses my cheek. I know how much he loves me. In fact, I love it! I just hope I can get to the place where I can express my love and affection for him. He deserves it.

We stop and take a few red-carpet photos and then head inside to make sure everything is ready for our guests. Blake spots us outside of the event hall and, as ever, is most dramatic in his greeting.

"Gemma. I've never in my life," he whispers, looking up at Brent and then giving Greta and I a hug. "Darling, if I ever doubted your showstopping appearance, let me be the first to ask for forgiveness. You are a goddess!" I smack him away as we head into the Great Hall. He gasps dramatically again, looking down at my left arm. "What in the hell is that on your wrist?" he asks as he takes my hand. "Brent! It's stunning!"

"She lost her watch. Plus, it looks perfect on her." Brent says as Blake turns his head dramatically to look at him.

"I agree. However, you do know it was an Apple watch that she lost, right?" Blake whispers, to which Brent shrugs his shoulders and turns to greet someone.

"You're making a scene!" I grit out to Blake, and he shoos me away.

"Maybe I need to lose my watch? Will you buy

me a diamond Rolex, daddy?" Blake says in his very best Marilyn Monroe-like voice. Brent laughs and takes my hand away from Blake. Intertwining our fingers together, he pulls me to his side.

"If she wants an Apple watch as well, we can take care of that too. Now leave her the hell alone!" Brent adds as Blake links his arm with my free one. Brent leaves to speak to someone, but not before he kisses my hand. After he's gone, Blake looks at me with a new appreciation.

"STOP!" I whisper, and he kisses my cheek.

"I'm proud of you," he whispers. I mouth *thank you* back to him as we turn the corner into the event hall.

It's like an expanded version of Versailles' Hall of Mirrors. I stop and Brent runs into my back. He places two hands on my shoulders as I walk up closer to the stage. A bunch of people are making toasts and speeches tonight, so I want to make sure that their teleprompter and speeches are already queued. The band is set up on a side stage near the dance floor. From what Blake tells me, they are ready to go. The I at the tables and chairs is to die for. The floral arrangements are over the top and the room is slowly being dimmed to different tones and light levels depending on where we will be in the schedule for the evening. The first is for our guests' arrival, with all lights on. The second is slightly dimmed with a rose gold overlay for dinner and cocktails. The next setting is for speeches toward the end of dinner and during dessert. The last setting is for dancing, with all overhead lights dimmed except for the chandeliers and candles around the room.

Greta is talking to our lighting guy, and I show her where I want the spotlight. They ask if I'll go up there to tell them when the spotlight is at the right brightness. I start to walk on stage and see Brent talking to a couple of people in the center of the room. It's an older couple and a younger gentleman. Greta asks me a couple of questions, but the lighting guy can't hear me so I point to the microphone. I look over to the sound guy, and he nods giving me a thumbs up.

"Okay, can we get this toned down? Maybe if this is a 10 let's go down to an eight. I want them to be able to see the teleprompter for their speeches. Right now, there seems to be a reflection. That's perfect!" I say as the lighting guy gives me a thumbs up.

When I look up, everyone in the room is watching me. "I'm not going to sing, guys. So everyone can calm down," I joke, and hear Brent laughing in the back. The people he's talking to seem to be his parents, or at least they look like the people in the photos in his office. He's beaming at me, but his parents aren't looking at me. They are looking at Brent's reaction to looking at me. His mom looks so happy as she grabs Brent's arm. I'm glad they are pleased with everything. The room looks perfect. I start to walk towards the stairs but see Blake running towards me. I shield my eyes from the spotlight to see what he wants as he runs up the side stairs. He grabs the microphone, and I laugh. "Yeah, I'm done," I say as I try to walk away, but he grabs my hand, pulls me into his arms and dances with me. The spotlight goes off, but Blake keeps dancing with me.

I hear someone yell from the crowd and look out to see Brent walking toward the stage. I know there are photographers here, and this is probably a good photo op for them. This is the company's big night to shine, so I give in. Blake dances with me dramatically until Brent walks up the stairs toward us. Blake runs off screaming, pretending to be scared of his brother. I laugh as Brent grabs my hand, pulling me into his arms. I sigh as he pulls me so close that there's no space between us at all. What first started out as a joke is now making my heart race inside my chest. He smells and looks so delicious tonight.

"Breathe," he whispers in my ear as I hear the singer of the jazz band get up and start singing. I see Blake standing there, and he winks at me. It's one of my favorites. Brent dips me when the singer sings, "And I'm feeling good!" We look over at Blake, who's living it up pretending to direct the band. They at least have the sense of humor to play along. Everyone is having a kick ass time, and then Greta tells us that our guests are starting to arrive. I pull back, but not before Brent pulls me into his side. I look up at him and he leans down whispering in my ear.

"I have some people I want you to meet." He walks down the stairs first, then holds a hand out for me. We make our way past a couple people from work who applaud and one who tells me I look like a fairy princess. I thank her, and then I'm standing in front of Brent's parents. "Gemma, may I introduce you to my parents. George and Regina King." His mother walks over and wraps her arms around me. I'm a little taken aback, but I wrap my arms around her as well.

"Gemma. We are so excited to meet you," she says and grabs my hand. I squeeze back, then his father steps forward, grabbing my other hand and placing a kiss on it. I smile kindly at him and see where Brent gets his gentlemanly manners.

"Gemma. It's an honor," George says in a strong Scottish accent.

"The honor is all mine," I reply as George releases my hand. Brent taps someone on the shoulder, and a mini version of Blake and Brent turns around. I gasp and then wrap my arms around him. I'm not sure why he makes me so happy, but he looks like a perfect mixture of both Brent and

Blake. The girl standing beside him doesn't look too pleased at me hugging her date. I don't blame her, but Brett smiles at me a little shyly. I find that funny considering that I'm around his age. He doesn't have the King swagger. Yet. I'm sure that comes with time, but I grin over at him as Brent starts the introductions.

"You must be Brett," I ask, and he nods.

"Please don't be Gemma. Dammit, Brent wins," he jokes, and I giggle. He's adorable. I love it. He's got a way to go to have the pizzazz of the older King men. I'll say this though -- genetics has been very kind to this family.

"Hey, King family," I say as they look over at me. I look down at my new watch and see it's 6:45PM. George and Regina look back at Brent when they see the watch, but don't say anything. Regina tries not to smile but doesn't hide it very well. Brent's beaming from ear to ear looking at me, and I can't help the flush that kisses my skin at his praise. "The party is officially in full swing, and we have 15 minutes until dinner is served. You guys have to be outside for pictures soon." Brent leans down, whispering to me.

"You're simply wonderful, darling! Thank you."

Brent and his family head out front to go back through the press line of photographers. Blake jogs by me, blowing me a kiss, and I laugh. I love this family. I haven't even started therapy, but the more I'm around this family the more I feel like I'm settling into myself and who I am now. Who I was doesn't have to be who I am now. I'm beyond excited for this new chapter. I know deep down in my heart I've got a hard road ahead. I feel like once I rip off the band aid I can finally start to heal the past I've been running away from for so long.

I walk over to some interns who are starting to look a little lost. I help them find their places and their tasks for the evening. I know it can be overwhelming. It was for me when I was in their shoes. There's a certain amount of pride that goes along with knowing you are a part of putting an event like this on. It's one of the most glamorous and notorious social events of the season in New York. I walk around, speaking to different people and I see Hugo. He's a head taller than everyone else, and he's walking towards me with Brent. He's one of only a few men that I know that are taller than Brent. Not as good looking, but taller. As they break through the crowd, I see Rhodes and Philip as well.

"Look at you guys. You clean up nice," I say as they take me in while ribbing Brent. I laugh as Hugo wraps his arms around me.

"Look at us? Look at you," he says picking me up, and Brent punches him on the arm.

"Put her down. You're going to mess up her

dress. Jesus, Hugo, you're such caveman. Were you raised in a barn?" Hugo puts me down, and I stand a little closer to Brent in hopes that he'll protect me from that happening again.

"Not a barn, but Texas. So, fairly close!"

We all stand around laughing for a few minutes, then I tell Brent he needs to get ready. He's opening and closing the night. I've already made sure that his notes are up there. I know the prompter works, but knowing Brent, he could probably wing it if it went out. I head to the back of the room and see Blake start walking towards me.

"You've made quite the impression, little lady," he whispers. He comes to stand next to me as he waves and smiles at people as they pass by him. "My parents are ready to trade one of us in in exchange for you, my mother in particular. She's already asked me to invite you to Sunday dinner at their house."

"In Connecticut?" I ask, and he rolls his eyes.

"Where else? Where did you think I went every Sunday? It's not a short drive" he asks, laughing and I punch him in the arm. "OUCH! My gosh, you've become very violent in your old age, Gemma. But yes, their house is very respectable. I think you'll find it very tasteful," he adds, joking with me. He holds up my left arm, admiring my new watch, and I have to laugh.

"If you're good, I'll let you wear it during

brunch Sunday!" I whisper, and he straightens up like a soldier. I giggle and shake my head as I see Brent walking up the stairs to the stage. They turn the spotlight on, and I see the interns are ready with the teleprompter feed behind the sound booth.

"Good evening," Brent says as he begins his welcome. His Scottish accent is amplified by the microphone, and it's a delight for all. I look around as women are literally drooling over the man of the hour. He really is Prince Charming, and your favorite superhero all wrapped into one absolutely delicious package. I should know first-hand. I smile up at him, and when I scan the room, I see his mom looking over at me smiling. She nods her head and then looks back up at her son proudly. That's the way it should be.

As he wraps up his speech, I head over to two older couples that are still looking for their table. I help them get seated and then hear Brent say my name over the microphone. SHIT! I looked over his speech. Hell, I'm the one who typed up the final copy. I know I wasn't in the speech. He's gone off script. The spotlight comes over to me, and I step away from the table as not to blind the guests. I hear Blake squeal from behind me somewhere, and when I turn to the left, I see him not only beaming at me, but laughing. He knows I will kill someone once the spotlight turns off me. Brent is very kind with his words. He also thanks the other countless staff who spent hours, weeks and months planning this event. He then thanks the interns as the spotlight moves back to the stage. I turn quickly and walk to Blake, who wraps me in his arms.

"Oh my gosh, that was horrible," I whisper, and he laughs.

"Well, you looked flawless, my dear. A little shocked, but at the same time absolutely stunning. Where are you sitting," he asks.

"I pulled my name from the seating chart when I knew I'd be doing a lot of behind-the-scenes stuff. I told Glen to save me some food. I'll eat once the dancing starts."

"What? No. You'll sit with me. I know the woman putting this show on, and she can get you a chair. Brent is not going to have any part of you not partaking. No ma'am."

"I'm not *not* partaking. I'm literally just eating after I make sure that dinner goes off without a hitch. Once the dancing starts, I'm golden. The interns and support teams are eating then. I'll join them in the kitchen. The caterers and vendors will start packing up, and we will have the entire evening to enjoy ourselves."

"Hmm…I'm not sold. Let me think about it, and I'll get back to you in four to six business days. Until then, plan on sitting with me," he adds as he walks away.

"Where are you sitting?" Brent asks as he takes

my hand and pulls me into the hallway. "Gemma?" he asks, and I lean in pretending not to hear him. I tell the intern standing near the door to help Mr. King to his table. He widens his eyes in disbelief as I wave goodbye to him, and he's ushered into the Great Hall. He turns back one more time, and the look on his face makes me laugh. He makes it to his table, and I see Blake point next to him. Everyone at the table turns to look at me. I give Blake a thumbs up, and he shakes his head, standing up and pointing next to him. He's pulled a chair up, and I shake my head no. I give him a thumbs up and then start making my rounds. I start at the back tables and ask how everything is. Most everyone is kind. I stop at one table and there are some rude girls, one being the girl in the red dress. Mindy, I think is her name. They all seem unhappy with me being the chick that is taking Brent's attention tonight. I can feel it, but I don't care. I smile at them and then move on to the next table. As I make my way around the room, I feel someone put a hand on my shoulder.

"Elaine!" I haven't seen her since the Hampton's.

"Gemma, you are a vision," she says as she turns to ask a photographer to take our picture. We wrap arms around each other's waists and get a few photos. She stands back and we talk for a couple minutes before Joseph pulls her back to their table.

I wave at Hugo, who blows me a kiss, and I giggle. I've almost made it to every table. Which is saying a lot since there are around 60 tables in the room tonight. I can't believe almost 500 people are here. Not including staff, the band, vendors and photographers. I can't believe we've pulled this off. It's one of the most extravagant evenings I've ever attended. The fact that I had a hand in making it happen is extraordinary and humbling.

As I make it to the last table, Glen comes out. I give him a hug, and he's ecstatic. This was a huge night for him as well. Everything tonight was incredible. Dessert is now being served. I'm so very grateful for this moment. I start walking toward The King family's table, sitting down next to Blake, but with my back turned to the table.

"Don't be angry. I have a job to do," I whisper as he leans over, kissing me on the cheek. He gives me a forkful of cake, and I smile. I catch Brent's eye, and he's taking a bite of his cake with a knowing gleam in his eyes. I think back to the cake we shared not too long ago and look down, blushing. I turn around in my seat, going back to my hostess role. I ask everyone how their dinner was, and everyone has raving reviews. Regina turns to me and places a hand on my arm.

"Darling, when do you get to sit down and enjoy yourself?" she asks sweetly, and I place my hand over hers.

"Very shortly. Once dinner is cleared away, I'm going to head back to the kitchen and eat with the support staff and interns. Everyone will be dancing by then. It will be a good time for me to sneak away." The wait staff starts to come around offering coffee and tea as the plates are cleared. I look at Brent and wink. "I'll be back shortly. You guys enjoy your dancing," I whisper as I stand up. For some reason the spotlight hits me at the same exact time, and I sit down and take Blake's hand. "What is happening?" I ask as he pushes me back up to standing. The band leader points to me, and I shake my head. Please no.

"Earlier this evening, I had the delight to lead these two ravishing humans in the first dance of the evening. Earlier it was just a rehearsal, but this time it's for real. Who wants to see them show off their dancing skills for the rest of us?" he asks as everyone cheers and applauds. I can specifically hear Hugo and the guys in the background being their obnoxious selves. I close my eyes, and when I open them, Brent comes around to take my hand. He buttons his suit jacket, and the smile he gives me could make me a puddle on the floor.

"Wake me up when this is over," I whisper, and he laughs.

"Don't you dare check out on me now. I need you!"

The intro to Feeling Good starts again. The

lead singer starts the song off, his voice a-cappella, and you could hear a pin drop in this place. As the band joins in, I feel Brent press me closer to his body. So close that there's really only one of us dancing. He leads so well, and it's a damn good thing because I don't think I could move otherwise. He places his lips against my ear, reminding me to breathe. I squeeze him tighter as he interlaces our fingers and pulls them closer to his chest. Eventually the song ends, and he asks me if I'm ready. I look into his eyes and know what he's going to do. I squeeze his hand as he wraps his arm around my back tighter. He slowly and easily dips me backwards as the guests cheer and applaud. When he pulls me up again, he presses his lips to the side of my head. I lean into his kiss wearily, then he walks me out of the spotlight. Others start to hit the dance floor as we exit, and I'm starting to feel a little faint. I haven't eaten since appetizers last night and a bite of cake from Blake. My energy is starting to wane. I feel Brent pull me closer to his side as we make our way to the back of the room to the kitchen. When we are out of view, he picks me up and I wrap my arms around his neck as he carries me.

"You don't have to do this," I say, and he shakes his head.

"You want me to let you pass out in front of everyone?" he asks as he places an apron down on a table and then sets me on top of it. He walks away for a second and then one of the interns brings me a water. Brent brings me a plate, followed by Glen who brings out a plate of desserts. I smile, and Glen comes around to hug me.

"It was perfect. We will be packing up once everyone has had a bite to eat. And Gemma, please call me for your next event. This was the most fun we've ever had at an event. You were so easy to work with." I take his hand, then Brent comes to stand in front of me. I eat a little, then Blake joins us. Brent is needed back in the event hall, so Blake and I eat some more cheesecake! After we've finished, we fix ourselves up again and go take some pictures.

We go out front to where the photographers are and take some serious and some funny pictures together. The press is gone for the most part, but we head out to the red carpet and have one of our vendors take some of us. Blake and I always have the best time together. Whether we are goofing off or not. As we head back inside, we notice that people are starting to leave. I look down at my watch. It's already after 11 p.m. Well, no wonder. Everyone except Brent has given their final speeches and "thank yous" for the night. He will shut down the event between 11:30 and midnight. It just depends on how many people are still around.

I spot Brent, but he doesn't smile back. He's

watching me like a lion hunting its prey. I move to the dance floor to dance with Blake, Hugo and the other guests from our weekend in the Hamptons. We have a blast dancing and laughing as the evening ends. I feel Brent behind me, and I twist my arm above my head to run my hands through his gorgeous hair. He places a hand on my wrist and then slowly drags his fingers down my arms until he reaches my hips. Blake was right. Brent's an amazing dancer. He grabs my hand, spinning me out and then pulls me into his chest as I laugh.

"You know your brother was right."

"Oh yeah? What about?" Brent yells over the music. I grab the back of his head pulling his ear down towards me.

"Your dancing does translate into the bedroom." He runs a hand around my waist and pulls me closer.

"Thank you for your hard work tonight, Gemma. You were such a kind and caring hostess. People love you," he whispers in my ear as I lean my head against his chest. A slow song comes on, and I'm grateful. My feet are starting to really hurt, and I could use a nap. "Are you sleepy, baby?" he whispers, and I nod. I'm not even able to move my head away from his chest. I hear a laugh reverberate from inside his chest and it's comforting, like my own sound machine. Brent wraps his arms around me, pressing his hand against my head to his chest and the other one around my waist. I keep my arms around his waist as if no one is around. I could literally fall asleep here. We move slowly together during the entire song. When it comes to an end I pull back, Brent's hand still cupping the back of my head, and I look up at him.

"This would be the perfect time for you to kiss me," I whisper sleepily.

"Anything for you, Pumpkin," he jokes before leaning down and kissing me tenderly.

"Did I turn into a prince?" he asks.

"Wrong fairy tale!" I scold playfully, and he chuckles.

"I thought you didn't believe in fairytales?" he whispers in my ear.

"Give a girl a chance," I say as he leans back down, kissing me more passionately this time. The people around us cheer as he heads up to the stage platform to say good night to everyone. He winks at me, and I can't help but blush. This must be the wooing he was talking about. Most of the staff is still here, and we get together for a big group picture after the guests leave. The photographer has to climb up on stage in order to get everyone in the shot. Brent, Blake and I get a photo, and then Blake says he's leaving. I give him a kiss and a big hug.

"I'll see you on Sunday for brunch," I remind him as he's walking away.

"Perfect. I've never been prouder of you, my

little gem," he yells back, and I smile. "Don't forget. Think about Sunday night family dinner in Connecticut." Brent comes over, wrapping a supportive arm around my waist, and I lean into him.

"In Connecticut?" I yell. Blake laughs as he walks down the hallway.

"YES! In Connecticut!! I LOVE YOU!" I hear him yell, and Brent looks down at me smiling. I blow Blake a kiss, and he disappears into the night. What a perfect night!

"Connecticut, huh?" he asks, and I shrug.

"I don't know. I was invited, but I mean, Connecticut?" I repeat, working the word out dramatically. Brent laughs as I smile up at him.

We call it a night about an hour later. I can barely walk to the car. The shoes aren't particularly uncomfortable. It's that I've been on my feet all day long. I step into the waiting town car, and Brent is right beside me. I sit down and take my shoes off. As we start heading back toward Brooklyn, I look up at the lights of the city as we drive away. It's beautiful. Brent places a hand on my knee, and I sit up.

"Please unzip me," I ask as he groans in acknowledgement to my request.

"Happy to, Pumpkin. Are you uncomfortable?" he asks as he unclasps my dress and unzips me until my entire back is exposed. I breathe out a sigh of relief and feel Brent's hands against my sore back.

"I'll say this. If you're worried about your posture, or want your girls to look nice and perky, this is the dress for you. There's no slouching in this thing," I add as he laughs.

"I'll keep that in mind," Brent says with a deep, resounding chuckle. "While we are on the subject. I thought your posture and your girls looked incredible tonight. So, job well done. Also, you were amazing tonight. Being with you this afternoon and tonight was like a dream for me." Brent runs his fingers gently up and down my spine as I sigh. He leans down, kissing my shoulder and my bare back. I want more than anything to turn around and kiss him, but I'm beyond exhausted. I feel him pull me backwards until my back is resting in his arms. I immediately fall fast asleep.

I wake up to Brent whispering my name quietly, and I groan. *NO!! I want to go back to bed.* I honestly contemplate having him take me back to his apartment, but I know that I need to go inside. Tomorrow is a big day for me. I need to be as prepared as possible. If I'm at Brent's, there's a good chance that I will get distracted. I don't want to have any excuses not to go tomorrow. I wouldn't be waking up at nine on a Saturday after an event like tonight if I wasn't serious about starting therapy. I have every excuse to cancel, but I won't. Brent apologizes as he rezips my dress halfway up. He steps out of the car, and I put my heels in my bag. Brent gently lifts me into his arms, and I smile gratefully up at him.

"You think of everything, don't you?" I state as he tells the driver he will be right back. Pretty sure I hear the driver mutter "yeah right," but that could have been my imagination. He carries me inside and up to my apartment. I open the door to my apartment, and he puts me down once we are inside. I reach up, bringing his lips down to mine. As our lips meet, we both sigh. I swear the kisses get better each time. He smiles adoringly down at me but tells me goodnight.

"I know I probably won't talk to you before your appointment in the morning, but I'm proud of you. If there's anything I want you to remember as you're going into your appointment, it's how much I love you. There's no rush where I'm concerned. I'm going to be here no matter what!" he adds as I wrap my arms around him. "I love you," he whispers as he leans down, kissing the top of my head. I close the door and walk into my room, locking it and taking my dress off. I throw on a tee shirt, set my alarm and then fall onto my bed. I don't think my feet will ever recover. I plug my phone in and see I already have a text from Brent.

I love you, Gemma.
Sleep well!

. . .

I'm waiting in the lobby 45 minutes before my appointment starts, and I can feel my nerves getting the best of me. I place my hands on the armrests of the chair and hold on for dear life. *I'm not going to run away! I'm not going to run!* I try to breathe through the fight or flight impulses I'm having and tell myself I'm going to stay and fight. I have to. I deserve a better life. One where I can truly live as freely as possible without my past trying to ruin everything for me. The receptionist is watching me, and I give her a small smile. She comes around the desk and hands me a small, bottled water. I thank her and take a small sip. Before I know it, I hear someone come into the waiting room calling my name.

"Gemma," I hear as I look up. The woman looks to be in her late 50's. Beautiful auburn hair and the softest blue eyes. "I'm Jesslyn," she says, and I smile up at her. "You ready?" She asks, and I nod, standing up. *I can do hard things*; I repeat to myself as I walk back to her office. Her office is set up like a den. I sit down on the plush sofa, and she takes one of the chairs facing me. She slips off her shoes and tucks her feet underneath her. "Showing up is half the battle. You know?" she states. I take a sip of my water and try to settle my racing heart. She's got a cup of tea in a mint green coffee cup, and I can see it's her favorite color from the decor around the room.

"I'm afraid I'm not going to be able to speak," I say hoarsely. My heart is racing so fast as I place a hand over my heart. She starts slowly by asking me a couple of broad questions, and I tell her about the last month. About meeting Brent and my tendency to run. My lack of experience in relationships, at least positive ones. She doesn't have a notebook, and her hands sit relaxed in her lap. I think I like that about her. I was expecting someone to be sitting across from me judging and writing all the things that are wrong with me down as I spoke. She smiles kindly and then she picks up her tea, taking a sip. After she places her cup down, she starts to talk to me like a friend would.

"We have all the time in the world. We aren't going to fix everything in one day, and some things can't be fixed. When you come to my office, Gemma, wear comfortable clothing. I have weighted blankets, tissue, waters, snacks, tea, you name it. This is supposed to be a safe space. I remember when I started attending therapy myself as a young girl. Just showing up was difficult for me. I'd get violently ill beforehand, my body revolting against me. I'd even have panic attacks during my sessions. I remember one time almost not making it to the bathroom in time. Our bodies and minds are connected, and if you take care of your body, you're also taking care of your mind and vice versa. I'm not saying you won't have episodes where you want to run. I'm simply saying you'll be more aware of what's happening in the future, and you'll be equipped to handle it. Our fight or flight response is meant to protect us. Our minds pick up on something and our bodies react. We're meant to have those responses. So, when you get into a situation and you want to run, ask yourself 'why am I running?' Learn to stop and take everything in. Sometimes it only takes a few seconds. Sometimes it takes a bit longer. You'll learn to be able to control it better."

Her words are comforting, like she understands that just being here is intimidating. She continues, "Between your intake forms and our conversation over the phone, I think I can help you. You sound like you're in a place where you want your past to not control you anymore. Not wanting your past to control your future is a big step. Most people suppress or numb it out with drugs or alcohol. I've found that's never the answer. It's a short-term fix with long-term consequences. From what I'm hearing, you tend to suppress. Let me ask you this: since meeting Brent, have you been more emotional? Been able to cry more? Let out some of the suppressed emotions you've trained yourself to control?"

"Yes. In fact, I've only had my breakdowns in

front of him. I was super embarrassed about it at first, but he was very supportive. I'm not used to that."

"He sounds like a safe place. I think it's a good idea that you're taking a small step back as you get yourself to a better place. I'm not saying you can't be with him while you're working through all of this. To be honest this is a marathon, not a sprint. Things will absolutely get easier with time as you get to know your true self better, but I think you've got the right idea. If he's a good sounding board and he's not pushing you to commit or make promises to him, then you guys are on the right track." She places her cup on the table and looks back over at me. "Okay. Let's start at the beginning. Can we talk about what you remember about your mom? Do you remember her at all? Any memories?" I sit back, taking a breath and I shake my head.

"No, I mean. Yes, we can talk about her, but no, I don't have any real memories of her. I think what I remember of her is through a few pictures. I want to believe she loved me. I have no reason to think otherwise. She died a little after my fourth birthday. I don't remember my father before that time either."

"That's okay. Four years of age is very young to have a clear memory of someone. However, with trauma sometimes we have flashbacks and moments where things come flooding back. From what you've told me, the verbal abuse and neglect by your father didn't start until after your mother died?" I take a deep breath, knowing I'm opening a door I can't close. I know what I'm fighting for, so I push through.

"From what I can remember clearly. My first memory, I think I was in 1st grade. I was waiting for him to pick me up from school. The office called him, and they waited with me for what felt like forever. Finally, he showed up, but it was much later, and the receptionist was very put off with him. I was working on my homework in the main office. He didn't look embarrassed or upset about forgetting to pick me up though. He seemed enraged that he got called out on it. He said it was my fault. I was supposed to go home with a friend or something like that. I didn't remember that being the plan. At least that's what he told the school receptionist. Whatever look he gave me as I packed my bag, I knew to fear him. We got in the car, and I could feel the anger coming off him in waves. He was gripping the steering wheel, and I kept looking over at him. I knew he was angry, and when we got closer to the house, he started to beat on the steering wheel. He screamed at me for embarrassing him. Told me I made him look like a bad parent. He told me I needed to ride the bus from now on. I needed to figure out how to get on a bus in the mornings and in the afternoon." I pause here to take a breath. Jesslyn gives me the time I need to collect myself.

"I didn't know what to do. I didn't know how to make a bus pick me up for school. He said that he never wanted a kid, so it was just ironic that my mother would die and leave him to take care of one. He was so angry that she had died, and I wasn't with her when it happened. I don't even remember where I was the night my mother died. I just don't remember her at all. This was what I heard from him over and over growing up."

Jesslyn urges me to continue, and I try to remember where I left off.

"I went up to my room and closed my door. I started crying. I was so scared. I was confused, and my father was never comforting or compassionate. Something had happened though. I laid on my bed in my room and cried for the longest time. I remember looking out the window and feeling as if the world outside my window was a big lie. I felt like such an inconvenience. That feeling never stopped while I lived in that house. I went downstairs that evening to get something to eat, and my father was sitting at the kitchen table drinking. I'd never noticed his drinking before that time. It's like anything before that day, I was oblivious to.

"It's like when the fear started to be my go-to emotion, I become more aware of him. He sat me down and told me where the bus stop was. Told me I was on my own during the day, that he had to work. When he got home, this was his house, and he would do whatever the hell he wanted in it. My room was the only place I was permitted to be once I was home from school. I asked him about dinner, and he said I'd have to learn to fend for myself. He would go to the grocery store when he got paid. I could always figure something out. After a couple of years, I started to cook for myself once I could reach the stove with a stepstool. Once he realized I could cook, I was responsible for making him dinner the nights he came home. Which was rare. If he was home, he was loud and angry. Most nights he'd come home really late. My bedroom was over the garage, and he'd be banging around and crashing into things. It wasn't until I was around 10 that he started bringing women home. He wasn't very kind to them. Maybe he was before he brought them back to the house, but he would scream and shout at them. I would turn on music in my room at night. I had a nursery rhymes CD, and I'd listen to that at night. It helped a little, but the songs always made me sad. I remember being able to cry back then. One night I was downstairs as he was coming in with some woman. She saw me and immediately was taken aback by my presence. I grabbed my hot pocket from the microwave and started to run upstairs. My dad grabbed my arm and my hot pocket fell off my plate and onto the floor. I remember just staring at it as he screamed at me. I wasn't supposed to be downstairs at this time, but I was so hungry, and he came home early. I started crying, and he pushed me up against the wall. He grabbed my face with one hand, squeezing so hard I thought he'd break my jaw. I could taste blood. I was crying so hard, and he kept squeezing and squeezing until I finally stopped crying. I forced myself to focus on the pain and to swallow down my tears. He released me, and I dropped the plate, running upstairs. After that, crying was something I didn't do anymore. I would remember the physical pain, but I could push it all down. I felt so strong when I did that. Like maybe I was stronger than him because he no longer had the power to make me cry." I lean over, take a sip of my water and continue on.

"I fell down at school one time and busted my knee up pretty bad while playing on the playground. I didn't cry and the teacher was surprised. I was used to the girls around me crying when they got hurt. Some of the boys, too. I wouldn't cry though. At that point I couldn't, even if I wanted to. I loved school but hated going home. I had girls ask me over to their houses on the weekends. Their family life was so bizarre to me. I felt like when their mothers looked at me, they knew. They knew that I wasn't being taken care of. Not like they were taking care of their little girls. I learned to do my own laundry pretty early. That was a bizarre journey. At first with just water until I got brave enough to try a little soap. I was so scared that I was going to mess up and he'd squeeze my face again. I can still remember the taste of blood in my mouth. Is that enough information for now?" I ask, exhausted, and she nods.

"We can stop there if you want. When was the last time you shared this information with someone?" she asks as she picks up her tea and holds it in both hands. "Sorry, I know I keep it pretty cold in here. Not because I like it cold, but because there isn't anything worse than a hot room when you're already sweating with nerves. Also, my patients tend to cover up with a blanket and get cozy when they arrive. Muggy rooms don't mesh well with cozy."

"I've never shared this information with anyone. I've told Brent and his brother a little bit. They know I had a rough childhood. I've probably shared the most with Brent though. I've never really gone into this much detail with anyone."

"Gemma, I'm sorry that you've had to keep these memories to yourself for so long. Or maybe more accurately carried this for so long on your own. So, we've covered let's say from your first memories up to maybe third grade? Is there anything else in those early years that you remember and are ready to share? Moments that maybe if you close your eyes, you try to mentally skip over?"

she asks.

"I came home from school one day, and my dad was hungover from the night before. I remember not knowing at first that he was home. He was supposed to be at work. I came in from the garage, and he was in the den watching TV. He was really irritable, and I could smell the alcohol and sweat on him. I avoided him, even though I usually first got a snack before heading upstairs to my room. I ran upstairs, and he caught my ankle on the steps. He was livid. I think maybe he was confused. He asked me where I'd been. I told him I was at school. He thought I was lying to him. He took his belt off and he kept whipping me over and over with it. I kept telling him that it was early afternoon. That I promised I'd been at school. I pleaded with him to stop. I begged him. He hit me with it on my lower body at first. Then it's like he blacked out. He turned into this monster just waving a whip around. He started screaming and taking all his anger out on me. Whipping my face and my arms. Then he started whipping me with the metal buckle. He busted my lip open. I remember when he fell trying to get to me, I kicked him away and ran upstairs. I closed my door and locked it and walked over to my mirror. He was banging at the door, and I moved a chair in front of it. I was so scared he would break the door down and kill me. I hadn't cried. I screamed, but the physical pain still didn't make me cry. I had blood on my new white shirt. We didn't go shopping often. We went to Goodwill or Salvation Army a couple times a year. A mom in the neighborhood gave my dad hand me downs from her older girls. It was my favorite shirt. This one still had the tags on it when I'd received it. I'd never owned a brand-new shirt, not as long as I could remember. I can still see myself looking in the mirror at the blood on my new white shirt. It had the prettiest Peter Pan collar with lace butterflies on it. I remember that was what was the most upsetting to me. I could handle the pain. The pain reminded me that I wouldn't cry. I would never let him make me cry. He didn't deserve my tears, I was stronger than him. He was a washed up, drunk, dead-beat dad. I took a bath that night, and my lip was so swollen. I remember being so concerned because of the bruises on my face. What was I going to say to my teachers? To my friends? I told them the next day I was in a car accident. I wore long leggings and a long sleeve shirt, even though it was so hot and muggy outside at the time. He had people so fooled. *We* had people fooled. I lied for him, and I hate liars. But I did lie for him. It's weird when I have nightmares or flashbacks, it's of that incident. I see that little girl so many times haunting my dreams."

I wipe a stray tear that falls from my eye, and she hands me a tissue. I take a small sip of water and grab a pillow so I can play with the tag as I continue on.

"In school we would learn about telling the truth and the honesty policy. I felt like such a fraud, like an imposter. I was keeping some deep, dark secret from everyone. That secret kept me from having any real friends. I was a great student. Never had bad grades, never missed a day of school, even when I was sick. I had a really high fever one time. My teacher sent me to the school nurse, even though I told her I was fine. She called my dad, even though I told her that he was at work and busy with important meetings. He had to take off work, and he sent me upstairs. He went back to work, and I remember looking through the cabinets for medicine. I'd seen my friends' medicine cabinets in their houses with cute little band-aids and those little cups for cough medicine. I remember thinking how unfair it was that we didn't have a cabinet like that. I was still in my bed that afternoon, feeling horribly sick. I was freezing, and no matter how many layers I had on I still couldn't get warm. My old tattered purple blanket was worn so thin. I wanted to crawl to the bathroom and take a hot bath, but I couldn't move. I just laid there shivering so hard my teeth were sore. My dad got home that night, and I remember calling out for my mom even though I knew she wasn't there." My voice breaks, and I look up at Jesslyn. She has tears in her eyes as well as she hands me another tissue.

"I wished and prayed so hard that she'd come save me, take me with her. How unfair it was for her to leave me with such a cruel man. She was dead, and I wished I was too. He never came to check on me. I remember the next morning I didn't go to school. I couldn't get out of bed. Apparently, the school called him and asked if I was still sick since I didn't show up to school. He didn't even know I was still upstairs in my room. I was in fucking elementary school. I was so sad and depressed. He came home after work screaming my name. I was never scared of him after that. I was no longer afraid to die. He came in my bedroom and was so disgusted with me. I just stared straight ahead. I couldn't even look at him. Part of me wished he'd leave. Part of me wished he'd just go ahead and put me out of my misery. He slammed my door, and I remember praying for death in that moment. I missed that entire week of school. I don't remember going to the doctor that often. When we did go, I wasn't allowed to answer questions. I was supposed to pretend to be really shy. My dad answered for me. I wasn't a shy kid though. At school I was active and social. Then I'd go home and that's when I had to be someone else. I was two people growing up. The unloved, abused child at home and the straight A's, outgoing kid at school."

"Was there ever an adult that you could trust?"

she asks, and I nod my head.

"My dad had a girlfriend maybe when I was in fourth grade. She was an exotic dancer and lived in a trailer park close to our neighborhood. My dad was so proud to be with her, and she was kind to me. My dad started to shape up around that time. I was allowed to come down and hang out with them. I didn't though, I thought it was a trick. I told them I had too much homework. When she came over, she'd cook dinner and the house wouldn't be such a dirty, disgusting mess. I still kept to myself. I remember she would go to the grocery store, and our pantry would always be stocked. There'd be fruit and snacks for me in the fridge. I was apprehensive because I knew it wouldn't last long. I didn't want to get attached to having someone kind like her in our lives. My dad always screwed things up with women. I remember he brought home another woman one evening when he was out on a bender. The girlfriend broke up with him after that. I don't blame her. He lured her back, but she didn't stay long. She would drop food by the house, and I remember one Christmas she left some presents for me. Gifts still make me uncomfortable. I always feel like I won't be able to repay someone for their kindness and generosity. Those attributes were never free for me. For years she dropped groceries and gifts by the house. I don't remember her name. Maybe Katherine? Kathy? I don't know. My father would call her 'Kitty-Kat.' I remember it was then that I learned not to judge someone by their occupation, title or where they lived. There were so many wealthy people who knew my family. People that I went to school with and who had to know my situation. I was friends with their kids. But it was the stripper from the trailer park who reached out with kindness and charity. Who lived paycheck to paycheck, but still was generous to me. It's not that the other families were mean, but they were very judgmental and would turn their noses up at my presence. Please know I don't blame her for eventually leaving him. I'm sure he was abusive to her like he was to me. The difference was she could leave. At the time I was bitter about it, but if I was her, I would have done the same thing. I wasn't her responsibility, and she didn't owe me anything." I stop for a second and place the pillow down beside me.

"I'm so sorry, Gemma. I'm sorry that there wasn't a teacher or neighbor at the time that picked up on what was going on with you at home. Or if they did, they didn't stand up for you. Your introduction to our world was so cruel. Is there anything else you want to add about your elementary school years?"

"No. That's really it. In middle school I started to develop physically. That made my dad really uncomfortable. Most of the abuse was over by the time I got into middle school. Honestly, my father was never around by that time. He stayed out or he stayed at a girlfriend's house. I was old enough in his eyes to keep house and live by myself. That was the arrangement until I went off to college. I never had friends over. I was scared he'd come home and embarrass me. I realized by then that it was him and not me. However, by that time the damage was already done."

She and I go back and forth for another hour. We discuss every single moment that I remember before my middle school years. I feel like I've drained every ounce of my memory from that time, not to mention every ounce of energy I have. It's not necessarily that she has some life-changing advice for me. I know what happened to me was wrong. I know my father failed me. The school failed to take action when they saw bruising or sus-picious behavior by my father. We didn't live in a big town by any stretch of the imagination. While people did know my father, they mostly felt sorry for him. He was a single dad doing his best to raise a little girl by himself while also working full time and trying to balance a social life. We weren't part of a church. Even though there was one of those on almost every corner. At some point, I'm no longer able to respond to her questions. Jesslyn reaches across the table and places a hand over mine.

"I think you've done amazing today, Gemma.

We've reached the three-hour mark. Here's what I want you to be prepared for, especially in these first couple of weeks unpacking everything. I think these early years are probably going to be the hardest. Especially since you've never really recounted these years of your life. I'd like for you to keep going next time we get together. Just keep talking, Gemma. Saying it out loud will take some of the power away that it's held over you all these years. I feel like this is a good direction for you. There's not one great way to get to the bottom of this. I think the first thing we do is to get all these memories out into the open. How do you feel after sharing these early memories?" I look down at the ground and then back up at her.

"Lighter. Tired. Surprised that I've kept all this inside for 24 years."

"For next week, do you want to pick up from where we stopped today?" she asks, and I nod.

"I do, actually. I do want to keep going. I feel drained, but I also feel like I can do this."

"Yes, and. I'm here to process all of this with you. Remember, this is going to take time. There's a lot to work through. We haven't even gotten to your middle school and high school years. There's a lot that you might possibly be suppressing. As we clear space, there's a possibility that you might start remembering other things. I know this might not sound fun, but what are your thoughts on keeping a journal or a notebook with you? If you have a memory, jot it down. If you have questions, write them down. I'm going to start a document of my own as we continue to press forward. If you're at work and don't want to take your journal with you, write a note to yourself in your phone and move it to your notebook when you get home. As we move forward we can always go back and address other things. You're a survivor, Gemma. You WILL get through this. I'm honored to walk with you. Thank you for trusting me."

We decide to meet on Thursday afternoons. I know I'll be able to make this work. The next couple of weeks will be intensives like today, and I know I can do this. I start walking to my car, and when I turn my phone on I see two messages from Brent. The first one was sent at 10:45 this morning.

Thinking about you.
I love you, Gemma.

And then another one around Noon.

Do you want to grab dinner tonight?

Laid back, somewhere in Brooklyn!

I smile as I look down at my phone. It's around 1:15 right now. By the time I get home, it'll be 2:00. I really want to take a nap. I'm so tired, but I'm good to grab something to eat with Brent. I get in my car and text him back.

> I can do that! How about we meet at King Cobra's. 6:00PM work for you? I want to go home and take a nap first. I'm exhausted after last night and therapy this morning.

> I'm game for that. Happy to meet there!

> Go take a nap and try to rest up a bit.

He sends me a bunch of sushi emojis, and I laugh. I stop by the store on my way home and grab a leather-bound journal and something small to eat. I plan on keeping my journal at my apartment. I don't think it would be the best idea to keep it in my purse. I can take notes on my phone and transfer stuff as I go. I really like Jesslyn. She's easy to talk to and very laid back. Her office made me feel safe. When I get to my apartment I go straight to bed. I set my alarm for 5:30 just in case I oversleep.

When I wake up, it's a little before five. I jump

in the shower and then dry my hair, putting on a headband, a sundress and flip flops. I want to be casual tonight. Before I leave, I send a text to Blake.

Thanks for recommending Jesslyn.

She was wonderful. I've got a long way to go, but it's a good start. Just woke up from a nap and heading to sushi with your brother.

We still on for brunch tomorrow?

LOVE THAT! And yes! Brunch tomorrow.

Same bat time, Same bat place! Can't wait to hear about everything. Tell Brent I said hello!

Sounds good!

See you in the morning! Love you, my Gem!

You too Blakey!!!

I meet Brent at 6:00, and he's already seated inside the restaurant. He looks casual in some khaki shorts and a tee-shirt. He wraps his arms around me, and I hug him back. I love the feel of being in his strong arms. We pull apart, and he pulls my chair out for me. I sit down as the waiter comes. We have an amazing dinner together. Relaxed, casual, and the food is amazing! We sit talking for a while and he asks me how I'm feeling. We talk a little bit about my session with Jesslyn, but mostly about how amazing Friday night was.

It's good to laugh and also to start to see a little bit of hope in my future. I feel lighter this afternoon, and I am proud of how far I've come. I know I still have some work to do but I feel like I'm on the right path. I know Brent and I both love each other. I'm still learning though. If I really want to show him how much I love him, I'm going to have to give him the best version of myself. I can't think of any other man who would give me the time, patience and space I need to work on myself. I need to learn to love myself first, and I will.

•••

Sunday morning, I head into Manhattan. I park in the garage near Perrone's and grab a table for two. It's been raining all morning, so it's really dark outside. I'm a little early, so I wait to order any mimosas. I don't want a repeat of the last time I had brunch here. I order an orange juice as I sit back waiting for Blake. I read a few articles that have come out from Friday's event, and I'm not sure how much time has passed, but I'm sure it has to be close to 11 a.m. by now. I look down at my phone for a missed call or text from Blake. The rain is really coming down now. It's 10:45, and I'm sure he's going to walk in at any moment. It's pouring, so maybe he's waiting for it to clear up. Or maybe he's still sleeping. He oversleeps all the time, and I didn't text him this morning. He has the tendency to go all out on Saturday nights, so he could have had a late night. He's stood me up before, and I'm not offended. Blake loves to party late. I decide to go ahead and text him though.

> **Hey Blakey!! I'm sitting here at Perrone's!
> Did you forget?**

Fifteen minutes later I still haven't heard back, and I'm starting to get a little annoyed. I swear if he stands me up over some dude, I'm going to let him have it the next time I see him. The waiter comes back, and I relent. I'm actually pretty hungry. I order a breakfast sandwich instead of our normal fanfare, and it arrives quickly. I take a bite and then decide to text him again.

Hey! Where are you?

Just let me know if you're not coming.

At this point I just want to know you're ok.

After I finish my breakfast, I pay and decide to head out. I look around the restaurant to make sure he wasn't sitting somewhere else the entire time thinking I stood him up. I go back through my texts to make sure I had the correct place and time. I do. I roll my eyes and call him. His phone goes straight to voicemail. Maybe he didn't charge his phone last night. Even though he's always getting onto me about charging mine. I leave a voicemail as I walk into the parking garage. His apartment is a couple blocks from here. I know if he remembered he would have shown up by now. I'm tempted to go by his place, but I won't. It's pouring down rain. I'm going back home to take a nap and watch a movie.

"Hey Blakey! I'm not sure what happened this morning. I waited at Perrone's for you. Let me know if you get this. Your phone went to voicemail so I'm assuming that you're still holed up in your apartment. Call me back babe!"

I get back to my apartment, and it's been another hour since I left. I figured he would have called me by now to tell me that he is so sorry he forgot, but he's got a great story about last night. I'm sure he does have a great story. He always has a great story or epic drama. I get in bed and check my messages and email one more time. I still have nothing. Maybe he went out to Connecticut and has no service. I laugh at our Connecticut joke, then sit back, turning my TV on. I'm searching for a movie when I start to feel like something's wrong. Certainly, Blake would have called me back by now. I leave him another voicemail, and I'm partially pissed and partially worried.

"Hey Blake. Look, just send me a text or call me. I'm starting to get a little worried. You're normally pretty good about getting back to me within an hour. Maybe something from work popped up. I'm not even mad. I'm just worried at this point. Call me please or I'm coming back into the city to find you! I Love you!"

I eventually come to terms with the fact that I'm not going to be able to concentrate on a movie until Blake gets back with me. I pull my laptop out and start working on my spreadsheets. My phone rings. It's Helen. My stomach sinks. I answer my phone, almost dropping it.

"Helen?" I whisper, and there's silence on the other end. "Hello, Helen?"

"Oh, Gemma. Have you heard? I'm sure you have," she whimpers, and I sit up, starting to panic.

"Gemma?" she says, her voice cracking. My eyes start to water, and I open my mouth to speak but nothing comes out.

"What?" I manage to get out. It comes out hoarse and I squeeze my eyes together.

"You don't know?"

"Know what?" I whisper.

"Blake…"

"Blake *what,* Helen?" I feel like the room is getting smaller.

"He was in an accident this morning. He was hit by a car as he stepped off the curb from his apartment. It was storming pretty bad here in the city. I'm so sorry," she says, her voice cracking. "He was pronounced dead at the scene. Oh, Gemma," she says hysterically as I scream. I drop the phone and curl up into a ball.

Brent

I'm standing outside of the hospital with my parents. The pain is almost too much to take. I look up to the sky as tears trickle down my face. I haven't stopped crying since I got the news earlier this morning. I was the first one here. They contacted my parents, then called me to come to the hospital. Seeing his broken and bruised body was excruciating. By the time my parents arrived I was outside. I couldn't stay in there any longer.

I just feel numb. I'm simply breathing in and breathing out. Our family attorney showed up to take care of the paperwork and documentation needed. I couldn't answer many of their questions I was so choked up with grief. I'm to the point now where it's been too long for this to have been a nightmare. My stomach rolling, I lean over, throwing up in the bushes. My mum and Brett are wrecked. Da's grieving but is still his stoic self. I sit on a bench as far away from the hospital as I can and place my head in my hands. Not Blake. Not my brother. What will the world be like without his love, kindness and humour? My Da comes to sit next to me, placing a hand on my back.

"Son," he says, and I sit up. "I want to take Blake back to Scotland. Bury him in the family plot. New York might have taken him from us, but I won't bury him here. I know he loved it here. It was his home, but I don't want him buried here." I nod my head and wipe the tears from my eyes. "I'll let you know when I have everything arranged. Take care of yourself, son. I need to get your mum home. This isn't a place for a grieving mother."

I stand up, hug my Da, then wrap my mum in my arms. She clings to me, and I hold her tightly to me. Brett walks off, and I understand. I don't know what to do with these emotions either. I get back in my car and realize my phone's been in here the entire time. Doesn't really matter at this point. I look down at my phone and see numerous missed calls and messages. I'm sure this is going to be all over the news soon. I lay my head back and scroll through my messages. I see I have one from Gemma, and I click on her name.

> Brent. I'm so incredibly sorry. I can't believe this. I'm not sure if you're still at the hospital or if you're with your family?

> Just please know I'm here. Whenever you need me. Please let me know if there is anything I can do. I'm so sorry.

I feel the tears fall down my face at Gemma's kind words. I know how gutted she must be, but I can't see past my own grief right now. I rest my head on the steering wheel. I absolutely lose it. The noises coming from me don't even sound human. I put my car in drive and head to my apartment to pack. I can't be here right now. I need to get the hell out of this town. They've stolen my brother from me. My chest burns, and my heart is completely shattered. I'm back to my apartment in no time at all. I grab my suitcase, my laptop and my passport. Then I start throwing clothes into my suitcase. If I end up getting there and need something else, I'll just buy it. I call my Da, and he answers on the first ring.

"Son," he says when he picks up.

"I have to get out of here," I choke out. "I've got a private jet on stand-by. I can't be in the city right now. I have to get to Scotland. I'm packing my bags now. Does mum want to go now or wait with you for Blake's body?"

"I'm coming with you," I hear Brett say in the background, and I nod even though they can't see me.

"Your mum wants to be with Blake. Brett wants to go with you. I'm turning around right now. I'll have him at your apartment in 45 minutes."

"That's fine. I'll wait for you here, Brett. Then I'm getting the hell out of here." I hang up and finish packing.

Brett and I pull up to the hangar and park my car. We get out and walk straight inside. There are people in the waiting area, but I keep my head down and walk toward our plane. They've got her out and ready to board. I shake Jerry and Fred's hands as I board, and they tell me how sorry they are. Brett and I take our seats. I press my head against the headrest begging for sleep to overtake me. We are sitting longer on the runway than I want us to be, so I pull out the bottle of Macallan I packed. I grab two glasses as Jerry turns to let me know we've been cleared for take-off. I'm sure at this rate we'll have finished the bottle by the time we arrive in Scotland. The way I'm feeling right now I could drink straight from the bottle. I pull out my phone and send Gemma a text.

> I'm heading to Scotland. I've got to get out of the city. I'll let

> you know when I've landed. I
> imagine it will be a while before
> I'm back. I'm sorry. I Love You,
> Gemma. I just cannot be there
> right now.

I pour another two fingers of whisky and toss it back. I lean my head back as we take off, praying we get to Scotland in one piece. In about 10 hours we'll have landed, and I'm not sure I will ever want to come back to New York.

Gemma

t 10:15 Monday morning, we are all called into a meeting with the other executives, HR and finance. Hayden has really stepped up, which I'm grateful for. He's going to be running things here until Brent gets back. Hayden's interim plan is well thought out. I know he wants to be sensitive, but the business must move forward. Clients will give us time, but there's only so much to spare. The hiring process is still on schedule and the offer letters have just recently gone out. We start to stand thinking the meeting is done when Hayden holds a hand up.

"Brent wanted to let you all know how extremely grateful he is for all of you. Please take the time you need. Regardless of what office you are in or what your position is. If we can be of any assistance during this time, please let us know. A statement has gone out from the King family as well as from our office to the media. Please refrain from speaking to the press during this time. Anyone who wants to attend the funeral is welcome to. Unfortunately, we can't fly everyone to Inverness on such short notice, but everyone is welcome. If you can go, please let Paolo know so that he can inform the family. They are more than happy to help everyone find lodging. The funeral will be held this coming Friday at the private family burial site at their estate in Inverness. You will not be able to attend the funeral without an invitation. Please email Paolo and he will ensure you are not only on the list but also have the correct documents to attend. Do not feel obligated to go. When the family returns, they will have a memorial service here in the city. I don't have a date for that yet, but that's the tentative plan. It could be next week or it could be a month from now. In the meantime, keep the family in your prayers. Thanks everyone," Hayden says, and I can't move from my chair. I immediately email Paolo that I'll be there, and he responds with my documentation.

Everyone heads to lunch as I sit looking at flights to Inverness. JESUS they are expensive. I know that I'm going to do it, but I'm not finding anything for this week. I close my laptop because

I feel the stress of the situation start to rise. I look down at my phone and see that I have a missed call from Jesslyn. I listen to my voicemail, and her calm voice is exactly what I needed to hear. She tells me she's moved me to tomorrow for a sit down.

I head to the staff kitchen to grab a water and literally run into Hayden as he's leaving the kitchen. He pulls me into his office, and at first, I think I'm in trouble.

"Hey. How are holding up? I'm actually surprised you're here," he asks as I nod.

"I'm not. This is a good distraction for me." I look up at him, and he's got a funny look on his face.

"Look, Gemma. Take whatever time you need. I talked to Brent last night. He sounds…" I hold my hand up, closing my eyes. "Okay," he whispers, and I swallow the lump in my throat. I slowly back out of his office and head back to my desk. I sit down and start typing up notes from the meeting earlier, trying to not get sick.

I'm sure Brent is devastated. I can't imagine anything otherwise. I understand why he's not able to speak to me right now. I'm sure everything is really difficult to process. SHIT! I don't know. Maybe he could be angry with me. He knew Blake was meeting me for brunch Sunday. I mean Blake died on his way to brunch with me. I close my eyes, and the nausea returns. I walk quickly to the bathroom knowing that I'm going to be sick. When I'm done, I sit back on my heels and press my hands to my eyes. The tears are flowing now as I sit here silently crying. I flush the toilet, and when I return to my desk, I feel people staring.

Now it's Monday. Here I am in the office, and my people are in freaking Scotland. I should be in Scotland with Brent. Even if he doesn't want to see me, I should be there. I can't find a damn flight. Most everyone here has access to a private plane. I know most of the executives do or they have connections to someone with a plane. The only people I know are in Scotland. Then I remember Ava Grant, but I haven't spoken to her in a month. The last we talked she was newly pregnant and vomiting everywhere. She was just returning from doing her scenes in LA last time we spoke. I wonder if she or Clark know of anyone with connections. I pull my phone out and send her a quick text.

Forgive me Ava. I've been a horrible friend.

I haven't checked on you or Clayton.

I hope you're feeling better.

Look, I know this is a long shot but do you or Clark have

connections in the aviation world?

My best friend just died, and his funeral is in Scotland this weekend. If you don't, please don't worry. DO NOT go out of your way with this.

I know it's a long shot. I'll figure something out.

I put my phone down, figuring that it'll be a while before I hear something, but my phone starts ringing. It's AVA.

"Hey, Ava," I say, my voice a little hoarse from getting sick.

"Hey, Love. I'm so sorry for not texting you earlier. Clark and I saw that Blake had passed. I'm so sorry. Look, Clark is right here, and he said that you are welcome to use our plane. We are back in New York from LA, so it works out perfectly. I just talked to Clayton and Brian to see if they can make sure you can have it for the entire weekend. How long are you going to be gone?"

"Oh, please don't apologize. I don't know how long I'll be gone. I imagine I would need to leave sometime this week. Thursday maybe? And then return Sunday. I haven't spoken to Brent, so I don't know what I'm walking into. That's my plan at least. The funeral is on Friday at their private estate in Inverness.”

“Under different circumstances, Scotland sounds like the most romantic place. Have you seen Outlander? OUCH,” she squeaks, and I smile. I’m sure Clark pinched her. “I know that’s so insensitive. I’m sorry. Pregnancy really has made me say the most indelicate things.”

“I haven’t seen it, but someone did recommend that to me already,” I answer.

“Listen. I’ll text you back with the details soon. It sounds like when you get back, we need to catch up. We are here, Gemma. Please let me know if there’s anything else we can do. If I wasn’t so pregnant, I’d come with you,” she adds, and I sit back closing my eyes. She really is a great friend.

“Thank you, Ava,” I whisper as tears of relief spring to my eyes.

“Aww, Honey. Gosh, Pregnancy has made me so emotional.” I hear her sniffle, then cough. “Take care of yourself, Gemma. I promise to do better with staying in touch. I’ll text you here in a bit. Bye, doll.” She hangs up, and I place the phone down. I head to the bathroom again, and when I’m done this time, I splash water on my face.

I’ve taken care of the flight. Now, I just need to figure out what the hell I’m going to do once I get there. I email Paolo once I get confirmation from Ava with the flight times. He tells me that the Regina and George have requested that I stay at the family's estate. I close my laptop and place my head on my desk. It's after 5:00 p.m. now. I've been in the office for 12 hours, and I'm pretty much alone. As much as I've been sick today, I think most people know if they speak to me, chances are I'll throw up on them.

I look up at the door to Brent's office, and know I shouldn't go in there, but I have to. I unlock his office with my key and step inside. CHRIST, it smells like him in here. I lean against the window to his office and close my eyes. He's got a suit jacket hanging in the corner and I go over to it, feeling the sleeves. I close his door and slip his jacket over my shoulders. I slide down the wall behind his desk and wrap the jacket around me. I need to go home, but I don't take Brent's jacket off, even though it's August and humid as hell. I need him right now. It smells just like him. If I close my eyes, I can imagine that it's his arms wrapped around me. When I arrive at my apartment, I walk into my bedroom and take my clothes off. I drape Brent's jacket over me and fall asleep. It's only 6:00, but I can't manage to care about things like that. If I can just make it to Wednesday, everything will be okay, right?

• • •

It's very dreary when we land in Inverness. Luckily, we flew through the night so that I'm literally waking up in Scotland. I know I probably look like hell run over! I restart my phone, and with the time change it is 8 a.m. Thursday morning. My appointment with Jesslyn on Tuesday went great. We talked a lot about Blake and Brent. I texted Brent when we took off last night just to let him know that I was thinking about him. I didn't tell him I was coming though. I was feeling a little unsure about coming, but here I am, so I guess I'm doing this. I gather my bags and step off the plane and into the waiting town car. The driver helps me with my bags, and I thank the flight crew before I leave.

Brent was right. Scotland is beautiful. I've only seen a small portion of it through my window. Between the water and the mountains in the distance, it's absolutely stunning. I planned for the temperature difference, but I'm still cold. The sun isn't out, but I'm sure that it will warm up once it does peek through the clouds. We make it to the King Estate, and I'm shocked. This isn't an estate, it's a castle. I mean it's a mansion in itself, but as I look through the car window, I shake my head in disbelief. I knew the Kings were billionaires, and this is probably nothing to them. However, to me it's something!

We pull through the gates and drive down the mile-long driveway to the front of the house. Everything is so green. The mountains are situated behind the house, making it look like a portrait. I open my door, and the driver brings my bags around. The butler comes out to take them and smiles kindly at me. People are very friendly here. In New York they would have thrown my bags to the curb and peeled off, leaving me to fend for myself.

This way Ms. Williams," he says as I follow him up the stairs to my room. I walk to the window and can see the back of the property. It's massive. It seems to go on forever. I'm not used to this much space. I hear a knock on my door, and a petite woman with the sweetest Scottish accent comes in.

"I'm Ms. Hall. You may call me Bitsy though. I'll be attending to the guests on this floor while you are with us. If there's anything you need, please let me know. Have you settled in okay?" she asks, and I smile.

"Not really. I'm kind of still in awe of everything."

"Scotland is bonny, isn't she," she adds as she walks to the fireplace in my room and checks the logs. "I can start a fire at any time if you start to get chilly. It's supposed to be a fairly warm day, but unfortunately, it's supposed to get colder this weekend. Especially at night."

"Thank you," I answer. "I'll unpack my things, and then where do I go?"

"You just make yourself right at home. There

are four other guests staying at the estate other than the family. Also, if you dial star on the phone, it'll connect you downstairs. We want to make sure your needs are taken care of while you're here."

"At this point I'd just like to use the restroom, unpack and change into something else." She shoos me into the bathroom and heads towards my suitcase.

"I'll help you unpack your things. I can take care of this while you freshen up a bit. The bathroom is right through those doors over there. You'll find everything you need is already in there," she says, pointing to the door on the other side of the closet. "This room has a private bathroom, so you won't be sharing with anyone else."

"Thank you, Bitsy," I say as I grab my carry-on bag with my toiletries and head into the bathroom. The bathroom is beautiful. No surprise there. I was going to tell her I could unpack my own things, but I decided against it. I wash my face and forgo makeup. I'm not sure wearing makeup is even worth it right now. I've cried more in the last few days than I've ever cried in my entire life. At least from what I can remember. Jesslyn was pretty proud of my emotional reaction to everything this past week. I'm not so sure. Mourning for someone else is different than mourning for yourself. When I leave the bathroom, Bitsy's already left. I walk over to where she's hung up some of my clothes. I throw on some leggings, a long-sleeved tunic and a sweater. I slip into some ballet flats and head to the window.

People are working in the garden area as well as setting up tables and chairs. I'm assuming it's for the lunch that they'll be serving tomorrow after the funeral. Sleeping in a chair, no matter how luxurious, still isn't the same as sleeping in a bed. I'm sure I'll sleep better tonight, possibly tomorrow once the funeral is over. What I'm going to do Saturday is beyond me. I guess if I still haven't heard from Brent, I could go sight-seeing. Maybe walk around town? Explore a little bit. I don't have a car, but I could figure it out. We're close to town. I look down at my phone and decide to man up and find Brent. I walk over to the phone and press star.

"Ms. Williams?"

"I was wondering if there was a rental place close. For a car," I ask, and then there's muffled talking in the background.

"Mrs. King has reserved a car for your use while you're here. It's one of the vehicles we keep on the estate. It's filled up and available whenever you are ready. Should I phone the valet to have him bring the car around?"

"Yes, please," I reply and hang up. A personal valet, Lord Jesus I am out of my element here. I want to head into town, and then I'd like to go by Brent's property. I know the estate is the size of a small town, but I'd like to at least try and find him. I walk downstairs, keeping my ballet flats on and decide I'll buy some boots in town to wear while I'm here. I pray my leggings, tunic and sweater will be suitable for the weather, especially since the sun is starting to peek through the clouds. I have my purse, my passport and myself. I pray that's enough. As I'm walking out the front door, I hear someone call my name. It's Regina.

"Gemma, I'm so glad I caught you. It's so nice to have you here. Thank you so much for coming. I'm sorry to hold you up from your plans, but have you driven in European countries before?" she asks, and I shake my head.

"I've never been out of the States."

"Oh, goodness. Okay, well we drive on the left side of the road. Are you heading into town?" she asks, and I see more questions in her eyes than she's asking.

"I am. I thought I'd do some shopping and explore the town a little bit. Then I'd like to try and find Brent's property. I'd like to stop by there, if I can, and check on him. I don't want to intrude though." She gives me a small smile, and I laugh. "I'm glad you reminded me about the driving. I think I knew that, but to be honest, this is kind of last-minute decision I'm making."

"Just take your time. Other drivers will pass you if they need to. In town, just park a bit away and do some walking through town. Once you're back out here, you'll be fine. Brent's property is 15 minutes from here. It's in the other direction away from town. If you have any trouble, please call me." I hand her my phone, and she enters her information. "I'm glad they pulled the Range Rover around. You'll possibly need it if you are going to Brent's. You'll also need the code for Brent's gate if it's closed."

"Is it the same code to his house in Brooklyn?" I ask, and she looks surprised, but she smiles.

"Yes," she whispers, and I nod.

"I remember it," I mention sadly. "Thank you, Regina. If I have any trouble, I'll let you know!

"Drive safe, darling," she says as I hop into the old Range Rover. I close the door and head off towards town. I've plugged the destination in my GPS. Luckily, I'm able to pick up quickly with the rules of the road before I get into town. I park at the first parking area I see outside of town then head toward some shops. I find some gorgeous black hunter boots and a Burberry scarf that's listed on sale. I make the purchase along with a couple other trinkets. I put everything on my credit card, as I've decided to splurge a little while I'm in town. I rarely buy myself anything, especially if it's expensive. I want to buy something that will help me remember my short time in Scotland. Something I can look back on when I'm back in the States. Who knows if I'll ever be here again.

I walk around until I find a cute café to grab a coffee and a breakfast sandwich. This place is beautiful. I could spend an entire weekend walking around here. The sun is shining, and the wind feels refreshing on my heated skin. The exertion of trekking around town is good for my body, but I know eventually I will need to sit down. I find a cute shop on the edge of town that I must have missed on my way in. Looking around a bit, I find a couple of dresses and jeans that I adore. At the check-out area I find a cute Scotland sweatshirt that I add as a keepsake item before paying for my clothes.

I walk back to the car with my new treasures and head toward Brent's. I at least know the direction I'm heading. There's only one property between The King Estate and Brent's property. It shouldn't be hard to find, but as I pass The Kings', I start to get nervous. I'm starting to think that maybe I've made a mistake being here. He's just lost his brother. Nothing will ever be the same as it was before. This was a bad idea, I think as I pull off to the side of the road. I close my eyes and will myself to stay on the path I'm on. You'll never know if this was the right decision until you follow through. My hands are frozen, but it's not just because of the cold. I feel like I've overstepped by being here. If the roles were reversed, I know he'd be there for me. So why am I so scared? We both loved Blake, we're both hurting, and we love each other. I know this, but I'm still apprehensive.

What if he doesn't want me here? What if he has a woman there with him? He wouldn't. Even in my distress I know Brent isn't that kind of man. Brent said in the Hamptons that he hasn't built anything on his property. I asked Bitsy before I left if there were any landmarks, and she told me to look for the beginning of a stone wall. That marks the beginning of Brent's property. His property goes on for miles. There are three different driveways on his property, but the one I need to use will be gated.

I see the beginning of the stone wall and follow it past the first driveway. It's really a dirt road. It takes me another five minutes to come to the next driveway. He must own a lot of property. I pull up to the closed gate. I type Scotland into the keypad, and the gate opens. I pull in and start down the long driveway. It's another five minutes before I come up to a small hill and see a cottage down in a valley area. It's on higher ground but hidden behind some trees. There's a gorgeous mountain and lake in the near distance, and I stop the car to look out my window at everything. I can't blame Brent for loving Scotland more than New York. This doesn't even seem real. It's like a painting. I pull next to a large truck and put it in park. I pull on my Hunter boots and hop out of the car.

I walk down toward the water first. I want to look around. I know I'm intruding, but I'm dying to see this. The mountains are so close that I feel like I could touch them. The sound of running water from a nearby stream into the lake is incredibly soothing. I close my eyes and feel so comforted. I know this is going to sound bizarre, but I feel like Blake is with me. He'd be complaining that there are bugs nearby and that his shoes were getting muddy. I giggle to myself but then immediately feel robbed of all the time we should have had together. It's at that moment that I don't feel like I'm intruding at all. Blake would want me here. Regardless if anyone else does. The breeze is freezing as the afternoon sun disappears behind the clouds. This is nature at its finest. I could stay here forever. I'm cold, but I'm nervously sweating. I'm out of my depth, and I've never stepped out this far of my comfort zone. However, knowing that Blake is here with me also gives me the encouragement I need not to run. I don't know what I'll find here, but I know I'll be okay.

Brent

I see her. I think I'm losing my damn mind, but I see her. Maybe it's because I've wished so many times since I've been here that she was here with me. I look out the window from the kitchen as I place my glass in the dishwasher. I'm not drunk, but I'm definitely not sober. At least that's what I've been telling myself since I arrived. I blink a couple of times trying to clear my vision. I swear it's her. If it's not then it's an angel, and I'm closer to heaven than I realized. I walk toward the front door looking through each window as if she'll disappear if I take my eyes off her.

I open the front door and pull my boots on. She's too far away to hear me, but I start toward her. I stop at a fallen log about 20 yards away from her and sit down. I can't believe she's here. This looks like a painting. Maybe one day I'll have one like this made. Sensing my movement, she turns around and stops dead in her tracks. She stands there staring as I prop myself on my elbows watching her with my hands clasped together.

"You know you can get into a lot of trouble trespassing on people's property here. We're a kind country, but we take those things very seriously," I say jokingly, but she looks down and her shoulders sink. She doesn't feel welcome here. I can tell, and that's my fucking fault. I look down, tears filling my eyes. I've messed up. I should have been in touch before now.

"I'm sorry," we say at the same time. She starts toward me, and I stand up and hold my arms out.

"Please don't be sorry, Gemma. This is my fault. I haven't been in touch, and you came all this way. I can see you were unsure of what you'd find here." She walks toward me, and I collapse down to my knees in front of her. She runs a hand through my hair as I softly cry against her warm body. She smells wonderful. Like her. Love, gentleness, kindness. Of a time that was so happy that I almost forgot what happiness felt like. She whispers soothingly to me and doesn't pull back as I cling to her. We stay like this for God knows how long. I didn't think I could cry anymore, but I was wrong. I move my head so my forehead is resting against her stomach. I pull her on top of me so she's straddling me. She looks me in the eyes, and I find my home. My comfort. My love. I've been such a damn fool. She has tears in her eyes as well.

"I love you," she whispers, and I close my eyes, looking skyward and then back at her. She's finally said it. My darling, Gemma. It's a soothing balm on my shattered heart.

"I love you too, Gemma. So damn much. I've been such a damned fool. Forgive me. I'm sorry I haven't returned any of your calls or texts. I don't know what to say other than please forgive me." I whisper as she leans forward, kissing me tenderly. I wrap my arms tighter around her, picking her up and carrying her back to the house, her legs wrapped tightly around my waist.

"I'm afraid I'm getting dirt on your clothes," she says as I laugh. My first real laugh since Sunday.

"I couldn't care less. I'll change when we get back up to the house." We walk up onto the porch, and I place her down. We take off our boots, and I head over to the fireplace in front of my couch. I place a hand on the mantel and realize that I'm much drunker than I realized. I let the dizzy spell pass.

"Brent. I'm so sorry about Blake," she whispers as I nod turning around. I'm ashamed that I've let myself get this far gone. Now that she's here,

I see my situation more clearly. I turn around and make my way towards her.

"Thank you, Gemma. I'm sorry for your loss as well. I know how close the two of you were. I'm sorry that I haven't been in touch. I've been…"

"Drinking?" she interrupts, looking over at the kitchen at the empty bottle of Macallan. I nod, and she gives me a sad smile. "I get it. I really do. I can't imagine how you're feeling. I know it must feel eternally painful. This kind of loss is devastating. I know the weekend will be terrible as well. There's no other way to describe it. Look, I wanted to tell you that I'm here. We both are going through something devastating. I've asked for time, and it's only fair for me to give you the same. I'm staying at your parent's estate. I know I'll see you tomorrow, but in the meantime, please take care of yourself, Brent." When she walks over to me, I sit down and pull her into my lap.

"I needed this. I didn't know I did, but I do," I whisper as we wrap our arms around each other. Her smell, her body, her heart. I've missed her. I didn't realize how badly I needed to hold her and have her hold me. I'm not surprised she's staying at my parents. I would expect nothing less from them. Blake would want that. Hell, I want that. I'm surprised my mum didn't tell me about it though. "I've been in a dark place lately. I have a feeling this is only the beginning. I talked to Hayden yesterday. I'm glad he's taking care of everything." I lean my head against hers as we sit wrapped up in each other's arms. The sun is starting to go down, and I ask Gemma about her plans.

"I should go," she says before I can speak. "Your mom has dinner plans for the house guests, and I don't want to be rude. I've already missed her lunch spread." I don't want her to leave, but I also understand. I'm a mess.

"Thank you for coming out here. I would love for you to stay, but there's only a twin bed and the couch is the most uncomfortable piece of furniture you'll find. I've never planned on anyone but myself being here."

"I'm only a few minutes down the road, Brent."

"Blake would want you to be here, with the family. He loved you so much," I say as tears come back to my eyes. She looks over at me, and I know she feels the same pain I do.

"I'm not just here for Blake."

"I know! I wish I was in better shape. I'm not in a great place, Gemma." I whisper as I stands up to walk out.

"Why don't you come to your parents? Get cleaned up and eat something."

"I'm not ready to be there yet," I say as I rub my hand over my face. "I need to get myself together before I go to my parents'. I also need to sober up." She nods as she pulls on her boots, and the wind whips her hair across her face. She tries to move it away, but the wind has really picked up. She's only in a sweater.

"Do you have a jacket?" I ask, and she shakes her head.

"I'll be fine. I have a scarf in the car." I walk back inside, grabbing one of my older jackets. It's a vintage Burberry trench coat that used to be my grand-da's. I know it's not much, but it's enough to get her through the evening. I smile to myself as this gives me an idea. I look at her expression when I walk back outside to slip it over her shoulders.

"This will help a little bit," I add as she smiles up at me like she always does. I lean down, kissing her gently and then grab her hand. It's starting to get a lot cooler in the evenings. Her hands are freezing, so I bring the one I'm holding up to my lips and kiss it softly.

"Thank you," she whispers as we walk back toward the Range Rover. I recognize it as one of the vehicles from the estate.

"I would drive you back myself, but that wouldn't be wise. I'll be back to my usual self, hopefully tomorrow," I add as she squeezes my hand. Something in her eyes tells me that she's not fully herself either. Maybe it's the drinking. I wish she wasn't seeing me like this, but here we are. This is me, in pain and mourning for my brother.

"Don't rush it, Brent," she replies as I open

her door and she climbs inside. "Take the time you need. Don't try to rush through this for me. I know tomorrow you'll have to be on top of it, but don't do it for me. I understand." I lean down, kissing her cheek as I close her door and then stand back as she drives back up my driveway. She's right. I can't rush through this, but I can do better. Be better, for her. The first thing I can do is at least shower and sober up. I throw away the empty bottle of whisky and then head to the bathroom to shave.

Gemma

After dinner, I'm exhausted and want to go curl up in bed. I pass Bitsy on my way up, and she asks if I want some tea. I tell her maybe tomorrow. I'm going to bed. She bids me goodnight, and when I get to my room I change into my pajamas and head to the closet. There's a plush robe behind the door that has an envelope in the front pocket. I open it and read:

Gemma, dear I hope you'll find a bit of comfort in one of my favorites the "Cozy Cottage" in town makes these, and I never go anywhere without one.

It's always been a warm re-minder of home, no matter where I may be.

Regina

I pull the robe off the hook in the closet and pull it on. It's a cream plush robe that reaches all the way to the ground. I turn the overhead lights out and curl up under the covers. These sheets are amazing, but not as great as Brent's. I pull a book from my travel bag and open it up. I only get through the first paragraph, and I'm out like a light.

The next morning, I turn over and realize that it's already 9 a.m. The funeral starts at 10 a.m. I jump out of bed, running to the shower. I don't wash my hair because I don't have the time. I do douse it with dry shampoo and pull it into a low bun. I pull on the black lace dress from yesterday and head into the closet for my tan Louboutin heels. Maggie was right, they do go with every-thing. I brought black shoes as well, but these seem to work better. I put on minimal makeup and then my new Burberry scarf. I grab the trench coat Brent lent me yesterday, and as I open the door I almost trip over a box on the floor. There's an envelope on top addressed to me. I pull the box inside my room and close the door. I open the card, and it's from Brent. I touch the rose gold Rolex on my left wrist and think fondly of my sweet and generous Brent.

Thank you for yesterday!
While the vintage trench coat I lent you looks
great on you.
I thought this one might suit you better.
I love you, Pumpkin.
Brent

I place the box on the bed, and when I open it there's black tissue paper. I unwrap the first bit, and it's tan leather gloves from Burberry. I think how nice they'll compliment my scarf. Unfolding the rest of the tissue, I gasp as I pull out a tan women's Burberry trench coat. It's gorgeous. I place my hands on the bed beside the box. God, this feels like it's way too much, but I'm so grateful. He's such a thoughtful and generous man. Ridiculously so when it comes to me. I go to the bathroom, snip the tags off and put the coat on. It goes perfect with my black lace dress and my tan Louboutin's. I'm sure that it goes with anything. I grab the gloves and place them in the pockets of my new coat with my cell phone.

I head downstairs, and there are so many people milling around the house. As I approach the bottom of the stairs, I find people are looking up at me in wonder. Maybe they recognize me from the event last week? Or maybe they're curious who would be coming down the private stairwell. There's a butler at the bottom of the stairs who looks like he could also moonlight as security.

"Ms. Williams," he says in acknowledgement, and I nod back politely at him. I am staying here at the family's estate. So, I'm assuming that generates enough questions in and of itself. Bitsy comes to ask me how my night was, and I place a hand on her arm.

"It was wonderful, thank you. I needed a good night's rest. I'm sorry I was so late getting up this morning. It must be the difference in time."

"Not to worry, Ms. Williams. The Kings were adamant that we let you rest. Can I get you a cup of coffee or a tea?" she asks, and I shake my head.

"No, thank you. I'm afraid there's no time for that, and we will all be keeping you quite busy today as it is. There are a lot of people here," I add as it's getting loud downstairs, and she laughs as I look around. As I join the flow of people, we start making our way out back toward the chapel. I notice they've set more chairs up outside of the chapel so I take a seat where I can find one. It's not too long before the rows are filling up.

As the minister starts to speak, I realize they've set speakers up so everyone can hear what's going on inside the chapel. It's a tearful service, very formal and somewhat shorter than I imagined. There's got to be over 200 people here. It's pretty chilly, so I'm grateful for my new jacket. It's over before I realize it, and people start to get in the receiving line. The Kings were just here saying goodbye to their grandmother, so it feels incredibly soon for the family to lose yet another family member they love and adore. One of the things I do notice is that there are numerous men and boys in kilts. I shouldn't be surprised but yet I am. I should know this is typical Scottish traditions but it's just very different. I head back inside to warm up and head into the family library. It's there I find Brent and Brett deep into a bottle of whisky. They too are in traditional Scottish attire. Brent turns around and gasps when he sees me.

"You look absolutely breathtaking, Gemma. The jacket really suits you. I'm sorry I'm such a wreck. As much as I'd hoped today would be better, today hasn't been kind to me, either." I put my hand in his, squeezing gently. He looks unsteady on his feet, and I can see why he and Brett are in here hiding from the crowds. They both look like they've been crying all morning.

"The receiving line after the funeral got me," Brett says as he sits down in a leather chair next to the fire. He has a blank and far away expression on his face. I can only imagine their agony.

"That's understandable, and thank you Brent,

as always you are too generous." I add as he wraps me in his arms. "Is there anything I can do?" I whisper to Brent, and he shakes his head.

"I'm afraid that we are just going to need time. I had every intention of getting myself together, but then seeing Blake's casket threw me over the edge. I'm going to stay in here with Brett. I'll join you in the sunroom here in a little bit. I feel like he needs to probably go to bed." I look back over at Brett, and he's swaying back and forth. Brent is looking at his younger brother.

When I make it to the sunroom, I see Hayden and a couple others I recognize. Most are higher ups, attorneys and associates. I look around the room and head over to where the coffee is. I pour some cream into my cup and feel someone place a hand on my shoulder. It's Helen.

"Helen," I say as she wraps an arm around my shoulder.

"Gemma, you look wonderful. Blake would approve. He would say that you looked like royalty avoiding the paparazzi. He always said when you were dressed up you looked as if you should be photographed. That trench coat suits you. Blake always loved Burberry, as you know."

"He would say that, wouldn't he," I say as I take a sip of my coffee. "Are you in town for a while?" I ask, and she nods.

"I'm staying at Culloden House with a couple

others from the office. I'm staying all of next week as well. I wanted to talk to you about something, though. I know you aren't planning on staying long, and I'm not sure I'll be back in the office." I nod as we walk out of the sunroom to the foyer. I take her toward the mudroom where there's a bench.

"You aren't coming back to K.B & Associates?" I ask as she shakes her head that she's not.

"I'm afraid not. It's too hard for me. I should have retired years ago. I stayed for Blake, and now that he's not there I'm not sure I want to be either. I'm sorry, Gemma," she says, and I place a hand on her arm.

"There's no need to apologize, Helen. I completely understand. I'm not sure Brent will come back either."

"He will. Listen, I know I'm not one of the attorneys for the family, but I want you to know Blake left you some things in his will. When they have the reading, will you promise me you'll go when they invite you?"

"Of course. If Blake wanted me to be there, I'll be there. He left me something?" I ask, shocked.

"He did. He updated his will after his grandmother passed. He finalized it July 10th. I was a witness."

When I walk back into the sunroom, I grab a small plate of fruit. I'm not sure I can stomach much more today. I take my plate up to my room, not wanting to socialize anymore. I'm not surprised by Helen's decision to leave K.B & A. I'm starting to wonder if I'll stay as well. I need to figure out what I want to do. I do love working there, and I'm excited about the new direction we are heading. However, I'm not sure it's my forever plan. I'm grateful I don't have to make any rash decisions at this point though. I have time.

I open the door to my room and see that Bitsy's made a fire. I place the plate of fruit beside the bed and kick off my heels. I take off my dress, hanging it in the closet, and then wrap the robe from Regina around my body. I'm not hungry, but I know I need to eat something. I lay down in the bed and look through pictures on my phone. I find so many happy moments from this summer with Blake. Some on set, the Hamptons and from the event last Friday. I cannot believe that was just last week. I feel like my heart cracks in two as I touch the screen, seeing Blake's beautiful and happy face. He was everything to me. The only family I ever had.

I wake up feeling someone place a warm hand on my shoulder. I must have cried myself to sleep. I look up and see Brent sitting on the edge of the bed. He looks at my face and crumbles too.

"My sweet Gemma," he whispers as he crawls into bed. The two of us fall asleep holding each other as we cry. When I wake up again, I'm alone in bed. I sit up, feeling a little better. I look around the spacious room and see Brent sitting in one of the chairs by the fireplace. He still looks lost, and I imagine he'll be feeling that way for a while. I walk over to him, and he takes my hand, pulling me into his lap. We sit there just listening to the logs in the fireplace crackle and pop. It's soothing and warm.

I stand up and untie my robe, letting it fall to the floor. I'm still wearing my black bra and thong. Brent groans behind me, and when I turn to look at him, he's studying my body as if it's a work of art. I start to turn around, but he grabs my hips, holding me firm in place. He stands up and starts placing small kisses down my neck.

"I've missed you like hell, Gemma. I've missed the smell of your skin. The softness of your body. The taste of you," he adds as he walks in front of me. "I want to memorize your body." He takes my hand and walks me over to the bed.

"These walls are thin," I whisper as he unfastens my bra and lets it fall to the floor at our feet.

"Then you'll have to use your inside voice," he says as he pushes me gently onto the bed. "I've been dying to be inside you again. To hear the little sounds you make when I touch you *here*," he emphasizes as he inserts a finger inside me. I feel my body flush all over from just his touch. "Yes!" he says as he leans over, kissing me deeply as he continues to work me over. I'm starting to breathe hard, and when I whisper his name, he stands up and pulls my underwear off. His clothes are off in no time at all and then he's inside me. We both groan as he starts to move in a steady rhythm. I've missed this too. More than I can even explain to him. I've missed him!

"I love you," I say as I feel hot tears stream down my cheeks. "I love you so much!" He whimpers my name hoarsely as he continues to move, placing a hand on my cheek. I kiss the inside of his palm, and I see him close his eyes as tears stream down his face.

"I love you, Gemma. More than anything in this entire world. I love you," he whispers as his voice breaks. He pulls me up so that our faces are touching, and I throw my head back as I feel the orgasm take over me quickly. He follows me shortly and the collapses on top of me as we both try and catch our breath. We fall asleep like this again, and when I wake up, he's gone. I look around the room and he's no longer here. If I wasn't naked, I'd think maybe I dreamed, it but I know he was here.

This morning is the private burial with just the family. The clock says it's a little after 8 a.m., and I'm not even sure what time the burial is. I take a shower, dry my hair and put a little makeup on. When I walk over to the bedside table to put my watch back on, there's a note sitting by the bed.

Gemma,

I didn't want you to think I just up and left, but I didn't want to be late for Blake's burial this morning. I'm sorry to run on you like this. Last night meant everything to me. You are, as always, the best thing in my life. You bring me such happiness and hope. By the time you are reading this, the burial will be more than likely over. I have a few errands I need to run, but I'd love to spend the day with you showing you why Scotland is my heart and soul. I will come and find you after lunch!

I love you, pumpkin!
Brent

Brent

I take Gemma to a few places around Inverness that I fell in love with as a child. I showed her where I went to school and my favorite hangout places as a teen. I also took her to Culloden House and gave her a brief history lesson of Scotland. I then take her to a hole in the wall diner that I always have to visit when I'm in town. It's nothing like she's experienced before, and I'm glad that she enjoyed herself.

After dinner we have about three hours before sunset. I want to take Gemma somewhere special. She was super interested in hearing about Scottish history, so I want to take her to see a couple of castles. We head out towards Castle Leod and make a couple stops along the way, but I really want to make sure there's enough daylight for us to walk around Leod. We don't stay at the other places long, even though Gemma is fascinated by everything. I wish she was staying longer, but I have hopes that this won't be the last time she'll be in Scotland with me.

When we arrive at Leod, we walk around as I tell her about the different clans of the time and specifically about the Mackenzie Clan. We talk about the mixture of clans that were still alive after the uprising that created the different family lines that still exist today. As we traipse around, I'm so glad I told her to wear her boots. She's trekking through terrain she wasn't prepared for. I always wear my boots, but that's just a habit when I'm here. We come to a sitting area and I have her sit next to me.

"Thank you for bringing me here," she exclaims as I wrap an arm protectively around her. The wind isn't as crazy as it was earlier today, but there's still a chill in the air.

"Of course. I'd love to show you everything Scotland has to offer, but then I'm not sure you'd ever want to go back to New York."

"Would that be so bad?" she asks, laughing, and I agree. It wouldn't be bad at all.

"Not really, no. However, I know there are things you want to take care of first. I'd like to stay in Scotland, but I know I need to go back, for now,"

I add as she nods, looking up at me with an understanding that I appreciate more than she'll ever know. The sun is starting to set, and she leans her head against my chest as we watch the sky change to different hues of pink and orange. I love this woman so damn much. "I know you have to leave in the morning, but I want you to know that I appreciate you coming. If you didn't, I'm not sure what would have happened. I'd like to believe I would have eventually come around."

"I'm glad I came as well. I was nervous at first," she whispers.

"That's my fault, and I'm sorry about that."

"We will get through this. That much I know." I take her hands in mine and warm them with my own.

"That we will. I want to be with you always, Gemma. I want you to know that, and I don't want you to ever question that again." She turns to face me, and I grin down at her. "I have something for you!" I add as she gives me a hesitant look. "I'm not proposing, Gemma. Not yet at least." She blushes, and I give her a wink to let her know she's safe. "I don't want you running into the river and getting eaten by the Loch Ness Monster." She gives me a confused look as I laugh. "It's a Scottish joke. We really need to get you some more information on Scotland."

"I wouldn't run off," she replies sarcastically,

and I don't even think she believes that. I grab the ring box from my back pocket, and she gasps.

"Gemma," I laugh, and she gives me a small smile. "This is a signet ring." I say, trying not laugh as I open the box to show her. Her facial expressions kill me sometimes, in the best way. "It's used for many purposes. In my family, it's been used as a promise ring. I have one with my family crest on it. I don't wear it all the time. Mostly when I'm at a work function, family event, or somewhere nice. I'd be honored if you would accept this gift from me. It can be sized when we get back to New York. I think it should fit though. I want you to wear this and think of me, of our time together, your time in Scotland. This time with my family, memories of Blake. I want you to have this as a reminder of how much I love you. How much you love me. We want to build a future together, and I feel like that's what we're working toward. I'd be honored if you would wear it. Cherish it for me," I ask as she wraps her arms around my neck, kissing me hard on the lips. I groan against her mouth, kissing her back passionately. When I pull away, she has tears falling down her cheeks. "I love you, Mo Ghrá," I whisper as she smiles through her tears. "That means 'my love'," I add as she kisses me again giggling excitedly.

"I love you, Brent," she whispers back as we both pull back. "Thank you! I will cherish it always. It's beautiful." I slip it on the pinky of her left hand as she smiles up at me. I pull her hand up to my mouth and place a chaste kiss on top of her ring.

When we pull back up to the house, I help her from the truck. She jokes that she likes this outdoorsy version of me, and I laugh. She's seen nothing yet if she likes this rugged Scotsman. We walk into the house, and it's very quiet. I walk her upstairs and kiss her goodnight then head back downstairs to grab the bags I left in the back of my truck. I'm taking them back to my apartment in New York for Gemma. I pray one day she'll end up living with me there. I smile to myself as I dream of what that will be like. I head back upstairs to sleep one more night with Gemma before she heads back to New York.

The next morning, I take Gemma to the airport. It was a teary goodbye between my family, Bitsy and Gemma. My mum loved Gemma's signet ring. Gemma was excited to show it off. I walk Gemma to the plane and kiss her passionately goodbye. I'll be back in New York in a few days. There are still some things I need to take care of. The memorial service is on Saturday in Manhattan, and although I'm not looking forward to it, I'm ready for Blake to be at peace everywhere he was loved most.

Gemma

Being back in New York and knowing Brent is still in Scotland is a bizarre feeling. I've lived in New York for years without him but not having him here in town now feels like something is missing. It takes me a few days to get settled back in. Between jetlag and staying up way too late binging the first season of Outlander, I'm barely functioning. Brent gets back into the office Friday, and he's ready to get to work. Friday morning, at our staff meeting, they unveil the new office re-structure. Everyone is thrilled, and then comes in-formation I wasn't expecting.

The Uptown and Downtown Staff will be join-ing forces in a newly renovated office building in lower Manhattan in TWO WEEKS! They're selling the other buildings later in the year. The new building is incredible. It overlooks the Hudson River. Different teams will occupy different floors. The breakdown is going to be epic. The first floor will be HR and finance. The second floor will house the downtown office. The third floor will house a new midtown office. The fourth floor is the uptown offices, and the fifth floor will be executives and their assistants. The sixth floor will be communal space with conference rooms, staff kitchen, dining tables, and an outdoor entertaining area with sweeping views of the Hudson River and lower Manhattan. Their hope is to create more of a team dynamic and culture.

This way, Brent can be with the entire company during the week, and we can build new relationships across all our offices. Hayden will be over the Downtown office. A new executive is coming from the West Coast to run the midtown office, and Brett will run the Uptown office. We will hear more about the new executive in the coming weeks, but that's all we know for now. I haven't been able to spend much time with Brent since he's been back. It's just been so busy with packing up the offices to move into the new building. I know eventually we will get around to spending some time together but seeing him smile again in the office with everyone is enough to hold me over. I'm just so glad he's back!

Saturday morning is Blake's Memorial Service. It's a wonderful celebration of his life, and I believe he would have felt honored by it all. Brent says he wants to take me somewhere special as we pull out of the parking garage leaving the service. We head back toward Brooklyn, and I have no idea where we could be going. He takes my hand after letting me out of the car and we walk toward the Brooklyn Bridge. I don't know what he's up to, but I always know I'm safe wherever he leads. I giggle as we walk to a small brick building under the Brooklyn Bridge. He grabs us two lobster rolls and two drinks. We find a little seating area, and we eat the most delicious lobster I've ever had. We are dressed in all black from Blake's memorial, but you wouldn't be able to tell it was such a somber occasion because we can't stop smiling at each other.

"This was one of Blake's favorite places to eat when he'd come out to visit me out here. It's one of the most special places to me, not just because Blake loved it, but because I'm now able to share it with you. Someone that I know Blake loved and loved him well in return," Brent says as I wipe a tear from the corner of my eye. This morning started out so sad, but now it feels so beautiful that I feel like Blake is here with us.

"I feel him still with me sometimes. I know that sounds bizarre," I reply. "I know he's gone, but at times I'm reminded of him, or I can hear something he would say or joke about, and I don't feel so alone. He's one of the most precious people I've ever met. Without him I wouldn't be at K. B. & A., and I know that I would never have had the opportunity to meet you."

"I know," Brent says, taking my hand. "I think about how lucky we are to have had someone like Blake in both of our lives. I owe so much to him. There's so much love here under the Brooklyn Bridge."

"I feel the same way," I say as I stand up and sit on Brent's lap. He wraps his arms around me, and I feel like this is such a sacred place. "I will always come here and think of him. And you, of course," I add as he leans over, placing a kiss on my shoulder.

"This can be our place. Somewhere we will forever think of Blake and the legacy he left behind. I love you," he whispers, and I can hear the emotion behind his words.

"I love you, too!"

We get back to Brent's apartment, and I'm grateful that the day turned out so beautiful. It makes me feel like Blake is smiling down on us. Shadow gets so excited when he sees me. I love this sweet dog. Almost as much as I love Brent. I turn around after Brent leaves his room. He's changed into something more comfortable, and I'm in a black sundress so I'm already comfortable.

He's smiling mischievously at me.

"It's so great to have you back here. There was a time I thought you might not ever come back." I walk around his kitchen island, and he meets me halfway so he can kiss me. The kiss is tender yet passionate, and I sigh against his soft lips as we pull away. He presses his lips to the top of my head, and I breathe him in. I'm so happy to be back here with him. I feel like I've grown so much and learned so much about myself since the last time I was here. He knows it and so do I.

"I'm glad to be back here," I add as I take a step back. I lean my back against the kitchen island as he crosses his arms in front of him. He's relaxed, and it makes me relax. "Listen, I finish my intensive in three weeks, and then I start normal therapy sessions after that. Why don't we celebrate then? It'll be around the first of September, and we can celebrate the end of my six-week intensive, as well as the launch of your office restructure. The next few weeks are going to be busy for the both of us. I need to finish what I started. I feel better each week, and I'm learning so much about myself. What do you think? Celebrate then? Maybe do a sleepover, over here?" I ask as he lifts me up, placing me on top of the kitchen island. I wrap my arms and legs around him, pulling him to me. As I lean forward to kiss him, he whispers sweetly to me.

"I think I'll order a cake!" he says. I giggle as

he kisses me tenderly, and I know that there's nothing sweeter in the world than this love between us.

"Sounds delicious!"

•••

It's amazing how fast three weeks flies by when you're busy! Monday through Friday I train the new staff with another associate. Monday evenings I have my friends' nights with Maggie and the gang. I'm getting to know everyone, and I really do enjoy adding them to my small list of friends. Nothing will ever be like what Blake and I had, but I'm starting to think I'll be able to figure it all out in time. Maggie's group could not be less judgmental and they're so welcoming. I love that we can sit back with a glass of wine and hang out as we talk about current issues and how to love people better. They are my kind of people. The last three weeks I've spent two hours each afternoon at Jesslyn's office in my intensives. I'm supposed to write a letter to my mother, father and my younger self for our last intensive. Wednesday evening after work, I go home and write the letters. Tomorrow night I'm supposed to bring them to share with my her in the office.

Thursday morning, we are all moved into the new building. It's incredible. Lucy and I grab lunch Thursday in the new dining area of the sixth floor.

It's her first official week, and I think she's doing well. We haven't heard what assistants will be assigned to which floor or executive yet. I know the executives are still making assessments on each new hire to see who will be the best fit.

Lucy is telling me all about a horrific date her roommate set her up on when she freezes. I look up to see what's made her so quiet when I see Brent and Hayden approaching. This happens every time she's around Hayden. I've caught Hayden stealing glances at Lucy and vice versa. There's nothing more exciting than an office romance. It's going to be fun to watch this dynamic unfold. Other than when Hayden is around, Lucy is always the most outgoing and brightest woman I've ever met. When Hayden is around, for some reason Lucy gets quiet. I try to tell her to just get to know him better, but she always looks at me like I've sprung a second head. I head back to my desk at the end of the day, and Brent approaches.

"Can I walk you out?" he asks.

"Yes, actually I had something I wanted to ask you." We get on the elevator, and I know I want him there with me at therapy tonight. That is, if he wants to go. I've been playing around with the idea for the last week.

"What is it? You okay?" he asks.

"Do you want to go with me? To my last intensive tonight with Jesslyn? You don't have to.

Please don't feel obligated to say yes. I know it could be weird, but I wanted to at least ask," I say quickly as Brent looks at me funny for a second, then starts to smile.

"Gemma, of course, I'll be there if you want me there. Are you sure?" he asks, and I nod reassuringly.

"Tonight, I'm reading out loud the letters that I wrote to my mother, my father and my younger self." He looks at me as if his whole heart could shatter.

"Sweetheart, yes. Do you want me to drive?" he asks, and I think about it for a second. Chances are I might be a wreck afterwards. Hell, he might be a wreck afterwards too.

"That's probably a good idea."

We get in his car and head straight toward Jesslyn's office. Brent asked if I wanted to eat a little something beforehand, but I don't think I can stomach anything. I'm starting to get a little nervous, but I know I can do this. Writing it was hard but reading it out loud I know will be the worst part. We are in the waiting room for about five minutes, and Brent places a hand on my knee. I didn't even realize my leg was bouncing up and down.

"If you want, I can wait out here, Gemma. If that would be easier for you. This is a big milestone for you."

"No, I want you with me. This will be hard,

but I think you need to be here for this," I place my hand on top of his, and he leans down to kiss the top of my head. Jesslyn comes out, and I think she's a little surprised to see Brent. She's also fully welcoming having him here tonight. She knows how I feel about him and knows how much I love him. I think she's also secretly a little impressed he's here.

Jesslyn says writing is therapeutic. She believes that reading something like a letter or journal entry out loud is a form of closure when a person has departed from this Earth or if you no longer have close contact or a relationship with them. There's not a chance in hell I'd ever reach back out to my father, so this is as good as it gets. I start with the letter to my mom. This one is the easiest of the three to read out loud. It's mostly about the lost hopes and dreams of a mother-daughter relation-ship. It's heartbreaking to read out loud, but at the same time it feels fulfilling.

When I pull out the letter for my father, I know this one will be harder. I start to read and feel Brent tense up beside me. He doesn't speak, he knows I need to do this. There are a lot of things in the letter he didn't know. When I get to the end, I forgive my father. The forgiveness isn't for him, it's for me. I take back control and leave all the abuse, neglect, and trauma in the past with him. I now know this should never have been on my shoulders or conscience to carry all these years. I also know I have a long journey ahead, but I owe it to myself to continue forward.

I take a sip of water and can tell Brent wants to touch or comfort me, but he doesn't know what is acceptable in Jesslyn's office. He's struggling, so she tells him he can react if he needs to. He stands up, walks to the window and looks outside as he places his hands on his hips. I imagine hearing all of this in one sitting is a lot to process. I've given Jesslyn full access to share anything with Brent. We want to be together, and I feel like it's better for him to know what he's getting himself into, in a way.

"We still have one more letter to read. Brent, how are you feeling?" she asks him. He looks a little green around the gills, and I appreciate his empathy. He turns around and comes back to sit down next to me.

"That was like drinking out of a fire hydrant going full blast."

"That's a great description," Jesslyn answers with a knowing smile. His eyes are red-rimmed, and I know he's trying to hold it together. I pull my last letter out. It's addressed to my younger self.

Dearest Innocent,

You are worthy and so deserving of love. One day you will meet someone who will love you the way you always deserved to be loved. You are worth fighting for, so don't stop fighting for yourself! One day you will conquer all your fears. You WILL survive this and it WILL make you stronger. There will come a day when you'll be able to shed real tears again and when you do, that will be ok. You'll learn to stand up on your own two feet, so don't worry if you trip and fall. I'm so sorry for everything you went through. You didn't deserve any of the pain and abuse. I'm so proud of you for not giving up. Your life is worth living and you have a purpose bigger than yourself.

Don't let the light inside of you die. Keep shining bright through the storms of life. You will eventually find your voice, and when you do, no one will ever be able to silence you again. I will never forget what happened to you, but it's time now for us to move forward together. I'll never forget your pain, but there are brighter and better days coming. You need only to reach out and take it! The future is yours and it starts now!

I will always love you!

Your Future Self,
Gemma

I crumble onto my side into Brent's arms, and he pulls me into his lap. He rocks me gently as I try to gain my composure. Jesslyn and Brent are wiping away tears of their own. It takes us all a moment, but we eventually come around. Jesslyn asks me what I want to do with the letters.

"Can I burn them?" I reply as I wipe my eyes with a tissue.

"You most certainly can," she answers as I smile. I fold the letters back up, putting them in my bag. I steal a glance at Brent. The love and adoration in his eyes for me makes me want to weep. The man beside me loves me so much, and I love him too. He steps out for a second as Jesslyn and I finish up. We set up our next appointments, and I'm so proud of myself. I feel so much lighter, albeit exhausted, but I'm ready to move forward.

Brent and I walk to the car hand in hand, and when we get to the passenger side, he picks me up. I wrap my legs around his waist and look deep into his eyes.

"I'm so proud of you," he whispers with tears his eyes. "I'm working on finding my words right now, but I'm in awe of you Gemma!"

"Thank you for coming. I know that had to be hard to hear," I add as he shakes his head.

"I'm so glad I was there. It was hard to hear but not as hard as imagining you having to experience that, and all on your own. You are one strong woman, Gemma. I love you!"

"I love you, too," I whisper as he leans his head against mine. He takes me back to my apartment since tomorrow morning we have an early meeting.

Honestly, I'm too tired to do anything else tonight.

When I get back to my apartment, I'm asleep before my head even hits the pillow. I have a dream that night about my mother. It's the first time that I feel like I truly can see, hear and talk to her. She's so beautiful, and she tells me how proud she is of me. She tells me about how much fun we had those first few years together. How much she loves me and how excited she is for what God has in my future. I've never been too keen on the idea of God, but I truly believe that she was with me in my dreams. I've never had a dream like that with her, but I'm grateful when I wake up. I cry as I retell it to Brent the next morning on the way to the King Family's Attorney's office.

I give George and Regina kisses on both cheeks when we walk in. I'm still not sure what Blake would have left me. When Brent picked me up this morning, we joked that it's probably a gift card to Perrone's. Blake left his portion of the company to Brent. His property in Scotland goes back into the family trust. I didn't realize that the property between The King Estate and Brent's was Blake's. I remembered passing it, but that's it. Blake left his condo in New York to Brett, which surprises even him. Now he has Brent and Blake's properties to choose from. I smile at him, and he laughs. Blake leaves half of his net worth and savings to help support the LGBTQIA+ community, as well some other local charities he was passionate about. The other half he leaves to his parents. It was expected. He inherited a lot of money this summer when his grandmother died. The attorney turns to me after they go down the stocks, portfolios and other uninteresting things. Wealthy people have a lot of shit to leave behind.

"Mr. Blake King is leaving his Land Rover and Tesla to one Ms. Gemma Williams. So that she can, and I quote, 'get rid of that damn clown car' end quote." Brent laughs beside me, and his mom slaps his arm. I'm not at all offended. I giggle as I can hear Blake saying it. "He also is leaving a lump sum of one million dollars to Ms. Gemma Williams." I nearly choke on my own saliva. Brent places his hand on my back, and I hold my hand up saying that I'm fine.

"I'm sorry, but I'm declining the money," I reply hoarsely as Brent laughs, and of course he has something to say about it.

"There's not chance in hell the family will allow that. These are Blake's final wishes. If we have to open an account for you and add the money to it ourselves, we will," I look up at him and can tell he's dead serious. The attorney hands me a letter, and I look at it, confused.

"Mr. King had a letter in case you tried to forfeit your inheritance. He went through a lot of trouble to have the correct documentation. It can be a lot of work to leave an inheritance to a non-family member."

"Well, tough shit." George states and we all look over at him. "She is a family member, and no one here will dispute that or what he's left for her." I look down at the letter and open it. The letter from Blake is short and sweet.

Gemma,

If you're reading this, then some serious shit went down. I think I'll probably outlive you anyway, so you probably won't ever read this. However, if you are please know how much I love you. I'm so proud of you, and I better see you up here in heaven, so get your shit together. It's going to be boring as hell up here at brunch if you aren't here to enjoy this with me. God has big plans for your life, Gemma. I know you don't believe it, but he does. Just like he has one for me. When it's my time to go, I'll go knowing that this isn't the end. This isn't good-bye, Gemma. It's just "see you in a little while." Please go to Scotland. You'll instantly fall in love just like you fell in love with Brent. Scotland is Brent. Brent is Scotland. You can't have one without the other. You are so worthy of him, Gemma. Stop fighting it and start living the future that's meant for you! You deserve it and so does he! I love you, Gem! I'll see you on the other side!

All my Love,
Your Blakey

P.S. Please donate that piece of shit car of yours. I'm leaving you mine. Deposit the damn money. Chances are you won't need it because you'll be married to one of the richest men in New York. Please do something with it. Chase your dreams and makes others' lives better because you can! The future is yours! You are the future!

I wipe my eyes as I hand the letter and envelope to Brent. As I do another folded up piece of paper falls out. I see it's addressed to Brent, so I hand it to him.

Brent,

If you haven't already put a ring on her finger, I will come back from the dead and haunt you! Don't be an idiot! She's not going to say no! Even if you guys don't ever get married. Just ask her!

I Love you,
Blake

He laughs as he hands the letter back to me. We all laugh and cry seeing Blake's handwriting. I will keep these forever. I will obviously donate my car. I don't have it with me, but Brent says he knows some great charities in Brooklyn that would accept it. As we are leaving, I hug Regina and George. They tell me they'll see me soon as Regina turns to take my hand.

"Your spirit seems so much lighter today. Whatever it is, I'm so proud of you. If you want, please come to dinner Sunday night." She smiles as she leaves, and I laugh to myself, thinking back to mine and Blake's Connecticut jokes.

"What do you have against Connecticut?" Brett asks before he leaves. I laugh and tell him absolutely nothing. It's just a joke between Blake and me.

"You want to go into the office? Grab some lunch?" Brent asks, and I nod.

"Lunch is good. Perrone's?" I ask.

"I can't think of anything more perfect."

After lunch we head into the office for a little bit. I've decided to stay over at Brent's for the weekend and both of us are giddy. It feels so different now. I'm not scared, I'm excited. It's almost 4:00 when I see I have a new text from Brent.

> **Meet me at our spot me under the Brooklyn Bridge at 6:00pm!**

I look down smiling like a fool in love, and Lucy giggles as she watches me over the copier. I look up at her and bite my lip.

"Sorry! I can't help it," I say as we make our way back to the conference room. We turn the corner, and Lucy runs smack into Hayden. She drops our copies and drops down to her knees to pick them up.

"So sorry," she apologizes as Hayden drops down to his knees as well.

"No, it was my fault. I should have been watching where I was going. Are you okay?" he asks, and she looks up into his face. He's like three times her size so he could have knocked her out. I giggle at their interaction as I pick up some papers. You can feel the attraction, and I have to say, this one is going to be so much fun to see play out. He stands up and then takes her hand to help her up. They stand there for a few silent moments just staring at each other. I clear my throat, and they both jump back into action. "Nice to see you, Lucy!"

"You too," she answers, blushing. When we get back into the conference room, I close the door behind us. "I'm such a dork. Did you see me back there! Oh my gosh," she squeals as she places a hand on her cheek. "Gemma, say something!"

"You're fine. It was an honest mistake. Don't think anything of it." We get back to work, and I finally text Brent back that I'll see him there at our spot.

It's Friday night and we're supposed to be celebrating. I had a cab drop me off near our spot. I walk down toward the waterfront and spot Brent in nice slacks and a dinner jacket. He told me to wear something fancy, so I'm excited about what he could possibly have in mind. I'm wearing one of the dresses I bought in Scotland. It's a red polka dot wrap dress and I wear my tan Louboutins. When sees me, he walks toward me. He's so incredibly attractive, and I hope I get to undress him tonight.

"I can't wait to unwrap you tonight," he says as he leans down, kissing me tenderly.

"I was just thinking the same thing. You smell incredible, as always."

"As do you. We will get into that later but are you hungry?" he asks.

"I am. What did you have in mind?"

"I have a lot of things in mind, Gemma. How about dinner at River Café, and then we head back to my place for dessert?"

"Perfect!" I answer as he takes my arm, and we walk the short distance toward the restaurant. It's such a beautiful night, and I can feel a slight chill in the air as fall begins to sneak in. Dinner is extravagant, and I'm in awe that this is my reality. When we get back to Brent's, we sit down on the sofa, and he moves to sit in front of me on the ottoman.

"We should go on a trip together," he says as he pulls my feet in his lap. "Would you want to do that?"

"Of course, what did you have in mind?" I ask, and he has the biggest smile on his face. I already know where he wants to go.

"Scotland?" He asks, and I nod enthusiastically. I've been dreaming of Scotland since we've been back.

"I'd love to go back to Scotland, Brent. Honestly, I didn't want to leave."

"When would you like to go?" he asks as I lean back against the sofa.

"Maybe for my birthday?" I answer slyly as he smiles.

"Your birthday is at the end of October, right?"

"That's right," I answer as he sits up and moves in between my legs.

"What's the date, Gemma?" he whispers as he pulls me forward off the sofa and onto his lap. He stands up, picking me up as if I weight nothing at all.

"October 24th! Can you make the arrangements?"

"Can I make the arrangements? Are you kidding me? Yes, I can make the arrangements, and I'm super excited. How's your Outlander watching going?" he asks, laughing. He lays us on the couch and rolls over to the side, so we are facing each other. I place a hand on his chest as he lifts my hand to place a gentle kiss on the inside of my wrist. God, I really could have screwed things up if Brent hadn't stuck with me. He really stayed with me through everything just as he promised he would. This is exactly where I want to be.

We take our slices of cake up to the roof and sit on the lounger together. The cake is just as delicious as the first time. I forgot how amazing the view is from up here. I love being with Brent. He plays some music from his bluetooth speaker. He holds his hand out, and I gladly let him hold me. We start dancing, and I will never forget how great of a dancer he is. He brings my hand to his lips, kissing my hand and looking down at my signet ring. I haven't taken it off since Brent gave it to me. I love it. It's beautiful. I haven't decided what I want to have engraved on it yet, but it fits me perfectly. Brent leans down, kissing me as I run my fingers through his hair, gently tugging it, as I feel his lips press softly against my skin. He runs his nose up the side of my neck before lightly kissing his way back down.

"This reminds me… remember when we were

dancing at the event? It would have been highly frowned upon, but I wanted to make love to you right there on the dance floor. You looked so regal and royal," he whispers, and I giggle.

"You mean like Queen Elizabeth?" he barks out a loud laugh, looking down at me.

"No, Gemma! Not like Queen Elizabeth. Although she was quite an amazing woman. I meant you looked so exquisite and untouchable. I felt like the luckiest man that night, and I still feel that way."

"You looked pretty delicious yourself, Brent! Speaking of the event I have something for you!"

We grab our empty dessert plates and head back down to the kitchen. I head over to where my work bag is. Maggie sent some 8 x 10's of me from the shoot with Morrey. They turned out amazing. I hope Brent likes them. I hand him the thick envelope, and he takes my hand, pulling me towards the sofa.

"What's this, darling?" he asks as he pulls them out and lays them out one by one on the ottoman in front of him. Most are in black and white except for the ones in the park and a couple of me topless. They are so tastefully done that I'm not embarrassed to show him. I probably wouldn't show them to anyone else, but Brent's a different story. He stops at the close-up of me in black and white wearing the veil but looking into the camera. It's one of my favorites as well. Brent is silent. He looks over at me, and his eyes are on fire. "These are incredible, Gemma. You are so fucking beautiful," he says as he lifts my chin up so he can kiss me. "Please tell me I can have these!"

"They ARE for you! There's a disk of the pictures as well. Maggie printed some of her and Morrey's favorites. I'm glad they were pleased with how they turned out. Matter of fact the studio loved them so much that they are going to use some of the photos. Not to mention Morrey had them on his website and Vogue has asked to use them in an article they are doing on Morrey and his career."

"Jesus, Gemma. You are everything. I need to order some frames for these. I want to put some in the bedroom. Thank you, Gemma. This is one of the best gifts I've ever received."

"Seriously? The Billionaire's favorite gifts are some pictures of his girlfriend?" I ask, and he turns to me smiling.

"Girlfriend? Yes, I love that. I love you, Pumpkin," he says, leaning over and pressing his lips against mine. I stand up, straddling him as my dress bunches around my hips. I kiss him deeply, my hands in his hair. His hands move up from my hips into my hair as well. He stands up, takes me into the bedroom and places me on my feet as he turns me around. He unwraps my dress, and it falls to the floor. I step out of it and turn around so I can start on his tie. He starts to unbutton his shirt as I go straight for his belt. I pull him closer to me by his waist band and he laughs. I giggle against his lips as I undo his pants and reach inside grabbing HIM firmly. He's no longer laughing. He pulls his pants off, then leans us back onto the bed. He runs a finger down my chest as he leans forward, kissing my shoulder.

He reaches behind me, unfastening my bra and throwing it to the side. He looks down at me reverently. He kisses one breast, and I whimper as he moves to the other. His hand moves from my waist to pull my underwear to the side. I gasp as he slips a finger inside me. He leans down, kisses me and pulls my underwear down my thighs. He moves down my body, and I know exactly where he's heading. I've dreamed about having this moment with him again. He spreads my legs, devouring me like he did the first time. I grab a handful of the duvet, overcome by being this intimate with him again. Closing my eyes, I know I'm getting close to climaxing. He starts moving back up my body and takes his sweet time. He kisses my breasts again, but I grab his hair pulling him up to my mouth. I pull his boxer briefs over his ass, and he kicks them off. He's back within seconds and kissing me with passion I've never felt. He looks down at me adoringly, and I return the sentiment.

"I love you, Brent," I whisper, and he pauses.

"I love you too, Gemma."

He pushes inside me, and I gasp. We start slowly, and by the time we are getting close to going over the edge, we are both holding tightly to each other. I cry out his name as he stills inside of me, joining me in our moment of ecstasy together. He whispers my name and places his forehead against mine, catching his breath. He picks me up and carries me into the bathroom. Brent turns on the shower, and we both stand under the hot stream of water. He wraps his arms around me, and I lean my head against his warm, wet chest. He washes my hair, and I wash his.

"Do you remember when you caught me naked in your shower?" I ask with a giggle.

"How could I forget? I was stunned, but also incredibly aroused. Once I found out you worked for K.B. & A. I think I felt like I needed to rein in my emotions. However, I think I was smitten by you from that moment. Also, the fact that you handled it like a champ. Then again, I was smitten before I ever saw you in the shower. That first night at Perrone's in that red dress. Jesus, I thought I'd died and gone to heaven. When you walked away, I was scared I'd never see you again. Then you winked at me, and I felt it in my heart. When I saw you were with Blake, I relaxed a bit. However, I was a goner from that first moment."

We both laugh at the crazy situation, one of

many such situations brought on by Blake. As we slowly and tenderly wash each other, I close my eyes remembering that time back in the Hamptons. He has always been so gentle and tender with me. I knew he loved me then, and I know without a doubt that he loves me now. I know I deserve his love. He deserves mine as well, and I'm thankful that I'm able to give him all of me. He turns the water off, grabbing towels and drying us off. I step out and remember I didn't bring anything to wear.

"I probably need to head to my apartment and grab some clothes," I mention as he gives me a mischievous grin. "Not running! Just need clothes!" He laughs, picking me up and carrying me to a door on the opposite side of the room from where his closet is. I open the door and see that it's another walk-in closet. He's bought clothes for me! I shake my head, turning around to wrap my arms around his neck.

"I thought you might need some clothes, as well. I bought these for you when we were in Scotland," he says, answering my unspoken question as we walk into the closet. There are a couple dresses, some pajamas and a few more separates. "If you don't like them you don't have to wear them. They made me think of you. Reminded me of what I've already seen you wear before. The pajamas look extremely comfortable. They're eucalyptus. The same material as the sheets you love so much!"

"Oh. Is that what they are? I still need to buy some of those for my apartment."

"Or you could just move in with me," he suggests nonchalantly, and I take my hand off of the pajamas looking over at him. "You know, I've wanted to ask you to move in with me since the first time you stayed here. I want you here with me, Gemma. Always. I want you to have the freedom to be wherever you want. If I'm traveling, then I want to know that you are here safe, sleeping in our bed and dreaming about me. If you're traveling, I want you to know that I'm missing the hell out of you in our place and praying you'll return home to me safe. I'm not sure what your plans are in life, Gemma, but I want to be with you. My home is wherever you are. If you decide you want to move somewhere else, I'll go with you. My places are your places. If we go to Seattle and you end up wanting to move there, I'll be the first one to celebrate. If you want to move to Scotland, you know I'll be right there beside you. If you want to continue acting, I'll move to LA."

"Brent," I whisper wrapping my arms around him. "I feel the same way. Of course, I'll move in with you. There's no place in the world I'd rather be. I don't know what I want to do, but whatever it is, I know I want to do it with you by my side!"

"I love you," he whispers against my lips, "so damn much."

I pull on my new pajamas, and they feel like butter against my skin. Brent pulls on some athletic shorts, then takes my hand. We head into his office, and I smile as we walk around his desk. He pulls me into his lap and wakes up his computer monitor. There's a blueprint for a house in front of me, and I turn around, looking at him in shock.

"Scotland," he whispers, and I smile.

"Seriously?" I ask, and he nods. The blueprints are amazing. Brent explains to me what he's thinking as I curl into his lap. He scoots forward, explaining the plans, and I can see it in my mind.

"I wanted something a little more 'homey' as I've been dreaming it up. My parents' house is formal looking, even though they try to be casual. So, you know where the cottage is currently sitting?" he asks, and I nod. "I'm going to leave it there until we're done with the build. If you cross over the river, there's about 10 acres to build on. Right now, there's only trees and brush. I'll have that cleared out, put a bridge from the cottage to the build site. It'll be a stone and wooden structure. I'm thinking around four bedrooms, four baths. Keep it cozy. A large open concept on the first floor. Great kitchen and dining area. A double study for us with built-in library. A heated pool area in the back, and I know we'll both enjoy that," he says, squeezing me, and I giggle thinking back to all our intimate moments in pools. "Master off the back of the house so we can have an incredible view of the mountains and water. Waking up to that every morning will be incredible. The second floor will have the other bedrooms. A detached four-car garage with storage and a gym on the top floor. A pool house in the back and a large entertaining space at the back of the house as well. Like at the Hampton House. What do you think?" he asks as I spin around to meet his eyes.

"It's perfect." He pulls up the drawings the architect and designer sent over as concept art for the outside of the property. He's right, it does seem so homey. It's such a masterful design with modern lines. It's very cozy and it looks like home.

"I want your input, Gemma. It will be your home, too." Tears spring to my eyes, so I close them. I've never really had a "home." A place to really feel like it's my own. He wipes the tears from my face and kisses me gently on the forehead.

"I love it, Brent! It's wonderful."

"It's ours, Gemma. The first of many spaces we will create together. I want you to make it your own. In all our homes."

"When do you break ground?" I ask, and he sits back so he can look at my face.

"As soon as I get my partner's approval," he answers, and I give him a confused look. "You, Gemma, you are my partner," he adds, laughing as I nod.

"Well, if that's what you're waiting for then you can give them the go ahead." He minimizes the blueprint pictures and types out an email response. I smile when he gives them the go ahead, and he signs it Brent King, proud boyfriend of Ms. Gemma Williams. I lean my head against his shoulder, and he wraps his arms around me. He picks me up, carrying me to the sofa and placing me down. He gets a bottle of Champagne from the fridge, the same kind we had at his old bachelor pad not too long ago. He walks over to me after he opens the bottle and pours some into the two flutes. He hands me one and places his on the table beside him. He turns on the TV and pulls up his saved TV shows. He chooses Outlander, and I laugh.

"I'm doing this for you!" he says defensively. "Let's start with the first episode of season one and see how we fare. Obviously, I want you to keep going as well. I've bought all of them, so don't get upset with me if I pause it to tell you the inaccuracies."

"I wouldn't expect anything less, my Scottish laird."

"Scottish laird?" he laughs as he takes a sip of his champagne. "I guess I am. I do own a large estate." I pick up my glass as he holds his glass out to me. We clink them, and he grins knowingly over at me. "Slànte Mhath, mo ghràdh. Welcome home!" The Outlander theme song starts as I cuddle up in the love of my life's arms. Finally, I'm home!

"Hey!" I ask as I take a sip of my champagne. "Is this you wooing me?" I joke. He laughs as he leans down, kissing me gently on the lips.

"Pumpkin, you've seen nothing yet!" he says as I snuggle in closer to him.

Epilogue

6 months Later

It's been a few months since I've seen Ava. She's been back in LA, so I sit down in my office space at Brent's. I take out some stationery that she and I both bought at a boutique in Brooklyn. She and Clark came over for dinner one night and we had a fun night shopping. Ava and I laughed about it and decided to become "pen pals" so we could use our stationery.

My Dearest Ava,

Brent and I are doing so well.

Things at work have been incredible in the new building and with all our new support staff. So much so that I feel like a weight has been lifted off Brent's shoulders. He's getting to know all the new hires as well as some of the staff he hadn't been able to spend any time with. It's been hilarious to see Lucy and Hayden's minimal interactions. Right now, there's an office rumor going around that he's an ex-James Bond. Like in real life he was the "real James Bond." When I told Brent about it, he laughed and asked, "Wasn't James Bond British?" He isn't technically answering my question, as I know they've worked closely together for many years. If anyone knows Hayden's background it would be Brent. I know he's ex-military, but that's all I've got to go on and Brent isn't sharing any more. If I find out more, I'll let you know!

Lucy and I have lunch almost every single day. I can't wait for you to meet her. I love hearing her celebrity stories from who she's worked with in the past. It's funny how you think you know how someone would be in real life, but then find out how they actually are when you work closely with them. If I was Hayden, I'd be throwing my name into the running. She has all kinds of admirers in the office, but no one comes close to interesting her when Hayden is in a 10-mile radius.

Regina and George sold their Connecticut home and moved back to Scotland. No one is surprised, but I did laugh when they offered their home to Brent and I. Blake would shit a brick and for real haunt us if we moved to Connecticut. Brett is adapting well in the office. I think he's coming around to the idea of staying in New York. Brent and I have been to Scotland twice in the last few months and I love the way his demeanor changes when he's "Home." We are still figuring out our relationship. Honestly, I think marriage is in our near future, but we don't want to rush into anything yet. We have everything we could ever want or need together already. Doesn't mean he doesn't drop an engagement hint every once in a while.

I received a letter the other day from an attorney in Savannah, GA. I about puked when I saw where it was from. Honestly, I haven't spoken to anyone from my past in years, so it was a little alarming. Brent opened it for me, and it was a notification from an attorney. Apparently, my father could afford one, but sadly for him he passed away with no one there to care for him. There's nothing financially I would ever want from him, so I had Brent handle it. Part of me was relieved that he's no longer on this Earth to hurt anyone. The other part of me was sad for him. He missed out on so many opportunities to make things right. He died a broken and pathetic man with no one to even attend a funeral. That has brought on some closure that I didn't even realize I needed.

I signed the contract with the

studio to do the Lana Turner biopic, but it's not for a few years. I can't wait to rejoin you for your Ava Gardner film. We are going to have so much fun. I can't believe our Sinatra biopic comes out in a few months. I feel like we are going to get in so much trouble. Give your new bundle of joy my love. I can't wait to snuggle again soon. Brent and I created a children's charity in the city, and I could not be more humbled to use the money Blake left for me toward something honorable and good. I split my time between K.B. & A and the charity during the week. This year we are having a huge event like we did with Mid-Summer's, but the money will go strictly to our charity. Brent is an absolute dream to be with and work with. I couldn't think of a better partner. I'm still seeing Jesslyn once a week as well as my "city girls" group Monday nights. You'll have to join us one night when you are in town. They'll love you!

Please know I'm praying for your sweet family. Brent and I adore you both and I'm so glad that we've become so close. Life can be a real bitch sometimes but it's everything to find people you can do life with. You've been there when I've needed you and I promise you that I will always be there when you need me. Give Clayton and Marco a hug and kiss! Hopefully they can come visit soon as well when you are all in town. Tell Brooklyn I found the most incredible candy store here the other day and I can't wait to take her!

Love you so much!
Gemma
(Your Lana Turner)

Afterword

I hope you enjoyed Brent and Gemma's love story! As you continue moving forward through my books there will be more of their story, as well as Ava and Clark's, sprinkled throughout. Gemma's story sheds light on chapters of our story that we don't always want to bring to into the light. I felt like this story fit Gemma, and I pray that you received some hope, healing, and light by seeing her story come to life.

If you need someone to talk to or share your story with I pray that you find the right therapist, community group, and/or counselor to talk to. It really does make all the difference in the world, and you my friend are worth it. If you or someone you know is in an abusive situation, I pray that you take the right steps for them and/or for yourself. Here are some resources:

HELP IS AVAILABLE

Speak with someone today

---

988 Suicide and Crisis Lifeline
Hours: Available 24 hours. Languages: English, Spanish.

SAMHSA's National Helpline is a free, confidential, 24/7, 365-day-a-year treatment referral and information service (in English and Spanish) for individuals and families facing mental and/or substance use disorders.

1-800-622-HELP (4357)

Acknowledgements

To my Husband, Brad – Thank you for loving me just as I am! A Dreamer, a Disney Nerd & so very "Extra!" I Love You!

John John & Gracie! – You keep me grounded and continue to inspire me to be more of myself and stand firm in who I am! Thank you for reminding me to dream big and I pray one day you'll feel empowered to go out and chase your dreams…just like mommy does!

To KP Simmon – this all started to take shape when you reached out like my fairy God Mother, pointed me in the correct direction and said, "GO!" I will never forget the direction and patience you extended to me! Lord knows I'm still learning as I go…but I'm going!!

To Alyssa Garcia, Stacy Garcia, Jen Rebecca, Tricia Crouch, Megan Addison, Karin Enders, and the entire Team of strong and empowering women at LitUncorked & Blush Magazine – You all have been invaluable sources of knowledge, direction, and support. It is because of incredible women, authors, editors, and writers like you that the rest of us are able to pursue and achieve our dreams.

To Julie Holt – My Editor and Partner in Crime (E.P.I.C) – Started with "We need more Cupcake Moments!" and have progressed with… "Let them eat Cake!" You were correct…we are seeing a theme here! Must be my developing sweet tooth! Who knows what we will cook up next! I could NOT do this without you and I'm so grateful that I don't have to! I see a hundred more books in my future! The story boards continue to grow and you continue to help my voice sparkle and shine! So, thank you! I love you dearly!

To my ARC Readers – Thank you for taking the time to read the words I've written. You play an invaluable role to authors and if someone hasn't already told you yet. THANK YOU! I LOVE YOU! Keep reading and stay inspired!

Finally, to my family and friends – We are continuing to do it! Thanks for letting me be the little girl who loved to tell "stories." She's the reason I'm here today and still sharing my love of storytelling! I love you all! Hope to make you proud!

As always! I could sit here and thank people "'til they start playing the music" like at an award ceremony! However, this is my reward! Having my voice heard and being seen for who I am and who I am becoming!

Let your light shine in the darkness! And remember…One act of kindness can not only change someone's day. It can change the trajectory of someone's life!

So Be Kind! Be Bold! Have Courage and LOVE Big!

www.ingramcontent.com/pod-product-compliance
Lightning Source LLC
Chambersburg PA
CBHW021335310726
48971CB00001B/141